LIGHT YEARS

LIGHT YEARS

KASS MORGAN

LITTLE, BROWN AND COMPANY

New York Boston

Little, Brown and Company
Hachette Book Group
1290 Avenue of the Americas, New York, NY 10104
Visit us at LBYR.com

Little, Brown and Company is a division of Hachette Book Group, Inc.
The Little, Brown name and logo are trademarks of Hachette Book Group, Inc.

The publisher is not responsible for websites (or their content) that are not owned by the publisher.

First Edition: October 2018

alloyentertainment

Produced by Alloy Entertainment
1325 Avenue of the Americas
New York, NY 10019

Library of Congress Cataloging-in-Publication Data
Names: Morgan, Kass, author.
Title: Light years / Kass Morgan.
Description: First edition. | New York ; Boston : Little, Brown and Company, 2018. | Summary: After centuries of exclusivity, the Quatra Fleet Academy finally accepts students from the settler planets, forcing four teenagers from different backgrounds, with different ambitions, motives, and missions, to work together to outmaneuver a mysterious alien enemy.
Identifiers: LCCN 2017061515| ISBN 9780316510448 (hardcover) | ISBN 9780316510455 (ebook) | ISBN 9780316510462 (library edition ebook)
Subjects: | CYAC: Space stations—Fiction. | Military education—Fiction. | Schools—Fiction. | Secrets—Fiction. | Prejudices—Fiction. | Science fiction.
Classification: LCC PZ7.M8249 Li 2018 | DDC [Fic]—dc23
LC record available at https://lccn.loc.gov/2017061515

ISBNs: 978-0-316-51044-8 (hardcover), 978-0-316-51045-5 (ebook)

Printed in the United States of America

LSC-C

10 9 8 7 6 5 4 3 2 1

For my father, Sam Henry Kass, the greatest playwright in the galaxy. Thank you for making me a writer.

CHAPTER 1

CORMAK

The airlock opened with a hiss, and Cormak shot off through the blisteringly hot, pink-tinged air. As his bike sped across the cracked red ground, he took shallow breaths until he was sure that his gas mask was working. Then he exhaled and jolted the roader into a higher gear, leaning forward to make his body as streamlined as possible. After spending all night delivering H_2O to the luxury towers in Sector 2, it was a relief to be out in the open. The air in the towers might be quadruple filtered, but it always felt more suffocating than the poisonous atmosphere outside.

Water was strictly rationed on Deva, and most Settlers barely had enough for drinking, let alone showering more than once a week. But for a steep price, anyone willing to risk punishment could buy it on the black market from people like Cormak's boss, Sol. Cormak had been making deliveries to the luxury towers for two years, yet the wealthy residents still eyed him warily, as if he were something that should've been caught in the filters. He'd learned the hard way not to let his gaze linger longingly on anything in their apartments—not on the fruit growing in the terrariums, not on the films playing on the monitors, and especially not on the books locked in transparent cases to protect them from the corrosive air. If there was one thing rich people trusted less than a dust-covered Devak, it was a dust-covered Devak who liked to read.

It was fairly clear today, and in the distance, the towers of Sector 23 loomed up through the faint pink haze. Cormak lived on the thirty-first floor of Tower B, one of the six hulking cement structures that comprised his scenic home. If he was lucky, he'd get a few hours of sleep before Sol called with the next set of deliveries.

Cormak switched on his helmet radio, banging his gloved hand against the side a few times until the static cleared.

"—officials said fourteen miners were killed in the blast. And now, the local weather report," a cheery voice chirped.

"The time is 27:40 in the morning. Air-traffic conditions are suboptimal due to a storm in the mesosphere. Today's high will be 212 centis. The low will be 199 centis. According to current atmospheric readings, breathing unfiltered air will kill you in two minutes and forty seconds. Have a wonderful day!"

Cormak cursed as he hit a rut. The deliveries were wreaking havoc on his roader, but he didn't have a choice. Making runs for Sol beat fourteen hours a day in one of the few remaining mines, even if it meant working for the biggest asshole on Deva.

He straightened his legs and lifted himself up for a better view. The path ahead looked clear save for the remains of abandoned mining equipment—some rusty drills, huge broken barrels, and whatever tanker pieces hadn't been snatched up by scavengers after the mine dried up.

The drone of the radio was cut off by an alert. "Incoming call from…*Cormak, you'd better accept this or you're in for a world of pain.*…Do you accept?" Cormak sighed and mumbled, "Accept."

"What the *hell* were you thinking?" a familiar voice barked. "You don't mouth off to clients."

"What are you talking about, Sol?" Cormak asked wearily.

"The way you spoke to Rella Hewitt was unacceptable. To say nothing of stealing product that *she* paid for."

Cormak stifled a groan. On his way into the Hewitts' building, he'd passed an exhausted-looking girl mopping the floor—a fairly common sight on Deva, where kids often dropped out of school when their parents grew too sick to work. Cormak had offered her a tiny sip of H_2O, just enough so she wouldn't collapse before her shift ended. He'd forgotten that the nosy, bored Rella Hewitt often watched her building's security feed, monitoring her neighbors even in the middle of the night. When he'd arrived at her door, she'd spent a good five minutes screeching at him before Cormak ended her tirade with a few well-chosen words.

"I gotta tell you, Sol. It's tough to feel bad for rich people who care more about their exotic plants than Settler kids." Unlike the Settlers, whose ancestors had arrived on Deva generations ago, most of the wealthy people were recent arrivals from Tri, the Quatra Federation's capital planet.

"Oh, so now you're gonna get all moral on me, asshole? Your job is to make deliveries and keep your mouth shut. You got it?"

"Got it," Cormak muttered.

"You're lucky I happen to have a kind, understanding nature. I'm going to give you one more chance. I have a pickup for you tonight at 29°22′ north, 99°48′ west.... Why don't I hear you pulling over to write that down?"

"29°22′ north, 99°48′ west," Cormak repeated dully. "Roger that, chief." He never forgot coordinates. He had a thing for numbers. He could see them rearranging themselves in his head into all sorts of combinations that allowed him to solve complex equations in seconds. Not that it had done him much good. Because he couldn't show his work on math exams, his teachers always assumed he was cheating. Their skepticism had made his brother, Rex, furious, but Cormak hadn't really cared. Good grades only mattered for people like Rex—the rare students smart enough to catch the instructors' attention and likable enough to justify the endless paperwork, favors, and bribes required to get into an off-planet university or training program. Though in the end, even Rex hadn't made it off Deva.

"If you mess this up, you're gonna be sorry. I mean it, Cormak."

"I got it. I'll be there tonight." 29°22′ north, 99°48′ west was in Sector 22, where Sol had a contact who imported stolen nanotech from Tri. While water comprised the bulk of

Sol's trade, he also dabbled in weapons and had a passion for interstellar cryptocommerce. There was a rumor that he'd even hacked the Tridian Bank.

"Shit," Cormak grunted as his roader hit another rut and flew into the air. He managed to keep the bike steady but landed hard enough that the vibrations coursed through his body. He glanced down to check that his pants were still tucked into his boots. Exposed skin allowed the poisonous air to seep into your pores, killing you over the course of a few hours.

Deva was naturally toxic to humans. The planet was blanketed with a thick cloud of gas—a combination of nitrogen, carbon dioxide, and just enough oxygen to be filtered and piped into vacuum-sealed buildings. It also happened to be rich in terranium, the metal that was once used to build the vast majority of the buildings on Tri.

A hundred years ago, mine owners and metal exporters from Tri had come to Deva eager to stake their claim. They had built enormous bubbles around their comfortable homes to protect themselves from the toxic atmosphere and traveled back and forth to work in customized zipcrafts with backup oxygen-filtration systems. Then they'd built towers for the hundreds of thousands of workers they lured to Deva with promises of high wages and a new start. The towers were close enough to the mines that the workers could walk there, trudging through the toxic pink fog in their company-issued gas masks. The masks, of course, didn't have backup systems.

Then, about twenty years ago, developers discovered an even stronger metal, fyron, on Chetire and the terranium market bottomed out. The majority of the mines shut down, but of course, the time the miners had already spent underground was more than enough to corrode their organs. Cormak's father had died at the ripe old age of thirty-nine with more tumors in his lungs than coins in his pocket.

Up ahead, something shimmered near the horizon. A pol in a zipcraft. Cormak cursed and veered sharply off the road and into the bumpy, trench-filled wasteland. He hadn't been doing anything illegal—nothing that could've been spotted from the air, at least—but the pols stopped anyone they felt like messing with. If they pulled him over and found the stolen water, he'd be screwed. Most people who got arrested on Deva didn't get citations, and they didn't get trials. They were simply never heard from again.

Cormak sped up and angled the bike on the most direct route to the canyon, a series of channels that the miners had created long ago. It was too narrow for the zipcraft to follow and too dark to allow the facial-recognition mechanism to identity Cormak from afar.

Over the roar of his engine came the distinctive buzz of the pol's zipcraft. Cormak forced himself to steady his breathing. The mask could filter only a certain amount of air at a time.

"Halt and dismount from your vehicle," a loud voice droned from above. "You have entered a restricted area and are required to show identification."

Restricted area my ass. The canyon hadn't been "restricted" for the past two decades. It was just a bullshit excuse the pols used when they felt like searching someone. Cormak leaned over even lower, urging his roader to speed up. Red dust churned up on either side of him, and every time he went over a rock or a dip in the road, the bike flew into the air.

The entrance to the canyon loomed up ahead, a narrow gash in the red-dirt hill. There was no way the zipcraft would fit through it. If Cormak could make it there in time, the pol would have to give up the chase.

"Halt and dismount from your vehicle," the voice commanded. "This is your final warning."

The canyon was a hundred mitons away. Now ninety. Cormak sped up even more. Seventy. He glanced over his shoulder and cursed. Why wasn't the zipcraft turning around?

The canyon entrance grew larger. Now he was forty mitons away. Thirty. The canyon was only about seven mitons across, barely wide enough for two roaders to drive side by side, let alone a zipcraft. The pol was going to pull up soon. He *had* to.

A sudden rush of hot air nearly knocked Cormak off his bike. The zipcraft had dropped closer to the ground and was now driving alongside him. "Pull over," the pol shouted.

In response, Cormak crouched even lower and slammed the accelerator as far as it would go. He aimed for the canyon entrance and held his breath, praying that the pol wouldn't try to speed ahead and block him, and end up killing them both.

He plunged into shadow as the canyon walls soared up on either side of him, then glanced over his shoulder just in time to see the zipcraft veer sharply to the left. A few seconds later, he heard the crunch of metal followed by a thud.

Cormak braked so hard that the roader spun out, slamming against the wall of the canyon. For a moment, he stayed there, slumped over and panting as dull pain throbbed through his ribs. But as he watched the pol's shadow emerge from the battered zipcraft, Cormak let out a long breath. There was no chance of that guy catching up with him now. He straightened up and revved the engine, smiling as it drowned out the echoes of the pol's curses.

It was early afternoon by the time Cormak returned to Tower B, which meant he'd only have time to sleep for an hour before heading out again. The second the airlock hissed shut behind him, he yanked off his helmet, sending beads of sweat everywhere. He locked up his roader and started trudging up the thirty-one flights of stairs without bothering to check whether the elevator had finally been repaired.

Cormak managed to make it into his apartment without running into any of his neighbors, thank Antares. Too much time had passed since Rex's death for them to offer more condolences, but Cormak could tell they didn't feel comfortable making normal small talk either. You'd think in a place like Sector 23, where grief circulated with the endlessly refiltered air, people would know how to deal with loss. He couldn't think of a single family that hadn't been touched by tragedy.

As usual, the tiny living room managed to look bare and messy all at once. Nutrition-packet wrappers were strewn across the floor and the threadbare couch, and dirty clothes were draped over the chairs. When Rex was alive, the apartment had been shabby but spotless. Even though he was only three years older than Cormak, Rex had often seemed more like a parent than a brother. After their father died, Rex had been the one to haggle over the rent, brave the finicky gas stove to cook an occasional hot meal, and encourage Cormak to complete his homework long after his teachers stopped caring about it.

Cormak closed his eyes and allowed the familiar cloud of pain to envelop him. He hadn't even known that Rex was working in the Hobart Barrens mine until he'd been notified about the accident. His brother had had a safe job as a janitor at the shuttleport and was studying for pilot school entrance exams. Why would he have given all that up for a short-term gig in the most treacherous region on Deva? Only the most desperate people went to work in the Hobart

Barrens, an enormous crater where earthquakes caused mines to collapse and boiling-hot steam shot up from cracks in the ground.

For the first few days after Rex disappeared, Cormak hadn't worried. Rex often took on extra shifts, and it wasn't unusual for the two of them to go days without running into each other at home. After the fourth day, though, Cormak began to grow anxious. And on the seventh day, he got the news that tore his heart into a thousand jagged pieces. Rex was dead. Cormak would never again hear his goofy, echoing laugh—the only noise loud enough to drown out the incessant whine of the air-filtration system. He'd never roll his eyes while Rex did one of his terrible impressions that all sounded exactly the same. He'd never again feel the comforting weight of Rex's large hand on his shoulder as he said, "Everything's going to be okay." Words that had always filled Cormak's chest with warmth. Words that had turned out to be a lie.

Cormak pressed his hand against the wall and forced himself to breathe through the pain until it subsided. He needed to catch a few hours of sleep before his next run. As he took a few weary steps forward, his stomach rumbled angrily. Work tonight was going to be brutal if he didn't eat something first, but the kitchen was completely bare. To his immense frustration, he'd had to buy a replacement gear for his roader yesterday—Cormak usually scavenged for parts, but after days of fruitless searching, he'd ended up shelling out for the gear—and now there was no money left for food. He needed something to sell, and over the past few months he'd already pawned every valuable thing he'd ever owned: the watch he'd inherited from his father; his grandfather's vintage roader; the one piece of jewelry his mother, who'd died shortly after Cormak's birth, had ever owned. There was only one room he hadn't pillaged.

Cormak stared at the door he hadn't opened since Rex died. The thought of rooting through his brother's things made his heart cramp, but Rex would be furious if he knew Cormak was going hungry to avoid selling Rex's belongings.

He forced himself to walk toward the door, then slipped into the second minuscule bedroom. The air felt as heavy and still as that of a tomb, and Cormak found himself holding his breath.

Everything was in perfect order except for a pair of boots that lay on the floor a few centimitons apart near the door. A new wave of pain crashed through him as he stepped gingerly over the boots, careful not to brush against them. Something about their arrangement felt vital, active, as if the person who'd kicked them off would be back any minute.

The bed was made, of course. Rex had tucked the sheets neatly under the mattress the last time he'd gotten up. Had there been a small part of him that had known he was heading off to die, and had taken extra care to leave everything tidy?

Cormak walked to the dresser and let his fingers hover over the top-drawer handle before pulling it open. There was his brother's collection of model fightercrafts, which he'd always let Cormak play with. A stack of old T-shirts. He ran his finger along the top one and shivered.

He shut the top drawer gently and opened the second drawer. It was empty, as was the bottom drawer. Cormak felt a strange mixture of frustration and relief as he looked around the room, and he was just about to leave when something on Rex's pillow caught his eye. He took a few steps forward and realized it was two separate items—an ID card and a battered portable link.

Cormak picked up the ID first, wincing slightly at the sight of his brother's smiling face. Why had his brother left this behind? He set it back down on the pillow and picked up the link. Rex had been so proud when he bought the used gadget; there had been a point when you never saw him without the link clipped to his belt. But reception on Deva was so bad, he eventually stopped carrying it around.

To Cormak's surprise, the message light was flashing.

He pressed the screen and it blinked wearily to life. Some of the messages were junk—discounts for shuttle trips Rex had never been able to afford and ads for "exciting career opportunities" at off-planet companies that hadn't hired anyone from Deva in fifty years. There were a few messages from old friends and acquaintances who must not have heard about Rex's death, and a few who *had* heard and had written anyway as a way to say good-bye.

Cormak was about to close the link when he saw something that made his whole body go rigid. It was an unread message with the subject line *To Cormak*. Hands shaking, Cormak managed to open the message and began to read.

C-man,

I'm sorry I ran off without telling you,
but I didn't want you to worry. This stint
in the Barrens is only ten days, and you

won't *believe* how much they're paying us. If everything goes according to plan, you'll never read this note. I'll be back before you start rooting around my room. But I figured I should leave something behind just in case.

You're probably wondering why I signed up for this job. Well, there's something else I haven't told you yet. I was accepted to the Quatra Fleet Academy. Crazy, right? I didn't tell you I was applying because it was such a long shot. And then when I got in, I didn't want you to worry about being left behind. That's why I'm here. I'm making enough money for you to get off Deva as well. You can go to university on Tri or pilot training school on Chetire—anything. I know you've never believed me, but you're a freaking genius, C-man. You're way smarter than I am, and you can do whatever the hell you want. This way, we'll both get off this

godforsaken planet. We're not going to stay
here and rot away like Dad.

This job isn't as dangerous as everyone
says, and I really doubt anything will go
wrong. But if you're reading this, I guess
something did....

For the love of Antares, I hope you're not
reading this.

If I don't make it home, here's something
you can do for me: I want you to take my
spot at the Academy. I left my ID on my
pillow. You're smarter than all those
Tridians put together, and I can't wait to
see a Devak put them in their place. Because
I'll be watching you, C-man, even if we
don't know from where.

Okay, I've got to stop because this is
making me pretty emotional, and I don't want

you to come home and find me all worked up.
You're never going to read this. I know
you're not. I'll be home in a few days. But
just in case—take care of yourself, Cormak.
I love you.

—Rex

The world disappeared into a blaze of white-hot pain as Cormak fell to the floor. Rex had gone to the Barrens for *him*. He'd chosen to risk his life rather than leave Cormak on his own. Cormak tried to breathe, but it felt like his rib cage had collapsed, his heart impaled by jagged bone. "No," he whispered as he hugged his knees to his chest. "Rex, no."

He shut his eyes as he replayed the final hours he'd spent with Rex: their last dinner together, their last round of stair ball—a game they'd invented long ago—their laughter echoing as loudly as it had when they were kids. The memory had been a source of comfort over the past few terrible months, but now it felt tainted knowing that Rex had been carrying this secret with him the whole time.

If only he'd found the link sooner. If he'd gone through Rex's things earlier, when he first disappeared, Cormak might've been able to do something. He could've hitched or stolen a ride to the Barrens and forced Rex to come home. He could've saved his brother's life.

His hands still shaking, Cormak read the message again. This time, a prickle of pride emerged through the pain. He couldn't quite believe it—Rex had been accepted to the *Quatra Fleet Academy*. It was the most elite school in the solar system, famous for producing legendary Quatra Fleet officers. Until recently, only Tridians had been allowed to attend. Cormak had heard something about the policy changing, but he hadn't paid much attention. The idea of a Devak being admitted to the Academy was too outlandish to imagine. Yet Rex had done it.

Forget becoming a pilot; Rex could've been a goddamn officer.

But it would never happen now. Because that's how shit worked on Deva. No matter how hard you tried or whatever good fortune you stumbled upon, something screwed you over. Frustration ran hot through Cormak's veins. Rex, the kindest, smartest person he knew, had won the chance of a lifetime—but that life had been cut short. Cormak wrenched his arm back and hurled the link through the air. It struck the wall with a satisfying *crack*.

He let out a long breath, then inhaled again, relaxing slightly as oxygen finally reached his lungs. Slowly, he stood up and, with trembling hands, reached for the ID on the pillow. Cormak stared at his brother's smiling face and thought about what Rex had said in his message. *If I don't make it home, here's something you can do for me: I want you to take my spot at the Academy.* That was crazy talk. Cormak couldn't just take his brother's spot. The location of the Academy was top secret; there was no way an imposter could just waltz in with a fake ID. If he was caught, he'd be put in federation prison or worse. And even if he somehow managed to make it inside, he'd be taking classes with the smartest kids in the solar system. It wouldn't be long until someone noticed that Cormak was out of his league.

He ran his finger along the ID photo. Cormak knew that smile so well, it was hard to believe he'd never see it in real life again. It's the smile that must've crossed Rex's face as he'd written, *You're smarter than all those Tridians put together, and I can't wait to see a Devak put them in their place.*

It was so risky, it was practically a suicide mission. A thousand things could go wrong, and the idea of Cormak's responsible, rule-following brother encouraging him to commit identity fraud was laughably absurd. Yet that somehow made it feel all the more urgent. Rex had wanted this opportunity for Cormak so badly, he was willing to send his little brother into danger.

This was Cormak's one chance to get off Deva. If he stayed, it'd be just a matter of time before he ended up riddled with tumors or a pol's bullets. For the first time in eight months, Cormak felt something other than anger, grief, or despair stirring in his stomach, something he never thought he'd feel again—hope. He couldn't bring his brother back to life, but perhaps he could, in a way, make Rex's dream come true. He was going to make Rex proud whatever the cost.

CHAPTER 2

ARRAN

"Wait! Don't eat that!"

Arran glanced up to see a girl with curly purple-streaked hair looking at him with alarm. He stared back, as startled by her sudden appearance as he was by the concern in her voice. Arran had arrived at the shuttleport almost two hours early and sat on one of the padded benches to wait. For security purposes, all commercial flights had been canceled that day. The only people allowed inside were Quatra Fleet cadets and their families, and the circular atrium had been nearly empty, silent except for the squeak of the sanitation bot cleaning the floors and the cheery voices from the monitors. The ads repeated so often that Arran could recite them all verbatim.

Blast off on the trip of a lifetime! The mountains of Urud are waiting for you. Just one parsec away!

It's always sunny on Loos, the planet closest to the sun!

Every three or four minutes, the exotic travel images were replaced by a peaceful image of space with relaxing music accompanying the gentle twinkle of the stars. Then the music would turn shrill and urgent as a huge fighter-craft appeared in the background, followed by another, then another. As the first one filled the screen, it released a hail-storm of exploding bombs. *The Specters are coming. Will you let them in without a fight? The Quatra Fleet needs you!*

Although it'd been two years since the last attack—the one that had targeted Arran's planet, Chetire—everyone knew it was just a matter of time before the Specters arrived again. But this time, Arran wouldn't be cowering at home. He'd be training to fight back.

Arran realized the purple-haired girl was still watching him, and he looked down at the roll his mother had tucked into his bag that morning. "Why shouldn't I eat this?"

"Because you're going to vomit the moment we hit escape velocity."

"Oh, right," Arran said, blushing as he carefully re-wrapped the roll in the cloth napkin. It was the one with the blue flowers, his favorite. He wondered if his mother had done that on purpose, sending him off with a little piece of home.

"Don't worry about it." The girl smiled kindly. "I've never been on a shuttle either. I just did a bunch of research on interplanetary travel."

Arran stood and ran his hands though his hair, a nervous tic he'd never been able to break. "That was a good idea," he said, relieved that he wouldn't be the only space-sick novice. He'd never even left F Territory—the remotest province on Chetire—let alone gone off planet. His family had always been miners, and when he'd received his acceptance notice from the Academy, he'd been days away from signing a ten-year contract with the mining company. Ten years of working twelve-hour days more than four hundred mitons below the frozen ground. He still couldn't quite believe his luck. Ending up in the mines had been his greatest fear, but no matter how hard he'd tried, he couldn't figure out an alternative. No one born on Chetire ever got off Chetire.

Until now.

He just wished he'd done more research himself. Arran was used to being the knowledgeable one; he couldn't count the number of times he'd been roughed up after school for asking "pointless questions" that kept the weary instructor from releasing the class early. Once, while applying ointment to Arran's swollen eye, his mother had gently suggested that perhaps it might be better to save his questions for the library, but he knew that would never work. When something sparked Arran's curiosity, it quickly consumed all other thoughts... including how easily he bruised.

A pale girl approached Arran and the purple-haired girl. "Are you also headed to the Academy?" she asked, looking slightly anxious.

"Yes." Arran bowed his head, the proper way to greet a peer on Chetire. "I'm Arran."

She returned the gesture. "Mhairi."

Once the girl with purple hair introduced herself as Sula, Mhairi cast a worried look over her shoulder at a man and woman, still bundled in their snow-covered wraps, hovering near the wall. "I should probably say good-bye to my parents. I don't want everyone to know they came with me."

Sula smiled. "Mine would've come if they could have afforded it. It's not every day the first group of Chetrians departs for the Quatra Fleet Academy."

"It sounds like you're reading from your memoir," Arran said, careful to keep his tone light so she wouldn't think he was mocking her. Because Sula was right. As self-important as it sounded to say aloud, they were making history. He just hoped he wouldn't let anyone down.

For millennia, Tri had been the only inhabited planet in the solar system. However, as technology improved, the Tridians terraformed the first settlements on tropical Loos and established mining outposts on toxic Deva and frozen Chetire. The poor Tridians who emigrated to work on these planets became known as Settlers. After a few generations, the number of Settlers far exceeded that of the Tridian business owners, and the Settlers began to push for self-rule, launching campaigns for independence that had ended fruitlessly but peacefully on Loos and resulted in violent wars on Chetire and Deva.

In the aftermath, the Quatra Federation had put strict rules in place to prevent further uprisings. Settlers weren't allowed to vote, attend Tridian universities, start businesses, or even take legal action against Tridians. And while they could enlist in the infantry, they couldn't hold any other positions in the Quatra Fleet, let alone apply to the Academy.

However, the Quatra Fleet commander had created shock waves last year with a new policy that allowed any Settler between the ages of sixteen and eighteen to apply to the Academy. Cynics on Chetire scoffed at the notion that the commander had suddenly become open-minded; they claimed that the Specter attacks had simply created a need for more officers. But Arran believed what Commander Stepney had said in his now-famous speech—that soldiers would have more faith in their leaders if their superior officers came from their home planet and that there were untapped pools of talent across the solar system.

Still, that hadn't been enough to bring everyone on board. There'd been considerable opposition on Tri, especially once it had been announced that, after centuries of admitting eighty new Tridians every year, the Academy would now accept twenty cadets from each of the four planets. The most vocal opponent was an admiral named Larz Muscatine, who claimed that opening the Academy to Settlers would weaken the Quatra Fleet.

Arran couldn't wait to prove him wrong.

Over the next half an hour, the other Chetrian cadets arrived. A few lived locally in Haansgaard, the capital city, but most had clearly traveled a considerable distance to the shuttleport. One boy was trembling so much the others assumed he had frostbite and all piled their coats on top of him. But it turned out he was just nervous.

"Do you know when we get our squadron assignments?" Mhairi asked from the bench where she'd slumped down surrounded by her bags. Arran felt a tingle of excitement. Long before he had even dreamed about attending the Academy, he'd heard stories about the tournament, an intense competition among cadets. Students were broken up into squadrons of four and assigned roles based on a notoriously rigorous aptitude exam: either captain, pilot, technology officer, or intelligence officer. The winning squadron was always featured in news memos around the system, heralded as the next generation of heroes training to fight the Specters.

"I'm not sure," Sula said. For the first time since her arrival, she sounded slightly nervous. "But I definitely want to be a pilot."

"Really?" Mhairi said, sounding impressed. "Have you actually flown before?"

Sula shook her head. "No, but I think that after the aptitude exam—"

A pale boy with shoulder-length brown hair cut her off with a snort. "You'll be lucky to *finish* the aptitude exam." He was the only one of them with a link, and he didn't look up when he spoke. Arran had considered asking the boy if he could borrow the link to send his mother a message—just to let her know he'd made it to Haansgaard safely. But after hearing him speak, Arran thought better of it.

"Excuse me?" Sula said, eyebrows raised.

"It's nothing personal," the boy said, finally looking up from his device. "But we need to accept the facts—we're in way over our heads. These Tridian kids have been preparing for the aptitude exam since *birth*."

A few of the cadets exchanged nervous glances while Sula shot the boy a withering look that cemented Arran's favorable opinion of her. "You can't prepare for the exam," she said. "It measures natural aptitude."

"Really?" the boy scoffed. "In that case, why do the wealthiest Tridians hire Academy instructors to tutor their kids? My uncle worked on Tri, so he saw it firsthand. You have no idea what we're going up against."

"Speak for yourself," Sula said, raising her chin. "Personally, I'm excited to put those Tri snobs in their place."

Most of the others murmured their agreement, and despite the knot of anxiety in his stomach, Arran nodded. He couldn't let himself be intimidated. Not after he'd worked so hard to get here, studying late into the night while his mother scrubbed floors for fourteen hours a day to support him.

With the time difference, it'd be evening in F Territory by now. Arran imagined his mother alone in their tiny cabin, warming her hands around a cup of tea as the clanking radiator filled the room with more noise than heat. What had she eaten for dinner? Arran's heart cramped as he pictured her setting the table for one—one plate, one fork, one knife, and one carefully folded cloth napkin. What would she do for the rest of the evening with no one to talk to? She'd never become close with any of their neighbors—her long shifts cleaning at the fyron mining company's headquarters didn't allow for much socializing. Arran couldn't remember a time when his mother hadn't looked weary. Yet when he'd suggested that he give up the scholarship and stay home, her eyes had grown fiercer than he'd ever seen them. "No," she'd said, trembling slightly as she placed her hand on his arm. "You have to go. You deserve so much better than this." She'd gestured around the sparsely furnished but spotless cabin.

"But what about you? Won't you be lonely?"

"I'll be fine." She'd forced a smile. "How can I be lonely when I have so many wonderful thoughts to keep me company? All I have to do is look up at the sky, and I'll be able to picture you at the Academy learning to be a hero."

Arran glanced around the crowd of new cadets. A few were visibly nervous; some affected an air of indifference, seemingly unruffled by the prospect of boarding a shuttle bound for the Academy's secret location; and a few stood rigidly, shoulders back as if awaiting inspection. Perhaps some of them *would* become heroes the next time they fought the Specters. And perhaps—Arran suppressed a shiver—some would sacrifice everything and become another name on the casualty list.

"Who's that?" Sula asked quietly, gesturing at a boy talking to a Quatra Fleet officer on the other side of the otherwise empty shuttleport. "There are already twenty of us here." Much had been made in the news about the twenty Chetrians headed for the Academy, though none of their names had been released.

Arran watched as the boy nodded, then began making his way toward the others. "Maybe they added one more at the last minute," Arran said. But as the boy got closer, it became clear that he wasn't Chetrian. Unlike the other new cadets who looked around the shuttleport with either wide-eyed wonder or forced nonchalance, he seemed genuinely relaxed. And instead of layers of wool and fur, he wore a thin black jacket that could only be thermalskin—material a hundred times warmer than fur and about a thousand times more expensive. The local mine owner wore a similar jacket on his yearly visit from Tri.

Arran automatically stiffened, bracing for the hint of disdain he'd come to expect from most Tridians, but to his surprise, the boy smiled warmly as he approached the group. He had fair skin, smooth dark hair, and—as Arran noticed when the boy came to a stop next to Sula—deep green eyes. "Are you all heading to the Academy?" the boy asked.

"We are," Sula said with a smile, though she looked a bit warier than before.

"Oh, good. I thought I was late. I'm Dash."

"Sula." She'd just started to bow her head when Dash extended his hand. Sula stared at it, startled by the gesture.

Dash's friendly smile faded a fraction as confusion flashed across his face. Arran remembered that customs were different on Tri, where most people didn't spend their days elbow deep in poisonous sludge—the by-product of fyron and the gas that allowed miners to extract it from the ground.

"I'm Arran," he said, grasping the boy's hand.

"Nice to meet you," Dash said. His smile returned and his green eyes brightened, making Arran's stomach tingle slightly. He wasn't used to boys who looked like Dash smiling at him like that.

"Where are you from?" Sula asked. She was clearly trying to sound politely curious but couldn't quite keep a note of suspicion out of her voice.

"I'm from Evoline, on Tri," Dash said cheerfully. "I was just here for pilot training. There's a school in the Chetrian tundra." He looked around the group, and when no one responded, he continued. "Less-crowded airspace."

A few of the Chetrians exchanged nervous looks while the boy with the link smiled smugly, pleased to have been proven right. "Thought you'd get a head start?" Sula asked.

Dash grinned sheepishly, revealing dimples that made the tingle in Arran's stomach spread to his chest. "I'm not sure it counts as a head start. I was there for three weeks, and I never managed to land without my instructor grabbing the controls. I didn't know there were so many colorful curse words on Chetire."

Sula tried to exchange an irritated glance with Arran, but he pretended not to notice.

"Good morning, cadets!" a deep voice boomed. A lean, white-haired man in a Quatra Fleet uniform strode toward them—the officer Dash had been speaking with before. "I'm Sergeant Pond, one of the deans at the Academy. I'll be escorting you on the shuttle."

Arran stood up straighter, and out of the corner of his eye he saw most of the others do the same. This was it. From this point forward, everything they said or did would be evaluated. Only a portion of the cadets would enter the Quatra Fleet as officers when they graduated in three years. At the end of their first year, anyone with middling grades—or who fared badly in the tournament—would be transferred to a less competitive training program. But it wasn't just Arran's future at stake; it was up to this first class of cadets to prove that Chetrians belonged at the Academy and in the upper ranks of the Quatra Fleet.

Sergeant Pond fiddled with a band on his wrist until a block of translucent orange text appeared in the air. A list of names and holopics of faces. Arran's heart began to pound. It was really happening. He was actually heading to the Academy. "All right, let's see who we have...." Pond said, waving his finger through the air to scroll. "Cadet Trembo."

Sula stepped forward. "Here."

Pond looked from her to the holopic of her face, then swiped her name, turning the text blue. "Cadet Feng."

A short boy with broad shoulders raised a muscular arm. "Here."

Again, Pond's eyes darted from the holopic to the cadet, confirming his identity. "Cadet Korbet."

Arran cleared his throat. "Here," he said, his voice slightly higher than usual.

Instead of looking at the holopic, Pond kept his gaze fixed on Arran. Arran shifted uneasily as worry knotted his stomach. Had there been some mistake? What if his acceptance notice had been meant for someone else?

Pond gave him an appraising look. "Interesting...so this is the Chetrian who received the highest score on the entrance exam. I'll be keeping an eye on you, Korbet." Pond smiled, and the knot of worry in Arran's stomach loosened slightly, replaced by a sensation he wasn't used to. Pride. But then his cheeks flushed as he heard the other cadets start to whisper as they stared at him curiously. He didn't want them to think he was conceited; there was a lot more to becoming a cadet than doing well on the exam.

Pond ran through the rest of the cadets, skipping over Dash, who'd apparently checked in with him earlier. "All right, cadets, time to go. Come with me," Pond said.

The cadets slung their packs over their shoulders and

followed Sergeant Pond through the atrium toward a door flanked by two uniformed women. They saluted him and stepped aside as the door slid open with a hiss.

"So what did you score?" Sula asked, falling into step next to Arran.

He glanced around before saying quietly, "Two twenty-three."

The whispers stopped, replaced by a heavy silence. *"Two hundred twenty-three,"* Sula repeated after a long moment. "Whoa."

A few minutes later, Arran had stowed his pack in the compartment below his seat and was doing his best to secure his harness without fumbling. The shuttle's cabin was circular, with about two dozen seats arranged around the perimeter. Arran had taken the first empty seat he'd seen, eager to escape the murmurs of the other cadets.

The buckle bounced out of the fastener, and Arran suppressed a groan. He tried again, still without success, as he wondered which of the other passengers would be the first to notice that the kid who'd scored a 223 couldn't work the harness.

Something soft brushed against his arm. "It goes in this

way," Dash said, yanking on the two shoulder straps and fastening the belt into the buckle at Arran's waist.

"Thanks," Arran said. Despite his relief, the heat in his cheeks intensified.

"No problem." Dash sank back into his own seat and fastened the buckle in one fluid motion.

A soft *ding* rang from the speakers, followed by a programmed female voice. *"Hello, and welcome aboard this intersystem shuttle flight to...destination classified."* A few of the cadets exchanged excited looks. *"Enjoy your journey."*

Arran grinned, his nervousness draining away. He forced himself to keep his eyes open during the jarring, rumbling launch even when it felt like every bone in his body was being jolted out of place. He didn't want to miss the moment when the shuttle shot out of Chetire's atmosphere, carrying Arran off the planet for the very first time in his life.

In the window across from him, the snow-filled skyline of Haansgaard shrank. The barren tundra spread out endlessly in all directions, sparsely dotted with the odd homestead or mining facility. An ache filled Arran's chest as he thought about his mother sitting at home in their tiny cabin a three days' journey away. He pictured her drinking her tea, staring at the gray sky out the window, trying to catch a glimpse of the shuttle.

The rattling suddenly stopped, leaving everything strangely still and quiet. The windows were no longer filled with swirling snow and clouds—they were full of stars.

The harness straps dug into Arran's shoulders as he floated up from his seat, his head spinning from the violent launch, the strange sensation of zero gravity…and something else. The hazy gray planet grew smaller until it became just another shape among the stars, and all at once, Arran understood what it really meant to live on the remotest planet in the solar system.

Out of the corner of his eye, Arran glanced at Dash. His eyes were closed, a peaceful expression on his face.

Arran smiled, realizing that for the first time ever, he felt completely weightless.

And completely free.

CHAPTER 3

ORELIA

"Proceed to the auditorium. First-year orientation begins in ten minutes. Based on your current location, estimated travel time is eight minutes." Orelia flinched as the voice rang in her ear. Upon arriving at the Academy, every new cadet had been given a link and fitted with a monitor that provided personalized instructions.

It was the most ridiculous device Orelia had ever seen. Surely anyone smart enough to gain admission to the Academy could get through the day without a machine telling them what to do.

She tugged at her strangely constrictive jacket with its two rows of buttons, then glanced down at the badge on the right side of her chest.

Orelia Kerr

Squadron: Unknown

Rank: Unknown

The brightly lit corridor was full of uniformed cadets. The second and third-year students, all from Tri, smiled widely as they jostled the crowd to catch up with friends. The first-years walked quietly in groups of three or four, sticking close to their new roommates, all in gray uniforms with badges like Orelia's.

There were people everywhere she looked, but Orelia had never felt so alone in her entire life. She could've walked to orientation with her roommates, but she was in no hurry to use her fake Loosian accent at length. So far, she'd managed to avoid speaking more than a sentence or two since boarding the shuttle to the Academy.

Despite years of preparation, she found everything about the Academy bewildering, from the taps that sensed your body temperature to the attendants zipping through the halls, their remarkably human voices at odds with their smooth, expressionless metal faces. She couldn't even walk down the corridor without feeling awkward. The Academy was built in a rotating space station with artificial gravity that was stronger than the gravity on her home planet. So, despite all the conditioning she'd done to maximize her strength and endurance, she was exhausted after just a few hours of wandering around the Academy.

Once she reached the auditorium, she took the first seat she could find and tried to catch her breath as she stared out the enormous windows, watching jagged chunks of ice zoom past, deflected by the Academy's shields. Eighty first-year cadets filed into seats facing a stage on which two men and a woman stood talking quietly among themselves.

Orelia felt a tremor of excitement. *I made it*, she thought. *I'm actually here.* On the shuttle from Loos, the windows had gone dark shortly after takeoff. Even the cadets weren't permitted to know the exact location of the Academy.

She watched the rest of the first-year cadets file into the auditorium. Some were so excited, they practically bounced down the aisle as they searched for an empty seat. Others moved more hesitantly, looking with trepidation from one chair to another as if this were a test they hadn't prepared for. One nervous-looking girl caught Orelia's eye and smiled, but Orelia kept her face placid as she turned away.

The woman onstage stepped forward, and the buzz of background noise died away.

"I'm Admiral Haze, superintendent of the Quatra Fleet

Academy, and it's my honor to welcome you to the Quatra Fleet. Today marks one of the most significant transitions of your lives. You're no longer civilians. From this moment forward, you belong to the most elite force in the solar system. Over the past few centuries, the Quatra Fleet has explored our world, organized the first settlements, and ushered in a new era of peace and prosperity." Next to Orelia, a few cadets exchanged wary looks. She assumed they were Settlers from the outer planets that, according to her tutors, hadn't experienced much peace or prosperity. The rebellions on Chetire and Deva had been subdued with ruthless violence. "But now the Fleet has been charged with the most important task of all: protecting our species from those who wish to destroy us."

Orelia's heart began to beat angrily, but after a few deep breaths, her pulse returned to normal. She'd spent years practicing relaxation techniques for just this purpose.

"We know it's just a matter of time before the next attack, and our best line of defense is *you*. The future commander of the Quatra Fleet is somewhere in this room. As is the engineer who'll design the weapons we need to win the war. There's a role for everyone in the fight against the Specters, though each person might be on a slightly different path.

At the end of your first year, we'll assess your performance and determine the best use of your abilities. Some of you will return to the Academy for two more years to train as officers, while others will be reassigned to programs better suited to your strengths."

Nervous whispers flew through the crowd. Admiral Haze cleared her throat sharply, and the room quieted down. "Classes begin tomorrow, right after the aptitude test. Based on the results of this exam, you'll be placed in squadrons, each with a captain, pilot, technology officer, and intelligence officer. You'll train in simulcrafts, and every term, your squadron will compete in a tournament designed to test your intelligence, creativity, temperament, and leadership skills. Each week, you'll go head-to-head against another squadron, and the victor will advance to the next round.

"At the end of the term, the winning squadron will have the privilege of carrying out a mission in an actual fighter-craft instead of a simulator. They will also be exempt from the usual review process and automatically continue their officer training at the Academy."

The other first-years exchanged anxious and excited looks. But for Orelia, the prospect of distinguishing herself to the fleet leadership meant nothing. And if she got her way, *none* of the cadets in this room would ever become officers.

"Your performance in the tournament matters, but your academic performance is equally important, and it's essential that you devote as much energy to your studies as you do to squadron training." Orelia looked around the crowded auditorium, cringing slightly as she imagined being locked in a tiny simulcraft with three other cadets for hours on end.

"With that business concluded, it's my privilege to introduce our special guest. Please welcome Horace Stepney, commander of the Quatra Fleet." Applause filled the room as the elder of the two men onstage stepped forward. "Thank you, Admiral, and welcomé, cadets. It's a pleasure to be here on this momentous occasion. After five hundred years of turning out some of the finest Tridian officers in history, the Academy now has the privilege of training cadets from all four planets in the Quatra System." He paused and smiled slightly as ripples of excitement passed through certain sections of the auditorium. "We've clung to outdated traditions for too long, and in doing so, countless talented individuals have missed the opportunity to serve the Quatra Federation. That's why I couldn't be prouder to be standing here in front of the next generation of fleet leaders from Tri, Deva, Loos, and Chetire." More applause broke out, and Commander Stepney nodded. "You've all worked incredibly hard to get here, and I congratulate you on your achievement."

He paused, and his expression hardened. "But the real challenge has just begun. Many of you are used to being the brightest students in your communities. Now you are among equals, people as intelligent and as driven as you are, and your instructors are leaders in their fields. They are not here to coddle you. They are here to challenge you, to push you to your mental and physical limits so you can achieve your fullest potential. The most important thing to remember is that you are not here to earn individual glory. You are here because the twenty billion people in our solar system have entrusted us with the survival of our species."

All around the auditorium, the windows darkened and grew opaque. The stars faded as a series of images flashed across the screens: Evoline, the capital city of Tri, shrouded in smoke as its famous skyline burned; a little girl on Chetire staring up at a massive starship hovering on the horizon; piles of bodies in the streets of Haansgaard. The whispers stopped as the room filled with a heavy, uneasy silence.

Dread and disgust filled Orelia's stomach. This was it. She knew she'd have to face this moment at some point, but she didn't think it would happen on her very first day.

"It's been two years since the last attack, but we know it's just a matter of time before the Specters return. Our enemy comes from a harsh system with severely limited resources a couple of light years away. The survival of their species is all that matters, and they don't care how many of their own they have to sacrifice to secure the resources they need. They certainly don't care how many of *us* they have to destroy. But the next time the Specters attack, we'll be ready for them. That's why you're all here. After three years of intense training, the best of you will be prepared to enter the fleet as officers and join the fight to protect our people." The grisly images faded, and the windows grew transparent again. But this time, the twinkling stars seemed more menacing than beautiful. "I've spoken long enough. I believe it's almost time for dinner. Is that right, Admiral Haze?"

She nodded curtly. "You are all dismissed."

Orelia stood up and followed the other cadets filing out of their row to join the crowd heading back toward the dorms. The mood had changed noticeably, and those who spoke did so in hushed tones.

"I hate it when they show those snaps," murmured a tall boy with dark skin and a serious expression.

Out of the corner of her eye, Orelia saw his companion's jaw tighten. "I think they should show them every day. Everyone gets so caught up in rankings and the tournament, they forget that we're not here to win prizes. We're here to learn how to kill Specters."

Murderers. The word flashed through Orelia's mind with such intensity, she couldn't believe it didn't escape through her skull.

"Hey, Orelia," a girl said, falling into step next to her. It was one of her roommates, Zuzu, a girl from Loos. "Are you heading back to our rooms to change?" Zuzu tugged on the sleeve of her uniform. "I'm glad we don't have to wear these to dinner. This is not a good look on me. What do you think we're having? It's not going to be weird Tridian food, is it? Because there's no way I'm going to survive on crystallized jellycrab for three years. Do you want to walk over together?"

"I'm not going," Orelia said carefully. She hated using her fake Loosian accent in front of real Loosians. "I'm not that hungry."

Zuzu's face fell, but Orelia refused to let herself feel

guilty. She wasn't here to make friends. All that mattered was her mission.

Orelia turned and began to walk in the other direction, exhaling as the sound of footsteps and chatter grew fainter. It was time to get to work. If she didn't start now, her entire mission would be in vain. Her head began to swim as she thought of all the people counting on her and what would happen if she failed. *Get it together*, she told herself as she placed a steadying hand on the wall and tried to take deep breaths.

"Are you all right?" A face was staring down at her. Her vision was still too blurry to make out the expression, but she could hear the concern in his voice.

"Yes...I'm fine...." she said carefully, hoping her accent sounded natural enough to avoid suspicion.

"Would you like me to walk you to the infirmary? You probably just need to lie down for a bit. These trans-system flights can be brutal." The boy was still staring at her intently, as if scanning for some ailment.

"I'm fine," she repeated, wishing she could keep her voice from shaking. She didn't like the way this boy was looking at her. Like she had something to hide. "You're right. It was a long trip from Loos." She prayed he was from one of the other planets and wouldn't start asking her questions about her supposed home.

To her relief, he nodded and said, "Get some rest. You'll feel better soon."

Orelia forced a smile and held it until the boy walked away, then let out a long breath. She'd memorized lots of facts about Loos, but she wasn't eager to put them to the test. Because Orelia wasn't from Loos. Or Tri. She was from a planet called Sylvan, though the boy wouldn't recognize that name. No Quatran would.

Despite all their talk about their enemy, the Quatrans knew nothing about the Specters. They didn't even recognize the one living among them.

CHAPTER 4

VESPER

Nervous chatter filled the corridor as the cadets headed toward the Hive for the aptitude test, but Vesper's heart was beating far too quickly to allow for conversation. The exam was designed to test natural ability, which meant that, technically, there was no way to study for it. However, in order to win a coveted captain assignment, you had to demonstrate both depth and breadth of knowledge, which is why she and everyone she knew had used a tutor. But unlike her fellow Tridians, Vesper didn't just *want* to make captain—her entire future depended on it.

As the cadets began to file into the Hive, an enormous room in the center of the Academy, the chatter gave way to whispers. The screens of hundreds of workspaces were glowing in the dimly lit, windowless room. The cadets' badges had also begun to glow, and Vesper stiffened, wondering who'd be the first to recognize her last name. But to her relief, it seemed like everyone was too busy choosing a workspace to notice.

You've taken hundreds of sample exams, she told herself as she slipped into an empty seat. *It's going to be fine.* Except that "fine" wouldn't be enough. Vesper closed her eyes as the words that had been haunting her for months grew louder.

You just weren't quite good enough.

The first few hours after receiving her Academy acceptance letter had been the happiest of Vesper's life. Her years of studying for the entrance exam had paid off. She was one step closer to her dream of becoming a Quatra Fleet officer just like her mother, Admiral Haze, who'd had a legendary career in the expeditionary force before becoming the superintendent of the Academy. But that night, her mother had called Vesper into her study and, with her trademark directness, explained that Vesper hadn't initially been accepted and that she had used her influence to overrule the admissions committee's decision.

"You just weren't quite good enough," Admiral Haze had said matter-of-factly while Vesper stood there trying to breathe as the world collapsed around her. She'd somehow managed to maintain her composure while her mother warned her that she wouldn't intercede on Vesper's behalf again. "If you don't do well enough to continue on to the second year, there's nothing I can do about it."

"I'll work harder," Vesper had said, trying to keep her voice from quavering. Nothing irritated Admiral Haze more than tears. "I'll prove that I belong at the Academy. I'll...I'll make captain."

Her mother nodded. "Good. Because if you don't stay on the officer track, it's going to reflect very poorly on me. It's one thing to pull strings for someone with potential—it's quite another to do so for someone in over her head."

"Cadets, please take your seats. The exam will begin in two minutes," an automated female voice announced. Vesper took a deep breath and rolled her shoulders a few times. This was it. If she made captain, her mother would have no reason to doubt her, and she'd stop feeling like a fraud.

The dim overhead lights went out, and darkness fell over the room. The Hive was designed to keep people from looking at one another's screens, but Vesper had no interest in what anyone else was doing. This was a competition with herself.

A prompt on the screen asked her to log in. *Cadet identified: Vesper Haze.* And then it began.

The test mixed all subjects together and adapted to the taker in order to produce the most complete picture of a cadet's ability. If you showed potential in one area, the test would feed you more related questions until they became too difficult to answer. The longer the exam lasted, the better, as it meant you had demonstrated a strong grasp of many different subjects.

Vesper breezed through the first few challenges: simple multivariable calculus, a geometric proof, and an activity that simulated landing a fightercraft in the middle of an anticyclonic storm.

Out of the corner of her eye, she caught a flash of movement and a snippet of conversation. "Sit down and start immediately," a voice whispered urgently. "You're already ten minutes behind."

That was enough to momentarily grab Vesper's attention. Who'd show up late to the aptitude test? In the darkness, she could just make out the shape of a boy looking slightly flustered. "I'm sorry. I got lost. Should I sit here?"

"Yes," the voice hissed. "And start *now.*"

Vesper turned her attention back to her screen as a new challenge appeared, and for the next two hours, she forgot about the boy. She was vaguely aware of people leaving as their tests ended, but she knew better than to look around the room to see how many remained. As she identified verbs in a made-up language, decoded an encrypted message, and calculated the escape velocity for Chetire, she felt the Hive emptying. There were fewer coughs, fewer frustrated sighs. She hazarded a glance around the room and was rewarded with the sight of a sea of vacant seats. All except for one.

The boy who'd arrived late was still there.

Vesper pushed her annoyance aside and spent the next ten minutes calibrating a long-range laser that had been hacked by the enemy. The boy didn't matter. She'd taken enough practice exams to know that she was doing extremely well, certainly well enough to secure a spot as one of the squadron captains.

She finished her calculation, pressed *Complete*, and the words *End of exam* flashed across the screen. She let out a sigh of relief.

Vesper hesitated before glancing around the room. What

if the boy had lasted longer than she had? She looked up—
and smiled. She was completely alone.

⌃⌃

Vesper grinned as she entered the first-year common room.
Circular star-filled windows lined one wall, while another
was hung with paintings of famous Quatra Fleet victories.
It felt both cozy and elegant, with upholstered couches
and chairs arranged in clusters. An attendant zipped back
and forth, delivering steaming cups of spineberry tea and
delicate, colorful sugar discs. It seemed so grown-up—the
common room at her prep school on Tri had always been
cluttered with discarded snack wrappers and sports equipment, the chairs covered with stains that defied explanation.

Most of the cadets milled about nervously, unsure of
where they were supposed to sit and whom they were meant
to talk to while they waited for their squadron assignments.
Luckily, Vesper was meeting some people she knew from
home, including her boyfriend, Ward. A few of the other
cadets did double takes when they spotted the name on Vesper's badge, but they were either too polite or too shy to say
anything.

"Over here, Vee!" a voice called. She turned to see Brill

waving to her from one of the couches. Normally, Vesper tried to limit the time she spent with the hypercompetitive Brill, but it was nice to see a familiar—if not wholly comforting—face.

Brill didn't even wait for Vesper to sit down before the inquisition began. "Were you the last one to finish?" she asked.

"I think so," Vesper said airily, as if she hadn't scanned every corner of the dark room before bounding out.

"What a wonderful surprise," Brill said in the syrupy sweet voice that always made Vesper bristle. Though for once in her life, Vesper was in too good a mood to let Brill get under her skin. Besides, it was hard to begrudge Brill for feeling resentful. Every kid on Tri grew up fantasizing about attending the Academy, making captain, and leading their squadron to victory in the famous tournament.

Vesper smiled at Brill and gave what she hoped was a careless shrug. "We'll see. I don't think it's healthy to get too worked up about this stuff," she said with a feigned nonchalance that she knew would drive Brill crazy.

Someone snickered, and Vesper turned to see a strikingly good-looking boy with dark brown skin, high cheekbones, and an amused grin. "Oh, really?" Frey said as he dropped into the empty chair next to the couch. "What about the time you shoved me off the track when it looked like I was going to beat you in drills?"

"That's slander, Frey," Vesper said with a small smile. "They cranked up the wind that day. It was a rogue gust that blew you off the track."

"A *rogue gust*. Right. Then why did I have an elbow-shaped bruise on my ribs the next day?"

"Frey, how'd you do?" Brill cut in, as she tended to do whenever the conversation veered away from her.

"I don't think I did too badly," Frey said, leaning back in his chair with a satisfied smile. "I had some help."

Brill's eyes narrowed. "Wait. Did you—"

"*Shhh*." Frey glanced over his shoulder, then lowered his voice. "Not here."

"You had some, and you didn't tell me?" Brill said indignantly, not bothering to speak any quieter.

"Had what?" Vesper asked, looking from Brill to Frey.

Frey closed his eyes and rubbed his temples. "We really, really can't talk about it here."

"Talk about *what*?" Vesper whispered. She knew she was being annoying, but she hated that Brill knew something she didn't.

"Fine," Frey said with a huff. "I gave myself a little boost before the aptitude test. It's not a big deal. We've been doing it for ages."

"Vega dust," Brill clarified, still not bothering to lower her voice.

Vesper stared at them, her brain racing to make sense of what she'd just heard. They'd been taking *vega dust*? Was this why she'd always felt like she was struggling? *Of course* she'd never been quite able to keep up; she'd been competing against people on enhancements.

Frey must've seen the look of surprise on Vesper's face because he smiled and said, "Though I have to say, it worked better than ever this time. It was like my brain went into hyperdrive."

"I can't *believe* you didn't offer us any," Brill said, narrowing her blue eyes.

Frey shot Brill a warning look. "You'd better be quiet or else I'm not going to share what I have left." He caught Vesper's eye and shook his head. "Look, we've scandalized poor Vee here. Don't worry, Captain Haze, it's safe to use once in a while."

"Greetings, fellow cadets!" Ward's voice boomed. Before Vesper realized what was happening, he'd scooped her off the couch and pulled her with him into one of the arm-chairs. "Isn't this place amazing! I can't believe we're really here."

"Ward," Vesper chided, trying to wriggle free as two peo-ple on a nearby couch exchanged amused looks. She wanted to make a name for herself as one of the promising cadets at the Academy, not as the girl who always sat in her boy-friend's lap. "Not now."

"What's the matter, Vee?" he asked, sounding hurt. "I ran all the way over here so we'd be together for the assignments. I want to see the look on your face when you make captain."

The assurance in his voice was enough to chase away her irritation. He knew how hard she'd worked, how much she needed this. She squeezed his hand. "Nothing's wrong. It's just that people are watching."

"I don't know that I'd call them *people*, necessarily," Brill said before turning to the attendant gliding by. "Can I have a spineberry tea?"

"Come on, Brill," Ward said with a mixture of exaspera-tion and amusement.

She tossed her blond curls over her shoulder. "I just mean you shouldn't worry what some Edgers from the outer plan-ets think about you."

"Brill, cut it out," Vesper said, cringing at the ugly word for Settler before glancing at the cadets on the nearby couch—a boy and a girl staring nervously at the blank squadron board. Despite the fact that they wore the same uniform as Vesper and her friends, she could tell at a glance they were from Deva. The girl's closely cropped hair and the boy's dry skin made it clear that they'd come from a planet with a severe water shortage. "They'll hear you."

"Relax, Vee," Brill said with exaggerated calm. "I think they have bigger things to worry about than eavesdropping on our private conversations."

"Yes, like their grooming habits," Frey whispered with a grin as he inclined his head toward the other couch.

"You should go say hello, Frey," Ward said, wrapping his arms around Vesper. "I thought you said you wanted to hook up with a Settler. Shouldn't you be off stalking your next conquest?"

Brill's curls swished around her face as she shuddered. "You couldn't pay me enough to hook up with a Settler."

Frey raised one of his perfectly arched eyebrows. "What about that time we all went on holiday to Loos?"

"That's different, and you know it," Brill said, blushing. At that moment, the attendant glided up with Brill's tea.

She smiled gratefully, clearly glad for an excuse to collect herself, and took a small sip before speaking again. "Loosians don't want to kill us all in our sleep."

"Neither do the Chetrians or the Devaks," Vesper said. "Dash just spent three weeks on Chetire and said that everyone was really nice."

"That's because the last Chetrian rebellion was hundreds of years ago," Ward said. "If he'd been training on Deva, he'd feel differently. A Tridian family was murdered *last year.*"

"Do we know what time they're posting the squadron assignments?" Vesper asked, eager to change the topic before the conversation grew too heated.

Frey's eyes suddenly darted toward the screen, which was glowing to life. "Right now, it appears."

Vesper leapt to her feet, her heart slamming against her chest. This was it. In a few moments, she'd know whether she'd redeemed herself by making captain or whether she'd be forced to hear those crushing words one more time—*You just weren't quite good enough.*

Grid lines appeared on the screen, forming a chart with the words *Squadron 1* at the top. A few seconds later, names began to populate the cells below.

The room filled with murmurs of pleasure and frustration. Out of the corner of her eye, Vesper saw a squealing girl embrace her slightly dazed but smiling friend while a nearby boy buried his head in his hands. "What do you think? Intelligence or tech?" Ward whispered, nodding at the boy. For reasons no one could quite articulate, intelligence officer and tech officer were seen as less prestigious than pilot or, of course, captain.

But Vesper couldn't spare more than a glance at the boy before turning her attention back to the screen. At any moment, her name would appear, cementing her future.

"Thank Antares," Frey said under his breath as the badge on his chest glowed to life and updated.

Frey Glint

Pilot

Squadron 3

Rank: Unknown

"Congrats," Vesper whispered. While she'd never be satisfied with anything other than captain, she knew this was what Frey wanted.

She took a deep breath and tried to savor the moment. Every famous military career had begun this way, with no-name cadets crowding around the screen in the common room desperate for the chance to prove themselves.

A minute later, the fourth name appeared under *Squadron 11*. Brill squealed when she saw her name in the captain slot. "Well done, my Brill-iant," Frey said, still grinning and jubilant over his own assignment.

Ward grabbed Vesper's hand and squeezed. "You'll be next." Moments later, his name appeared under *Squadron 13*. He was the captain. Ward let out a *whoop* and dropped Vesper's hand as he pumped his fists in the air. "Yes!"

"That's great!" Vesper tried to give Ward a hug, but he was jumping up and down too enthusiastically. She grinned at her goofy yet incredibly clever boyfriend and prayed that she was moments away from a similar celebration.

A few minutes later, *Squadron 20* appeared on the screen. This was it.

Arran Korbet—Technology officer

Orelia Kerr—Intelligence officer

The third name appeared, and Ward cursed under his breath. But Vesper barely heard him. She couldn't hear anything. She couldn't even breathe. It was as if someone had opened the airlock, turning the common room into a vacuum.

Vesper Haze—Pilot

Her stomach sank, then twisted itself into a knot. *No*, she thought, praying that it was a mistake. She'd done so well on the exam. This had to be some kind of system error.

Rex Phobos—Captain

Ward tried to wrap his arm around Vesper, but she pulled away as her head started to spin. She tried to take a deep breath, but something seemed to keep the air from reaching her lungs. *No*, she thought again. *This can't be happening.* After all her hard work, the months and months of constant training, she still wasn't good enough and never would be.

⮙

"I don't know what happened," Vesper said, doing her best to keep her voice steady. "The exam went really well."

On the other side of the desk, her mother surveyed her with an inscrutable expression. Vesper shifted in her uncomfortable chair but managed to stay quiet. She'd learned the hard way not to fill the silence with nervous chatter.

Admiral Haze's office was even more impressive—and even more intimidating—than Vesper had imagined. The shelves were full of her mother's Quatra Fleet medals, and there was an enormous glass case full of antique weapons, including a Chetrian ax and a beautiful old-fashioned laser pulse with an ornately decorated handle. Though the most striking feature by far was the glowing holomap of the Quatra System hovering in the air just above the desk.

Just when Vesper thought she'd have to give in and speak first, Admiral Haze broke the silence. "I'm not sure what to say, Vesper. You assured me that you'd do what it took to make captain."

"I thought I had," Vesper said quietly. Once she'd learned that her mother had orchestrated her acceptance to the Academy, Vesper had put herself on an even stricter training schedule that included two hours of physical conditioning followed by six hours of tutoring in cosmophysics, mechanical engineering, and advanced abstract algebra. But apparently, it hadn't been enough. "I was the last one in the Hive," Vesper continued, taking care not to sound emotional or defensive—two traits Admiral Haze despised. "I thought that meant—"

"Enough. It doesn't matter now." Her mother's expression hardened. "To continue on to your second year, you'll need excellent grades *and* your squadron will have to perform extremely well in the tournament. The admissions committee let you in as a favor to me, but you'll have to prove to them that you belong on the officer track."

"I know," Vesper said, unable to keep her voice from trembling. Her mother's disappointment was even harder to bear than her anger. "I won't let you down again."

"See that you don't," her mother said. "Now, if you'll excuse me, I have a meeting I have to get to."

Vesper rose from her chair and left the office without another word. But as she walked back to her room, she felt her disappointment turn to resolve. No matter what it took, she'd prove that she deserved to be at the Academy, that she deserved to become an officer—and that started with winning the tournament.

CHAPTER 5

CORMAK

This was a huge mistake, Cormak thought as he wandered down the empty corridor. Just a few minutes ago, it had been packed with the cadets who'd spilled out of the common room after the squadron assignments were posted. Most of them had broken off into groups and headed to the canteen, the simulcrafts, or wherever else kids went for fun during the free period before dinner. But now they'd all dispersed, leaving him to explore on his own.

It was Cormak's second day at the Academy. After he'd discovered his brother's message, he'd gone through Rex's link and found departure instructions for the shuttle from Deva. He'd thrown a few things in a bag, jumped on his roader, and raced to the launchport, arriving just seconds before the doors were sealed. He and Rex were close enough in age and looked so much alike that no one could tell from the ID that they were different people. Still, Cormak couldn't quite believe he was here, and he certainly didn't understand how everyone had made friends so quickly. Classes hadn't started yet, and he'd barely spoken to his roommates—a girl from Chetire, a boy from Loos he'd seen once, and a Tridian boy who seemed harmless on his own but unfortunately had a crew of idiotic friends from home who thought it was funny to ask Cormak how gas masks factored into the "mating practices" on Deva.

But Cormak wasn't going to let some shitty Tri kids get to him. He glanced down at the word *Captain* on his uniform badge and smiled. He'd had no idea what to expect from the aptitude test Admiral Haze had mentioned at orientation, but after a slight hiccup that caused him to arrive late, he'd found it surprisingly easy. And now he was captain of his squadron, which was apparently a big deal at the Academy. He wished everyone on Deva could see him now—the teachers who thought he was nothing but trouble, the snobs in the luxury towers who sneered at his dusty clothes. Even Sol, who only thought of him as a good-for-nothing delivery boy. Maybe Rex had been right. Maybe he was smarter than anyone ever gave him credit for.

⋀⋀

Cormak stepped back to admire his handiwork. After a little fiddling, he'd managed to reprogram the attendant to clean dishes instead of pour drinks. He smiled as he watched the battered, slightly rusted machine disinfect ten glasses in under a minute, leaving Cormak free to serve customers. As long as he put the attendant in sleep mode before he left for the night, no one would ever notice.

Rex had pulled a lot strings to get Cormak this job, which was a hell of a lot safer than the other options available to dropouts like him, and it almost paid enough to cover half the rent. But instead of letting Cormak serve drinks—and collect the much-needed tips—the bar owner, Ineke, forced him to clean glasses, claiming that it would cost too much money to reprogram the attendant that'd been pouring drinks for the past ten years. Cormak had offered to do it himself, prompting a warning from Ineke to keep his filthy hands off her most valuable possession.

He'd followed orders for a few weeks, growing increasingly frustrated as he watched customers pocket the change that could've been going to him. If he and Rex didn't pay their back rent this month, they were going to get kicked out of their apartment.

"Did you do that yourself?"

Cormak turned to see a man on the other side of the bar gesturing toward the attendant. He was bald, with heavy eyebrows and unusually smooth skin, as if he didn't spend much time outside with a gas mask strapped to his face. Something about him seemed vaguely familiar, but Cormak wasn't sure why. "Do what?" Cormak asked, feigning confusion.

"Don't pull that shit with me, kid. I can tell that attendant was reprogrammed by an amateur—a pretty talented amateur, though."

Cormak shot a quick glance over his shoulder at the attendant that was now stacking the clean glasses. "Looks fine to me."

"It has the wrong attachments for cleaning. I bet you've never seen a real sanitation bot, have you?"

"Can I get you anything to drink?" Cormak asked, eager to change the subject before any of the regular customers walked in.

"Double nitro spirit."

Cormak poured the drink and set it down in front of the man. "Four skyor."

The man placed a few coins on the bar. "Keep the change."

"Thanks," Cormak said, pocketing the extra coin.

The man gave Cormak an appraising look. "You know, I could use someone like you. A problem solver who's not afraid to take risks. You'd make better money than you do in this shithole."

Cormak felt a thrill of excitement. If the pay was really good, then maybe Rex could quit his job and finally focus on studying. "What would I be doing?"

"A little of this, a little of that," the man said with smirk. "Deliveries, mostly. I need someone who's quick on his feet and can come up with creative solutions, especially when the pols are around."

The excitement drained away, replaced by a much more familiar sensation—disappointment. That's why the man looked so familiar. He was Sol Fergus, the black market H_2O dealer. Working for him was lucrative, but a staggering number of his runners ended up in prison or worse. Yet no matter how many of Sol's employees they arrested, the pols somehow never managed to snag him. If Cormak were on his own, he might try his odds. But there was no way he'd risk leaving Rex in the lurch. They were the only family each of them had, and that was worth far more than anything Sol could pay.

"Thanks for the offer," Cormak said, trying to sound as friendly as possible. From what he'd heard, Sol wasn't someone you wanted to offend. "But I think I'm going to stick around here."

"Suit yourself, kid." Sol downed his drink and set the empty glass back on the counter. "If you change your mind, you can reach me here." He passed Cormak a card with no name or address—just a number.

"Will do," Cormak said, placing the card in his pocket. He'd have to get rid of it as soon as possible. If he got pulled over by the pols tonight, just having Sol's number on him would be reason for arrest.

During the next few hours, the bar became increasingly crowded, and Cormak's pocket grew heavy with coins. If he kept this up, he'd have a real shot at paying the back rent in time to avoid eviction. The idea of handing that much money over to Rex filled Cormak's chest with warmth. All he wanted was for his older brother to have a break from worrying, even if the reprieve was a brief one.

By the time he normally started cleaning up for the night, the bar had emptied out except for a drunk Tridian couple—a man and a woman—who seemed oblivious to the fact that they were the only ones left. Even worse, they hadn't tipped all night, explaining that they were friends of Ineke and she'd told them never to bother. "Can I get you anything else?" Cormak asked pointedly.

"We're fine," the woman said with a tight smile before turning back to her companion.

Cormak suppressed a sigh and went to switch the attendant to sleep mode. Ineke only came in the mornings to do the accounts and would never notice Cormak's upgrades. He reached for the power button, but instead of shutting off, the attendant spun around and sped toward the bar. "Shit," Cormak said under his breath as he watched it pouring glasses of nitro spirit at a frantic pace. He must've made some kind of error during the rewiring. He pressed the power button again, but it only made the attendant move faster. "Shit, shit," he said again. He needed to open the back panel to manually override the program, but that required a special tool in Ineke's office.

Luckily, the Tridian couple didn't seem to notice that the attendant had poured twenty glasses of nitro spirit and showed no sign of stopping. Cormak just had to move quickly, and everything would be okay. He sprinted to Ineke's office, grabbed the tool, and started to run back to the bar.

A shriek pierced the air, and Cormak reached the bar just in time to see the Tridian woman leap to her feet, her face red with rage. "That idiotic machine just poured an entire bottle of nitro spirit on me!" she shouted at Cormak.

"I'm sorry," he said breathlessly as he lunged for the attendant, pried open the panel, and yanked out the wire. The attendant fell still, and the bottle in its hand dropped to the floor with a loud crash. Cormak let out a sigh, then turned to the woman. The front of her expensive-looking white dress was drenched with the pale green liquid. "I'm so sorry," he said again. "I think there's some H_2O in the back. Do you want me to get it for you?"

"H_2O?" she spat. "My dress is ruined. What the hell just happened?"

"I don't know.... The attendant must've malfunctioned," he said.

"This is ridiculous. I'm calling Ineke," the man said, fiddling with his link.

"No, please. That's not necessary. H_2O will get that stain right out. Just give me a chance to—"

"Ineke? It's Dobb. So we're at the bar, and your attendant went haywire. One minute, it was cleaning glasses, and the next, it was pouring nitro spirit all over Leesa.... What? Yeah, he's here.... Hold on." The man extended his wrist toward Cormak. "She wants to talk to you."

Cormak's stomach clenched as he scoured his brain for some plausible explanation. But before he got the chance to speak, Ineke's voice rang out from the man's link. "I told you not to mess with my property. You're fired, moron. And you better leave all your tips in the safe before you go, or I'll have you arrested for theft."

"But I—"

"I'll be over in ten minutes, and if you're still there, I'm calling the pols."

The man smiled smugly as Cormak turned without a word and stomped toward Ineke's office, trembling with anger and shame. How could he have been such an idiot? Rex had called in countless *favors to get Cormak this job, and now he'd let him down. Forget making up the back rent—he wasn't going to have nearly enough to cover his own share. They were going to end up on the streets, and it was all Cormak's fault.*

He reached into his pocket for the money, then stopped when he felt his fingers brush against Sol's card. He'd almost forgotten about their unexpected encounter. Maybe working for Sol wouldn't be so bad. Perhaps he could do a few runs—just until he caught up on rent. With a glance toward the door to make sure the Tridians weren't watching, he reached for the link on Ineke's desk and entered the number.

"Who is this?" Sol said irritably.

"It's Cormak. You met me at the bar tonight."

"What do you want?"

"I've reconsidered your offer."

There was a long pause, and when Sol spoke again, Cormak could hear the smile in his voice. "They always do."

"Are you lost?" Cormak turned to see a pretty girl with brown skin and amber eyes staring at him. He was still getting used to the sight of girls without gas masks, and for a second, he couldn't do more than marvel at her thick lashes and the golden freckles on her nose. "Where are you trying to go?" she asked kindly.

"I'm not sure," he said, too flustered to come up with a lie that would keep him from looking like a loser. "I guess I was just looking around."

"You're a first-year, right?" she asked. Cormak nodded. "Don't worry. This place takes some getting used to. Though—" Her eyes darted to the badge on his uniform, and she smiled. "It seems like you're off to a pretty good start, Captain."

Cormak felt heat rise to his cheeks.

"Classes start tomorrow, so try to have fun while you can," she continued. "Have you been in the zero-gravity room?"

"There's a *zero-gravity* room? Where?" Why, for Antares's sake, were people hanging out in the common room when they could be *floating*?

"Just ask your monitor to direct you."

Cormak's hand went to his ear where the monitor had been affixed yesterday. So far, he hadn't found much use for it. "Directions to the zero-gravity room," he said, feeling slightly self-conscious.

"You are operating at suboptimal capacity due to insufficient

sleep. *Consider returning to your dormitory instead. For more information, say* healthy sleep cycles."

"Zero-gravity room directions," he said again as his cheeks grew warmer.

"Is your monitor being annoying? Don't worry about it," the girl said with a smile. "I'm heading in that direction. I'll walk you. What's your name?"

"Cor—" He stopped, catching himself just in time. "I'm Rex."

"Nice to meet you, Rex. I'm Ellee. Now follow me. You're going to love it." As he fell into step next to her, Cormak glanced out the window, at the stars that his brother had never gotten to see, and thought about everything Rex had done to make this possible for him. His older brother was still looking out for him, just as he always had.

Ten minutes later, Cormak was tightening the strap of his goofy helmet, part of the required safety equipment for the zero-gravity training room. He was also wearing knee-pads, elbow pads, and shin guards. He could barely walk and knew he looked ridiculous, but it didn't matter. In just a moment, he was going to be freaking *weightless*.

After a gleaming attendant—the first one he'd ever seen

that wasn't covered in rust—had confirmed that Cormak was properly outfitted, it opened the sealed doors. The space beyond was dark and seemingly vast, although it was hard to determine the actual dimensions. Shouts and laughter echoed from all directions. There was a large handle on each side of the entrance, presumably to hold on to while you positioned yourself. "Anything I should know?" Cormak asked the attendant.

"Try not to vomit. People tend to be squeamish about coming into contact with bodily fluids."

"Thanks for that image," he said, wondering who'd thought it was a good idea to program the machines with sarcasm.

Cormak took a deep breath, grabbed on to the handles, rocked back on his heels for momentum, then pushed off into the darkness. Holy shit, he was *flying*. He stretched his arms out, unable to keep himself from letting out a dorky, joyful *whoop* as he floated through the air, completely weightless. *Rex would've loved this*, he thought, bracing for the inevitable twinge of sorrow.

He felt his shoulder bump against something. No, someone. "Sorry!" Cormak called cheerfully.

"Watch it, moron," a male voice snapped.

"I said *sorry*," Cormak said, an edge creeping into his voice.

"Sorry," another boy repeated, shortening his vowels to imitate Cormak's Devak accent.

Cormak grabbed on to one of the handholds, then turned to see two Tridian boys floating toward him.

"Leave him alone," a girl said, sounding more bored than concerned.

"Leave him *alone*?" the second boy called over his shoulder. "Didn't you say you wanted to find out what Devaks smelled like up close?"

"*Definitely* didn't say that."

"Don't be shy, Keeli," the first boy said. "I'm sure our friend here won't mind." As the boys approached the wall, they stretched out their arms to grab Cormak.

He ducked away and reached for a different handhold. "Don't you assholes have anything better to do?"

Even in the dim light, he could see one boy's face harden. "Didn't anyone ever teach you what happens to Edgers who don't mind their manners?"

"No, but I'm happy to teach *you* what it feels like to have your nose bashed in." Cormak raised his fists, hoping that the boys were too stupid to know that you couldn't land a good punch in zero gravity.

"Come *on*," Keeli called. "You don't want to get expelled on your first day."

"You'd better learn some manners, space trash," one of the boys muttered under his breath.

Cormak ignored him and pushed off against the wall. A moment later, he was airborne again. He looked around but couldn't see far enough ahead of him to spot anyone. The vast room also seemed quieter than before; he couldn't hear any shrieks or thuds.

Cormak decided to take advantage of the extra space to try a zero-gravity somersault. He tucked his knees to his chest, and nearly completed one perfect rotation when, all of a sudden, he wasn't weightless anymore. He was falling. Panicked, he flailed his arms, desperate to grab on to one of the handles, but he was too far from the wall and plummeting too fast. It was as if a magnet were yanking him toward the floor.

He landed with a *crack* that jostled every bone in his body. "Shit," he muttered. He wasn't sure if he was hurt, and if so, how badly. The wind had been knocked out of him, and he couldn't breathe, let alone move. He wiggled his toes, followed by his fingers. Then, head pounding, he sat up slowly. He was sore all over, but nothing seemed to be broken, thank Antares. What the hell had happened?

"Impact detected," his monitor said. *"Remain in place while we assess damage."*

"Not now," Cormak groaned, rising unsteadily to his feet.

"Damage assessment interrupted. Please hold still."

"Deactivate," he said wearily, knowing that it wouldn't work. He limped toward what appeared to be a service door that led into a narrow hallway. Cursing to himself, he eventually found his way back into the main corridor where, to his irritation, the Tridian boys were standing. "Everything okay?" one of them called while the other smirked.

"Fuck off," Cormak said, wondering why no one else in the zero-gravity room had fallen.

"Damage assessment failed. Report to medical center immediately."

"I guess you still don't see the *gravity* of the situation," the boy said. He had wavy hair and the kind of face you just wanted to punch regardless of what he was saying. The kid could've offered him a thousand skyor, and Cormak would *still* want to punch him in the nose.

A realization fought its way through Cormak's pounding head. "Did you turn on the gravity in there? I could've been killed, asshole."

"Stay where are you. Help is on the way."

The two Tridians laughed. "And what a loss that would've been," the other boy said.

Before Cormak could respond, two attendants zoomed up with a stretcher in between them. "Wait," Cormak said. "I'm fine. I can walk to the medical center myself."

"An order cannot be overridden once we're dispatched," one said.

"Oh, come on," Cormak groaned. "You can follow me there. Just don't make me get on that thing."

"Refusal to follow orders will result in disciplinary action."

Cormak sighed. Being dragged in front of Admiral Haze certainly wouldn't help with his headache. "Fine," he said through gritted teeth, ignoring the laughter of the Tridian boys as he lowered himself onto the stretcher.

A few minutes later, Cormak found himself in the medical center standing next to a full-body scanner. "I think this is overkill," he said to the doctor, a young woman with red hair.

"Just need to scan you quickly," she said, fiddling with

a control panel on the wall. "The sensors in your uniform wouldn't be able to detect a concussion. Now hop in, please."

Cormak stepped into the scanner, and a moment later, a three-dimensional image of his body appeared on the screen next to the doctor. His bones glowed green, and it looked like his organs were color coded. "What's all that?" he asked as long lines of data scrolled down the sidebar.

"Just your vitals. Heart rate. Iron levels. Blood-oxygen content. Antibody levels."

"I thought you were checking me for a concussion?"

"The scanner collects this information automatically," the doctor said. "You might feel a slight pinch now. It's going to take a very small blood sample for a genetic analysis."

"Sure, because I might be genetically predisposed to concussions," Cormak said under his breath.

"Now, let's see.... I don't see any signs of a concussion, so it looks like you're all...oh, wait.... That's strange."

"What? What's wrong?" he asked, feeling a prickle of fear. On Deva, it was just a matter of time before your body began to revolt against the toxic air. Kids younger than he was were transformed into walking masses of tumors. It'd be just his luck to finally make it off planet only to discover that it was too late.

"It's saying that your DNA doesn't match the medical records we have on file." She leaned forward and squinted for a better look.

Cormak's heart lurched against his rib cage before starting to race. "How do you have my file?"

She glanced over his shoulder to shoot him a confused look. "From the mandatory physical you had on Deva."

Cormak's head was spinning. *Of course, Rex would've had to submit his medical records. How could I not have thought of that?*

The doctor sighed. "We're going to have to contact the Sector 23 medical clinic and ask them to send your *correct* records. I didn't realize it was possible to make such a careless mistake, but that's Deva for you." A beep sounded, and the doctor turned toward the screen with a frown. "Is everything all right? Your heart rate just climbed significantly."

"I'm fine," Cormak said, trying to keep his voice steady even though he felt his whole body starting to shake. "Can I go now?" He stepped out of the scanner without waiting for an answer.

"Yes. I'll contact the clinic and get this sorted."

Cormak nodded and forced himself to walk normally, willing his legs not to give out before he made it far enough away from the medical center. When he reached the empty corridor, he gasped, then stretched his arm toward the wall to steady himself. When the Academy received his medical records—or, more accurately, *Rex's* records—they'd realize that the discrepancy in the DNA wasn't an error and discover the truth: that Cormak was an imposter trespassing in the most highly guarded facility in the Quatra System. The punishment for unauthorized entry was twenty years in a high-security prison on Chetire. But Cormak wasn't simply trespassing. Impersonating Rex could conceivably count as treason, the punishment for which was death.

He let his head slam back against the wall, cursing under his breath. No one like him made it off Deva. He'd been an idiot to think he deserved better, and now he was going to pay the price.

CHAPTER 6

ORELIA

"Orelia, stay there!"

Orelia froze. She'd taken cover under the table once the walls began to rattle, but she was scared and wanted to be with her mother. Half the roof was missing, and the room was quickly filling with smoke. "Mama!" she called.

"Don't move," her mother ordered, her voice growing hoarse. Through the swirl of smoke and ash, Orelia could just make out her mother lying on the couch. She'd placed her hand on her stomach, but it wasn't large enough to cover the dark red stain blooming on her shirt.

"You're hurt," Orelia said. "Let me help you."

"Orelia, you have to stay where you are," her mother said in a harsh tone Orelia had never heard before. "It's not over yet."

The walls began to shake again just like Mama said they would. Because Orelia's mother knew everything. She knew exactly which night the moon roses would blossom; she knew how to dive into the lake from the highest ledge without making a splash; and she always knew what was bothering Orelia even when Orelia didn't have the words to explain it to herself.

Orelia hugged her knees to her chest as the rattling grew stronger until it felt like the ground was trying to swallow their house. Through the hole in the ceiling, she could see the sky, though it was a strange color—dark gray with jagged streaks of red, like a piece of torn animal hide. Somewhere nearby, a woman was screaming.

There was a flash of light, and the ground shook even harder than before. "I'll come to you," her mother whispered. With a groan, she slid off the couch and began to crawl toward Orelia, still holding her stomach with one hand.

"Mama," Orelia called, reaching out to help. She stretched as far as she could, but her fingertips weren't long enough to reach her mother. Orelia started to creep out from under the table, but her mother shook her head.

"No," she pleaded. "Orelia, you have to stay right there."

There was another flash of light, and it tore an even larger hole in the sky. Bits of white-hot metal rained down on them, followed *by more chunks of their roof. "Mama!" Orelia shouted as the room filled with dust and smoke.*

This time, there was no one to tell her to stay under the table, but Orelia hugged her knees to her chest anyway. It was what her mother wanted her to do, and she was always right. When the smoke finally cleared, Orelia crawled out to touch the hand she'd been reaching for.

It was already cold.

>>>

"Is anyone sitting there?"

Startled, Orelia looked up to see a boy gesturing at the empty seat next to her. She shook her head, hoping that he wouldn't try to initiate any further conversation—at least not until her memory of the Quatran attack on Sylvan faded and her anger subsided.

Orelia had been at the Academy for three days, and at first, everything had gone according to plan. Sylvan hackers had secured her admission to the Academy by creating an entire dossier of fake Loosian documents, and none of them seemed to have sparked any confusion or suspicion. She was free to focus on her main objective: obtaining the coordinates of the Academy's top-secret location and transmitting them to the Sylvan military.

Ever since the first unprovoked attack fifteen years ago, the Quatrans had been bombing Sylvan with increasing frequency. It had become clear that the only way to defeat the Quatrans once and for all—and keep them from destroying every single person on the planet—was to wipe out the next generation of military leaders. And so, once Orelia's commanding officer received the coordinates, the Sylvans would launch a massive preemptive strike at the heart of the Quatrans' military operations: the Academy itself.

But soon after Orelia arrived, she'd realized that the transponder she'd been given to communicate with the Sylvan base was blocked by whatever cloaking system the Academy used to conceal its location. The Academy-issued links could only transmit outgoing messages within the Quatra System, so although she could receive messages from Sylvan, she couldn't respond, let alone capture the school's coordinates. She'd need to figure out another way.

In the meantime, Orelia's objective was to act like a normal cadet. The first-years had received their squadron assignments the day before, and they were all anyone could talk about. To her amusement, Orelia had been named intel-ligence officer, the position responsible for strategic plan-ning and monitoring external threats—like the Specters.

The boy leaned over. "I can't believe Lieutenant Prateek is our instructor," he whispered, nodding at the empty desk in the front of the room. "He's the one who thwarted the attack on Evoline a few years ago."

Orelia wasn't sure how to reply. She hadn't practiced small talk with her tutors. But the boy didn't seem to be waiting for a response. "I heard he's kind of terrifying. He's really young—I think he only graduated from the Academy three years ago, but he's already won a bunch of medals," the boy continued, his voice a mixture of awe and apprehen-sion. "No one knows why he gave that up to teach. What's your theory?"

That he'll find it hard to thwart the next *Specter attack,* she thought before wracking her brain for a more appropriate response. To her relief, the instructor entered a moment later, cutting off the buzz of conversation.

"Welcome to Advanced Counterintelligence," the in-structor said as he strode toward his desk at the front. "I'm First Lieutenant Zafir Prateek, but addressing me that way wastes time we can't afford to lose, so call me Zafir."

The instructor was indeed young, or he looked young to Orelia, at least. He had dark curly hair, smooth beige skin, and intense, nearly black eyes that scanned the room as he spoke. His gaze hovered on Orelia for a moment, and her skin prickled with heat. Her new instructor was the boy from the corridor, the one who'd stopped to help her during her dizzy spell after orientation.

"Each of you was placed in this class because of your score on the aptitude test, but that doesn't guarantee you'll *stay* in this class. If it seems like you're out of your element, you will be transferred to the introductory course. Counterintelligence requires a special combination of skills, and it may turn out that your time and talents are best spent elsewhere."

Zafir leaned back against his desk and stretched his legs out. Between his trouser hem and polished shoe there was a glint of metal—the rod of a bionic leg Orelia hadn't noticed during their brief encounter. His pose was relaxed, but there was something about him that suggested coiled power. "We'll spend most of the semester discussing intelligence-gathering techniques and their applications for military strategy, but for the next few weeks, I'd like to spend some time on the Specters and what we know about their technology and culture." Zafir pressed a button on the desk that dimmed the lights and projected a holomap on the screen behind him. "The species we call the Specters comes from a solar system nearly six parsecs away. Every planet in the system has a pronounced elliptical orbit that suggests long seasons and dramatic temperature fluctuations, and having evolved in such an extreme environment, the Specters likely developed dramatically different features from Quatrans."

Orelia suppressed a smirk. The physiological distinctions were very minor—her people had slightly increased lung capacity and more red blood cells, which allowed them to hold their breath for longer. This was how the ancient Sylvans had survived the summers, when the oceans swallowed up most of the planet.

"Even if we never make it to the enemy's home planet, even if we never capture one alive, there's still plenty we can learn about them. The most powerful tool you have—" Zafir raised an eyebrow. "Yes? Do you have a question?"

A girl with long dark hair lowered her hand. "I was just wondering—have we ever tried communicating with the Specters?"

Zafir nodded. "That's a good question, one we're going to discuss at great length next week, but the short answer is yes." He went on to talk about communication drones, but his explanation barely registered with Orelia. She was too distracted by what Zafir had just said. What did he mean *if* the Quatrans ever made it to the Specters' home planet? They'd been launching vicious attacks on Sylvan for years. She looked around the room, searching for signs of similar confusion on the cadets' faces, but none of them seemed to have noticed.

"Of course, direct contact would be ideal," Zafir continued, "but since the Specters attacked us unprovoked, we have to assume that they wouldn't take kindly to unexpected visitors."

It took all of Orelia's finely honed self-control to stay silent despite the fury building within her. It was the *Quatrans* who'd attacked the Sylvans unprovoked. Fifteen years ago, the Sylvan military had detected a foreign probe collecting fyron samples and destroyed it. But the probe had apparently already transmitted all the data the Quatrans needed. A few months later, three battlecraft had darkened the skies above the capital city and released a massive bomb. Half a million Sylvans were killed instantly, and nearly two hundred thousand succumbed to their injuries over the following weeks. The Quatrans had returned again the following year, although this time the Sylvan military was ready for them and destroyed two of the ships, forcing the third to retreat. Sylvan intelligence determined that the attackers came from the Quatra System and were after the fyron on Sylvan, forgoing diplomatic means in favor of genocide. In order to save their species and their planet, the Sylvans began launching attacks of their own—mainly on military targets and a few cities with strategic and symbolic value.

Was it possible that Quatran civilians knew none of this? Had their leaders convinced them that the first Specter attack had been an unprovoked massacre instead of justified retribution? The truth was that if the Quatrans had their way, they'd massacre every last Sylvan and then slowly butcher the planet with the precision of a sadistic surgeon. The Sylvans had a moral obligation to defend themselves, to subdue the Quatrans by any means necessary.

Zafir clapped his hands together. "Of course, the first rule of intelligence is not to assume anything before you have evidence to back it up. You have to learn the difference between observation and conjecture, and that's going to be the focus of our first exercise. We're going to divide into pairs and write down inferences about our partners based on specific observations. Everyone stand and find a partner."

Orelia stood up along with the others but didn't move from her desk. Her mind was still reeling from the revelation that the Quatran government was lying to its people about the Specters. By the time she glanced up, the other cadets were all paired off. She felt a brief flicker of relief. Perhaps, since there was an odd number of students, she'd be excused from the exercise. But then, to her dismay, she saw Zafir walking toward her.

"You and I can be partners," he said, pulling up an empty chair and lowering himself into it in one fluid movement. "What's your name?"

"Orelia," she said, relieved that he didn't recognize her from the other day. The last thing she needed was to catch the attention of the Quatra Fleet's most celebrated counter-intelligence officer.

"Would you like to go first?" he asked. It was the nearest she'd been to a Quatran since arriving at the Academy, and her heart wouldn't stop racing. "Or I can start us off if you prefer."

"I'll go," Orelia said hoarsely. She bit her bottom lip and glanced at him again. Up close, his dark eyes were even deeper. He was clean-shaven, but a hint of shadow clung to his sharp jaw. Heat rushed to her cheeks, and without thinking, Orelia closed her eyes and took a deep breath. A pleasing scent filled her head, a familiar combination of salt, sand, and the minerals unique to the sea. "You like to swim in the ocean."

When Zafir didn't respond, Orelia opened her eyes and saw him staring at her in surprise. "How did you know that?"

No, no, no. She'd spoken too quickly, forgetting that Sylvans had evolved a keener sense of smell than the Quatrans had—a necessary survival mechanism on a planet where venturing too close to certain toxic summer blooms could kill you on the spot. "Your deltoid muscles," she said, grasping for an excuse. "It looks like you swim often...in rough conditions."

"Ah, I see," he said, eyeing her in a way that did little to assuage her anxiety. "Nicely done. Okay, it's my turn."

Just stay calm, she commanded herself as his eyes flicked over her. *You're dressed like a cadet. You've been trained to speak like a Loosian. If you're careful, he won't notice your accent.* But he *would* notice if she seemed anxious, and the last thing she needed was to rouse the suspicion of a counterintelligence expert.

After a long moment, he smiled. "I *infer* that you have a high tolerance for pain."

"Why is that?" she asked, mimicking the light, carefree tone she'd heard Zuzu use.

"Because you're not wearing your monitor, and I know from personal experience that it hurts like hell when you remove it yourself."

Orelia's hand flew up to her ear. She'd taken the monitor off last night so she could explore the Academy without anyone tracking her movements.

"I won't tell anyone…this time," Zafir said with an amused smile. "Just be sure to wear it tomorrow, or people will suspect you're trying to hide something."

He's just joking, Orelia told herself. But this time, her breathing techniques weren't enough to slow her racing heart. Was it possible that she'd somehow made him suspicious? Zafir's training had likely taught him to notice details others missed.

"Okay, class, let's wrap it up so we can go over your assignment for tomorrow." Zafir got up and began walking back toward his desk, then glanced over his shoulder at Orelia. "Glad to see you're feeling better."

Orelia felt her blood turn to ice, as if she were a hibernating frost python back on Sylvan. He recognized her from the hallway the other day. It was too late to lie low. She'd already caught the attention of the most dangerous person in the Academy—the person best equipped to discover a spy in their midst.

CHAPTER 7

ARRAN

Arran stopped in front of the engineering lab to collect himself. He'd been a little nervous before all his classes, but this was different. He was going to be his squadron's technology officer, which made his performance in engineering class all the more important.

"Elevated heart rate detected. Consider resting and taking a few deep breaths. For more information on relaxation techniques, say relax. *For information on cardiovascular disorders related to these symptoms, say* diagnostics."

"Ignore," Arran said under his breath, glancing around the crowded corridor. While he knew that the other cadets couldn't hear his monitor, it was still unnerving.

"For more information on—"

"Stop," Arran said. "Please, I don't have time for this."

"For more information on time-management strategies, say time management."

"Cancel. Mute!" Arran whispered as a few passing cadets turned to stare.

"Say *dismiss*," a deep voice said. Arran turned to see Dash watching him with an amused expression.

"Dismiss," Arran said under his breath before giving Dash a sheepish smile. "Thank you."

"You're welcome." Dash nodded at the door to the lab. "Are you also in this class?"

"Yes," Arran said, hoping his face didn't betray his excitement. He'd been waiting to run into Dash and had felt a pang of disappointment every time he'd walked into a new class without seeing him. But then a dispiriting thought hit him. What if Dash didn't remember meeting him on the shuttle? Unlike Arran, he probably hadn't replayed their interaction a hundred times over the past three days. "I'm Arran."

Dash gave Arran a puzzled look, as if he couldn't tell whether or not he was joking. "Yes, I know. We were on the shuttle together. I'm Dash."

Arran blushed. "No, of course. *I* know that. I just wasn't

sure that *you'd* remember it." The moment the words left his mouth, he regretted them.

"Ah, I see." Dash nodded thoughtfully. "Should I be worried that I struck you as someone with major short-term memory loss?"

"No. You didn't. I just…" There was no way Arran could possibly explain to Dash that he'd spent the past few years trying to make himself invisible. It was the only way for someone like him to survive on Chetire. When he'd done well on an exam, he'd been branded a show-off. When he'd skipped booze-filled snowshoeing jamborees to study, he'd been called stuck-up.

Dash grinned, and the embarrassment welling up within Arran turned into a different kind of warmth. "Should we head in?"

Arran followed him inside, and for a moment, all he could do was stare in wonder. So far, every room he'd seen at the Academy had been more spectacular than the last, but nothing could've prepared him for this. The lab was gleaming white with workstations scattered throughout. Holographic models hovered above each desk—schematics of weapons and vehicles Arran had never seen before. He took a few steps forward to watch a simulation of a streamlined zipcraft making hairpin turns through an asteroid belt.

"Everyone take a seat, please." Sergeant Pond, the instructor who'd accompanied them from Chetire, stood in the middle of the lab in his uniform, surveying the nervous-looking cadets. Across the room, Sula waved at Arran and gestured to a seat next to her. Arran looked to see where Dash had sat, but his workstation was already full. Fighting his disappointment, he made his way over to Sula and greeted her with a smile.

"Welcome to Advanced Engineering," Pond said, pacing as he spoke. "Before we dive into the curriculum, I want to get a sense of your mechanical-engineering abilities, so we're going to start with a simple exercise. You'll pair off into teams and design a prototype for a rover that can traverse all three of Deva's moons." He tapped his link, and a schematic for a basic rover appeared in the air above each workstation. "This will get you started."

Sula caught his eye and Arran nodded, relieved that he wouldn't be stuck searching for a partner. Pond must've noticed other cadets making similar gestures because he said, "And I'm going to divide you into pairs randomly. The sooner you all start working together, the better." He fiddled with his link, and glowing letters suddenly appeared on each workstation. "Go find the person with the same letter as you."

"I'm *F*. What are you?" Sula asked, peering at Arran's desk. "Oh well," she said with a sigh when she saw the glowing *K*. She got up to find her partner, and a moment later, someone else slid into her chair. It was Dash.

"It looks like we're partners," Dash said, extending his hand. "I'm Dash. I'm not sure if you remember, but we met about three minutes ago."

Arran laughed. "Yeah, I have a vague recollection."

"So, let's see.... Deva's moons.... There's the icy one, right?"

"That's one of them, yes," Arran said with a smile.

"And then the one with the underground ocean?"

"That's the same as the icy one. Victorine. Then there's Kaloo, which is mostly covered with volcanoes, and the red moon, Rola, the one with the high iron content."

Dash cocked his head to the side and gave Arran an appraising look. "Very impressive, 223."

"I'm pretty sure any eight-year-old in the solar system could name the moons," Arran said, secretly pleased that Dash had remembered his score.

"Hmm... I'm taking ten points away for your attitude. Henceforth, you shall be known as 213."

Arran nodded, suppressing a grin. "Noted."

"And we're going to start by doing this…" Dash's fingers flew across the desk, and a moment later, their transparent rover schematic turned bright red except for the number 213 emblazoned along the side.

Arran laughed, then ducked his head when a few people turned to look. "Not exactly suited for covert missions, is it?"

"At least one of Deva's moons is red. This is perfect!" Dash smiled, revealing the dimples Arran had been thinking about for the past three days. An unfamiliar feeling came over him. In the past, whenever something made Arran's heart flutter—a glimpse of his crush's toned chest or a shared knowing smile—he'd have to remind himself that it was all in his head. That no boy would ever fall for an awkward, studious loner like him.

"Jandro likes you," Evie said, not taking any particular pains to speak quietly. The school hadn't been able to find an advanced physics teacher this year, so their class was being taught by a buggy, rusted attendant who'd been programmed to deliver lectures and grade exams but couldn't process human voices. Not

only could their "instructor" not answer questions, it couldn't tell when the students weren't paying attention, which meant that most people spent class goofing around with their friends.

"What? That's ridiculous," Arran said quietly, his dismissive tone belying the flutter in his stomach. Jandro was new—his family had recently moved to F Territory—and although he was serious and studious during class, he'd started hanging out after school with Mace, Grover, and the other boys who liked to torment Arran when they couldn't find anything better to do.

"It's true," Evie insisted, ignoring the film the attendant was projecting onto the wall—an animated diagram explaining centrifugal force. "He likes that you're smart and that you care about your future."

"Then why doesn't he talk to me himself?" Arran whispered, wishing Evie would do the same. Although the cavernous classroom—housed in a former drill factory—echoed with laughter, you never knew who was eavesdropping.

"He's shy. You know something about that, don't you?"

Arran ignored the jab while he considered how to respond. He and Evie weren't friends exactly, but after four years of taking the same advanced classes, he knew her fairly well. She was nosy, gossipy, and not particularly nice, but he'd never known her to lie.

"Do you like him?" Evie prodded.

Arran glanced down at his desk so she wouldn't see him blush. The truth was he did like Jandro. Despite the droning robot instructor, physics had suddenly become his favorite class since it meant he could watch the new student. He liked how carefully Jandro took notes and how thoughtful he looked whenever he glanced up.

"What does it matter? Thirteen is too young for a boyfriend," Arran said, repeating what his mother had told him.

Evie rolled her eyes. "He doesn't have to be your boyfriend for you to have fun together. Don't you want to kiss someone eventually?"

Arran opened his mouth to give some indignant response, then sighed and closed it again. It was pointless to try to lie. Everyone knew everyone else's business in F Territory. He couldn't lie about having a secret love life and get away with it. "I have other things to focus on right now."

"Suit yourself. I'm just telling you what he told me. I said that if he wanted to talk to you he should go to the library after school. I assume you're going later, right?"

Arran shook his head. "I can't. I told my mom I'd feed the ironhooves."

"Your call," Evie said with a shrug. "Though if you're not there, he'll think you're avoiding him, and he'll be too embarrassed to try again."

Arran spent the rest of the day growing increasingly anxious as he deliberated about what to do. He watched Jandro carefully, but nothing about the boy's behavior confirmed or contradicted Evie's information. It couldn't be true—to the best of Arran's knowledge, no one had ever had a crush on him, let alone a popular new boy with soulful eyes. Yet there was a first time for everything. And what did he have to lose? He could feed the ironhooves later; his mother would understand.

By the time school let out, Arran was a jumble of nerves and excitement, but he did his best to act normally as he headed to the library—a storage room with an old but working link and some donated or discarded books. As usual, it was empty when Arran arrived, but he didn't let that discourage him. There was still plenty of time for Jandro to arrive.

He got to work right away, since he didn't want to look like he was expecting Jandro. He'd been teaching himself Cyrilia, a dialect used by early Settlers on Loos. Arran had only planned to learn the basics, but he'd found it so fascinating that he'd continued, and now he could read fairly fluently. He picked up where he'd left off, and by the time he looked up, nearly forty minutes had passed.

Disappointment hardened in his stomach, but as he glanced out the darkening window, it quickly turned to guilt as he imagined the confused ironhooves bleating for their dinner. He stood up with a groan, stretched his arms above his head, and had just begun to repack when the shrill wail of a siren made him jump.

Although the Specters hadn't attacked Chetire in years, there were still regular emergency drills. When the alarm blared, you had five minutes to scan into the nearest bunker, or else you had to pay a crippling fine. With a sigh, Arran headed for the school's bunker knowing he'd be on his own. None of the human teachers, to say nothing of the students, ever stayed a minute longer than they had to.

Why were they having a drill now? It'd only been two weeks since the last one, and drills normally occurred every five or six months. Arran swiped his ID against the sensor, then clanked down the metal steps. To his confusion, the door slid shut behind him. That was strange. The doors weren't supposed to close during drills—only in real attacks.

Dread began to seep down his spine. What if this wasn't a drill? What if it was a real attack? He went back up the stairs and pressed his ear against the door. He didn't hear anything— no explosions, no panicked screams. But that didn't necessarily mean anything. The last attack had been more than four hundred mitons away. They hadn't heard anything in F Territory, but later watched in horror as plumes of black smoke spiraled into the air like the ghosts of destroyed buildings.

His heart lurched as he imagined his mother searching frantically for him, calling his name out the door. What if she came looking for him instead of seeking shelter herself? Arran winced as a jolt of pain shot through him. If something happened to his mother, he'd never forgive himself.

Just as tears began to sting his eyes, he heard voices on the other side of the door. He was about to shout for attention when a familiar sound made his breath catch in his throat. Mace's laugh. The sound that had accompanied every humiliation Arran had suffered during the past few years.

"Do you think he's in there?" someone asked. It sounded like Mace's friend Grover.

"Of course. You really think he'd skip a drill?"

"But how do you know he was in the library at all?"

"I guarantee you he's here," a girl's voice said, sounding gleeful. It was Evie. "You should've seen the look on his face when I told him about Jandro."

No. The word tore through Arran as his heart began to race.

Mace laughed, and even through the solid door, the sound alone was enough to make Arran cringe. "I don't know why everyone thinks he's so smart. Like Jandro would ever go for someone like him. He's the one who figured out how to isolate the alarm to the library. I have to go tell him that it worked."

"What about Arran?" Evie asked, slightly less excited than before.

"Someone will find him tomorrow."

"I don't know if that's a good idea. What if something happens to him overnight?"

"If you're so concerned, we can lock you up with him and you can take care of each other." Evie must've given in, because the voices disappeared after that.

"No," Arran called, his voice cracking. "Wait! Come back!"

But it was too late. He was trapped alone in the empty, dark bunker. Silent except for the sound of his breath and the crack of his breaking heart.

⌃

Arran had learned the hard way not to let his imagination run away with him, yet looking at Dash's warm smile, he allowed himself to wonder if perhaps things could be different at the Academy.

They spent the rest of the class period customizing their rover with wheels that could navigate the craggy surface of Kaloo and churn through the dust on Rola, but they couldn't figure out how to make it work on Victorine.

"Maybe it's a test?" Dash said, rubbing his temples in a manner that Arran found oddly endearing.

"It *is* a test," Arran said. "A test of our engineering skills."

"You know what I mean." Dash smiled. "Maybe Pond's actually testing our ability to deal with impossible situations."

"This definitely isn't an impossible situation," Arran said, squinting at the schematic. "You know what? We won't need to worry about adapting to the different environments if we use a form of propulsion that doesn't require contact with the moons' surfaces."

"That sounds easier said than done."

"No, I think I've got it," Arran said as he zoomed in and began to adjust the engine. "We can make the rover levitate by using ducted fans where there's enough atmosphere, like on Victorine, and we can use repulsing magnets on Rola. If we polarize the magnets and place them on the underside of the rover, they'll react against the metal."

They worked quickly to redesign the rover. For all of Dash's feigned ignorance, he could perform lightning-fast calculations that, by the end of class, Arran found even more alluring than his dimples. After adding the ducted fans and the magnets, they tested the vehicle on all three surfaces. It worked beautifully each time.

Dash clapped his hand on Arran's shoulder. "You're a genius, 223!"

Arran blushed. "Come on."

"Are you *embarrassed*?" Dash's tone was more incredulous than teasing, but that didn't stop Arran's cheeks from growing even warmer. He hadn't realized it was possible to feel embarrassed about being embarrassed. "Listen, being modest isn't going to help you here. You've got to own being a genius."

Pond came over to their workstation to watch their rover in action. "Nicely done," he said with a nod before glancing at the time. "Okay, that's it," he called out. "If you didn't finish, you and your partner should arrange a time to meet before our next class."

Arran found himself wishing that he and Dash hadn't finished the assignment so quickly so he'd have an excuse to meet up with him later. But maybe he didn't need an excuse? Perhaps Dash would suggest hanging out later just for fun. Arran felt a flutter in his stomach and tried to come up with a response that would convey enthusiasm but not too much excitement.

"Great job, 223," Dash said after Pond had dismissed them and they were walking toward the door. "I'll see you around."

"Oh…" Arran said, trying not to sound disappointed. "Yeah, see you." He forced himself to smile even though it felt like someone had jabbed his chest with a dull ice pick.

Dash took a few steps, then stopped and turned back around. "Do you want to meet up for dinner later?"

"Yes." The word shot out of Arran's mouth before he had time to feign nonchalance.

"Great," Dash said with a grin that made every inch of Arran's skin start to tingle. "I'll see you later."

As he watched Dash go, Arran exhaled and grinned.

"Elevated heart rate detected. Consider—"

Arran closed his eyes and laughed. "Dismiss."

"What's going on?" Arran spun around to see Sula looking at him with concern.

"Nothing. I'm fine. My monitor was just acting up."

She glanced from side to side, then lowered her voice. "Don't you know who he is? That boy you were paired with?"

"Yeah. That's Dash, from the shuttle. He seems a lot nicer than the other Tridians, doesn't he?" Only a few of the

Tridians had been outwardly hostile to the Settlers, but they hadn't exactly been welcoming either.

Sula frowned and pulled him into the hall, waiting for a group of laughing girls to pass before she spoke again.

"Right. Dash *Muscatine.*"

"What's your point?"

Sula stared at him incredulously. "His father is Larz Muscatine."

"That's impossible," Arran said quickly. "Muscatine is a really common last name on Tri. He can't be Dash's father."

"Trust me. It's him. The man who's trying to reverse the new policy and close the Academy to Settlers."

The warmth in Arran's stomach crystallized into jagged ice, sending cold dread seeping through his body. "No… that can't be right…."

"I didn't realize it back at the shuttleport, but I've already heard lots of people talking about him, including some of the instructors."

"But he seems so *nice*," Arran said weakly. His brain strained to process this information, but he couldn't sort through the tangle of thoughts.

"Remember what his father's like. You've seen him in the news memos. He never raises his voice. Never stops smiling.

He seems so charming and polite, you can almost forget that he's calling us parasites and criminals."

There had to be some mistake. Dash had been flirting with him. He'd asked Arran to meet him for dinner. Why in Antares's name would he do that if he were some kind of hateful bigot?

Unless...

Arran winced as a painful idea wormed its way through his brain. What if Dash had only been flirting with him so he could go laugh with his friends afterward? Or worse, tell his father that the Settlers were even more stupid than anyone had realized?

He blushed and glanced away so Sula wouldn't see the hurt in his face. It didn't matter that he'd gotten the highest score on the entrance exam. It didn't matter that he was a tech officer at the Quatra Fleet Academy. He was still the sixteen-year-old who'd never kissed anyone. He was still the boy who'd never be anyone's favorite.

CHAPTER 8

CORMAK

Ever since leaving the medical center the other day, Cormak had been fighting waves of terror and nausea. It was only a matter of time before the Quatra Fleet found out he wasn't really Rex and came for him. He needed to get out of here. But how? Stow away on a cargo ship? Maybe even *steal* a ship? Except the punishment for that was probably even more severe than the punishment for trespassing. He'd have to worry about it later, though. He needed to be at his squadron's first practice session in five minutes, and he didn't want to be late and draw any more attention to himself.

The corridor echoed with shouts and the thud of footsteps as people jostled to catch up with squadron mates. But as they spilled into a darker, narrower hallway, the laughs and jeers died away, and the cadets began speaking in hushed tones. The only light came from the glowing numbers on the doors, and the crowd thinned as people quietly peeled off into their simulcrafts.

When Cormak reached number 20, he pressed his hand to the scanner like he'd seen the others do, and the door slid open. He found himself in a small, dark, round room that looked like the cockpit of a fightercraft. Three chairs faced various control panels, and in the center behind them was a single chair. The captain's chair.

Above the panels was a wraparound window. No, not a window, Cormak realized. It would be impossible for such a small room in the middle of the Academy to have windows on all sides. It was the simulcraft's screen, one with such high definition and dimension, it was hard to believe he wasn't really looking out into space.

This is incredible, Cormak thought, feeling a brief flash of excitement before it was subsumed by a new wave of anxiety. He hoped the practice session wouldn't last long. The sooner he got out of here, the sooner he'd be able to come up with an escape plan. He looked around the empty simulcraft with a mixture of confusion and irritation. It was a little strange that he was the first to arrive. He'd never been early to anything in his life.

But then, to his surprise, he noticed the top of someone's head peeking up from the captain's chair. "Excuse me, I believe you're in my seat," he said, forcing a playful note into his voice. The more relaxed he acted, the better.

The chair spun around, revealing a girl with long black hair, a smattering of freckles across high cheekbones—and the frostiest glare Cormak had ever seen. "Sorry," he said quickly, raising his hands in surrender. "It was just a joke."

She gave him a strained smile. "Hilarious," she said in a Tridian accent.

So far, the Tridians weren't doing much to dispel the idea that they were all humorless snobs. Then his gaze fell on the girl's badge and it hit him. This was Vesper, the admiral's daughter, the cadet he'd heard the Tridians talking about. Apparently, her mother was pissed that Vesper had been made pilot instead of captain.

"Listen, I know this must be awkward for you. If it makes you feel any better, this captain thing doesn't matter to me," he said. He wasn't going to be at the Academy for long. If being captain meant so much to this girl, then he'd let her have it.

She stared at him, as if unsure whether he was an idiot

or just being cruel. Cormak bristled. He was many things, but a cruel idiot wasn't one of them. Forget about offering to swap roles. She was clearly another spoiled Tridian used to getting her way. This would be good for her.

The door slid open, and two people stepped inside—a lanky boy with thick, dark hair and a pale blond girl with her hair pulled back severely from her face. "Welcome to Squadron 20!" Cormak said as cheerfully as he could manage given the growing knot of anxiety in his stomach. Seemed right for the captain to make everyone feel at ease.

"I'm Arran." The boy dipped his head, then jerked it back up and extended his hand for Cormak to shake. He had a thick accent—Chetrian, Cormak thought.

The blond girl stood oddly rigid as her eyes darted between Cormak and their two other squadron mates. There was a long moment of silence before she finally spoke. "I'm Orelia."

Cormak raised his hand in the air. "Rex," he said with a smile, hoping the girl would find that less intimidating than a handshake.

She nodded. "Orelia," she said again.

"Yes, I think we've got that part." Vesper clapped her hands together once. "Now let's get to work. The first—"

"Aren't you going to introduce yourself?" Cormak asked, enjoying the look of frustration on Vesper's face. He hoped all the Tridians were this easy to rile up; if he could take these snobs down a notch before he left, his risky trip to the Academy would've been worth it.

"Vesper," she said in a tone that suggested it was taking all her self-control to be polite.

"A pleasure to meet you," Cormak said, extending his hand.

She ignored him and continued. "The first battle is next week, and if we don't do well, it'll be really hard to climb back up in the rankings. Now, does everyone understand the responsibilities of each role?"

Cormak cleared his throat. "I'm pretty sure that the responsibilities of being *captain* include asking questions like that."

A look of pain flashed across her face, and for a brief moment, Cormak considered apologizing. But then she smiled at him. Or what would've counted as a smile if she hadn't followed it up with a patronizing "All right then, Captain. Proceed."

Arran looked at him expectantly. Orelia wasn't making eye contact with anyone, which Cormak vastly preferred to

Vesper's look of apprehension, as if afraid to see what ridiculous thing he'd do next. "Well," he said, stalling because he didn't actually have anything to say.

The lights darkened suddenly, and the control panels began to glow. *"Hello, Squadron 20,"* said a voice that Cormak recognized from his monitor. *"Welcome to your first training session. Please take your seats."*

Vesper spun around and marched over to the pilot's chair. Without waiting for further instructions, she started to adjust the controls with well-practiced movements.

"That one's probably the tech seat, right?" Arran gestured at a chair in front of a screen glowing with a schematic of the ship's engine.

"Right," Cormak said, figuring he had a fifty percent chance of getting it right.

Silently, Orelia settled into a seat that faced a large radar screen, then folded her hands in her lap, apparently waiting for further instructions.

Cormak lowered himself into the captain's chair, and despite the anxiety churning in his stomach, he grinned. He had to admit, it felt pretty good.

"There are three types of missions," the voice continued. *"The first is exploratory, in which the objective is to gather intelligence*

about a specific location without alerting the enemy to your presence. The second is rescue, in which the objective is to retrieve someone who's been stranded or captured. The third is combat, during which you'll face an enemy intent on destroying your craft."

"Everyone got that?" Cormak asked. Arran glanced over his shoulder and nodded. Orelia nodded without turning. And, to Cormak's delight, Vesper twisted around to glare at him. "Okay, good," he said.

"Today, you'll be performing an exploratory mission. An asteroid has been detected that could contain valuable minerals. Your objective: Locate the asteroid, land on the surface to collect soil samples, and return to your base. Your score will be determined by speed, fuel usage, and the condition of your craft."

"Soil samples?" Cormak repeated. "I wanted to destroy some Specters!" He was getting into this captain thing and figured he should enjoy it while it lasted.

Out of the corner of his eye, he saw Orelia flinch. What was with these girls?

"Your mission begins in 5 ... 4 ... 3 ..."

"Okay, everyone, we've got this," Cormak said. "Orelia, how far away is the aster—"

"143, 817 mitons."

"Efficient. I like it. Arran, what's the landing zone look like?"

"Commence mission."

The stars on the screen came into even sharper focus. It really felt like they were in the middle of space. It was pretty incredible, actually.

Arran pulled up a schematic of the asteroid. "Let's see.... The asteroid is on the smaller side, which means low gravity will be a challenge. It's going to be hard not to bounce."

"We can use reverse thrusters," Vesper said without turning. "It'll be fine."

"All right then, take it away, pilot."

Vesper yanked back on the throttle, and the simulcraft lurched forward. Arran gasped in surprise, and Cormak gripped the arms of his chair. He hadn't realized just how realistic these simulations were.

"The asteroid is located at the far edge of the Peel Asteroid Belt," Orelia announced, still facing the radar screen. "The safest route loops around and has us come from behind. There will be fewer obstacles that way."

"But we'll use a lot more fuel," Arran said, frowning.

"It might be smart to do the safer option for our first

mission," Cormak said slowly, still mesmerized by the sight of the stars. "What do you think, Orelia?"

"*You're* the captain."

Cormak was slightly taken aback by her hostility, but he was used to people snapping at him and decided to focus on her deference instead.

"We're not going the long way," Vesper said as she flipped a switch on the dashboard with one hand while turning a knob with the other. "It's a waste of time."

Well, that settles it, Cormak thought. "I disagree. I think it's wiser to play it safe this time. Please send Arran the coordinates for our new trajectory so he can calculate how much fuel we'll need for the longer route."

For a few minutes, silence filled the simulcraft as everyone focused on their tasks—Orelia kept watch on the radar, scanning for obstacles, while Arran monitored the craft's engines and life-support systems, and Vesper piloted.

Arran cleared his throat. "Vesper, did you send those coordinates?"

"I did."

"Okay..." Arran sounded slightly anxious. "Because it looks like we're still taking the more direct route."

"That's correct."

"Vesper," Cormak said, borrowing the same slow, patronizing tone she'd used with him earlier. *Antares, this was going to be fun.* "Did I not instruct you to take the longer route?"

"You did, Captain."

"So I take it you're disobeying orders?"

"Section 4 of the Quatra Fleet doctrine, paragraph B," Vesper recited. "Crew has the legal and moral authority to overrule a commanding officer's orders in exceptional circumstances including but not limited to mental incapacity, physical incapacity, and gross incompetence."

"Which one of those applies to me?" Cormak asked, trying to keep the amusement out of his voice.

The simulcraft shook violently as bits of rock began bouncing off the windows. *Simulated ice,* Cormak reminded himself as the craft rumbled again.

"Too late to turn around now!" Vesper called cheerfully as she steered deftly around the jagged chunks of ice hurtling toward them, some larger than their ship. Cormak didn't have a ton of experience in this area, but they seemed to be traveling at an alarming speed.

Orelia muttered something under her breath as Vesper narrowly avoided a jagged piece of ice, then swerved in the other direction, missing the obstacle by a hair.

The surface of the asteroid appeared—an endless stretch of craggy peaks and dangerous-looking crevasses that grew larger as Vesper began to descend. *Come on*, Cormak urged, despite himself.

"Which of those craters has the best landing surface?" Vesper asked.

Orelia quickly pressed a few buttons, and the craters on her screen turned different colors. "That long narrow one."

"Watch it!" Arran called as a huge stream of gas shot up from one of the cracks in the asteroid's surface.

With one fluid movement, Vesper turned the craft horizontal, sending blood rushing to Cormak's head, then straightened up again.

"Nicely done," Arran said hoarsely.

Somehow, she managed to find a patch of level ground nestled in between the ridges. Arran deployed the drill that collected the soil sample, and a few minutes later they were off again, speeding through the minefield of the asteroid belt.

"*Mission complete*," the voice from earlier announced. "*Calculating final score. Your score is... eighty-seven.*"

Vesper sprang to her feet, grinning. To Cormak's surprise, she looked nothing like the tense, rigid girl who'd greeted him. Her face glowed, and her dark eyes sparkled with triumph. She beamed as she looked at the score flashing on the screen, oblivious to the sweaty strands of hair clinging to her flushed face.

"Great job, everyone!" Cormak leaned back in the chair and placed his hands behind his head as he surveyed his squadron with a smile.

"Aren't you glad we took the shorter way?" Vesper asked.

"I guess it depends. Is eighty-seven a good score?"

Vesper tossed her hair over her shoulder. "Yes. Eighty-seven is *very* good." She took a deep breath, as if summoning all her self-control. "Great job, everyone."

"Not too shabby," Arran said, clearly delighted. "So what now?"

Vesper seemed to relax. "We get to do a victory lap around the common room," she said with a smile. "Who's in?"

"I'm definitely in," Arran said.

Cormak knew it was petty, but he couldn't wait to see the look on those Tri assholes' faces when they found out how well they'd done. "I suppose I could drop by for a minute," Cormak said. This could be his last chance to show off before he got the hell out of here. "Orelia?"

"I need to study," she said curtly.

They filed out into the hall and walked in silence toward the main corridor that led to the center of the Academy. Cormak racked his brain for something to say—back on Deva, he'd mostly interacted with people he'd known his whole life and rarely had to make small talk. But before he could speak, Arran inhaled sharply. Cormak spun around to see him staring at something written on the wall—a message that hadn't been there when he'd arrived.

Go home Edgers.

Cormak's stomach curdled with anger and disgust. He'd heard the hateful word before, of course, but this was different. This was directed at him, his squadron mates, and all the Settlers. It wasn't an offhand insult—it was a threat.

"Who...who would do this?" Arran asked quietly.

"I don't know," Vesper said, her jaw clenched. "But they're not going to get away with it."

Like hell they're not, Cormak thought as he pictured the smug faces of the boys who'd pulled the dangerous prank in the zero-gravity room. If they hadn't done this, some other assholes had. The Tridians couldn't keep getting away with stuff like this. Cormak might be days away from being arrested for treason, but that didn't mean he couldn't go down swinging.

CHAPTER 9

ORELIA

The corridors were full of anxious chatter as Orelia made her way back to her room. Word of the graffiti had apparently spread quickly. The cowardly act of vandalism had confirmed everything Orelia had ever heard or suspected about the Quatrans. Her tutors hadn't taught her a great deal of Quatran slang, so she wasn't entirely sure what *Edger* meant, but from the looks on Arran's and Rex's faces, it was clearly an insult. If this was how the Quatrans treated one another, it was no wonder that their leaders showed no qualms about annihilating a foreign population on a far-flung planet.

By the time Orelia had left the simulcraft corridor, a small crowd had formed to gawk at the message despite the instructors' best efforts to keep everyone moving. "The administration is investigating the infraction," an instructor had said to a trio of anxious-looking Loosians. "Whoever's responsible will face disciplinary action." The Loosians hadn't seemed convinced, and neither was Orelia. The Quatra Fleet was lying to civilians about its secret attacks on Sylvan—it was hard to imagine anyone getting worked up over a crude message scrawled on the wall of the Academy.

"You've left the simulcraft earlier than expected. Consider using this extra time for cardiovascular conditioning. For directions to the gymnasium, say directions.*"*

"Dismiss," Orelia said testily. She'd spent the past three years training twelve hours a day for this mission. She was probably in better shape than anyone at the Academy. But that wouldn't help her with the next step in her plan—she had to find another way to capture and transmit the school's coordinates. As the shuttle from Loos took off, the windows had darkened for security purposes. However, the windows of the Academy itself were transparent, and if Orelia managed to collect enough data about the position of the stars, she could use them to triangulate her location. Then she'd just have to find a way to transmit that information back to Sylvan. It was a far more complicated plan than the original, but she'd figure out a way to make it work. She'd already received two messages from her commanding officer asking for updates on her progress. Orelia hoped that General Greet would give her the benefit of the doubt and realize that the technology she'd been given had malfunctioned.

Orelia placed her hand against the scanner outside her suite, and the door slid open. To her surprise, Zuzu was in the living room. "Hi there," she said, glancing over her shoulder to smile at Orelia. "Do you mind if I put this up in here?" Zuzu rose onto her toes to drape a deep purple silk wall hanging.

"No," Orelia said without stopping.

"Oh, good. This room could use some cheer. And I don't think either of the boys will care. Karrl spends most of his time off with his Tridian friends anyway."

Cadets were assigned rooms in clusters of four, with a shared living space and communal bathroom. In addition to Zuzu, there was Karrl, a boy from Tri she'd only seen twice, and a boy from Deva named Quint, who spent most of his time with two fellow Devaks who lived down the hall.

Zuzu finished affixing the wall hanging, then turned to Orelia with a smile. "Where on Loos are you from again?" Zuzu asked.

Do it just like you practiced. "I'm from outside of Usgard, in the northwest quadrant."

Zuzu brightened. "Really? That's where my cousins live. What sector?"

"Forty-two," Orelia said, her heart beginning to pound. She wished she'd created a fake Chetrian identity instead. The Chetrians seemed to ask fewer questions.

"It's beautiful there. Do you have any pics? I love seeing people with their families."

"No," she said curtly. Orelia had never had any friends or family to take pics with. After her parents had been killed in one of the Quatran attacks, she'd been placed in a government home where she'd had few friends. Once the directors learned about her gift for mathematics and languages, she'd been shipped off to a military base to be trained as a special operative. There were others like her, but the children were kept in isolation lest they form too many bonds among themselves. It was a harsh way to grow up, but Orelia understood the reasoning. Having no one she cared about made it much easier to leave everything behind...especially when there was no guarantee she'd ever return.

"That's okay," Zuzu said hesitantly. "We can take lots of pics next week. Do you know what you're going to wear?"

This is ridiculous, Orelia thought. She had to focus on her mission; she couldn't waste time making frivolous small talk with Zuzu. Part of Orelia wanted to ignore the question and march straight into her room, but she didn't want to raise any red flags. She had to blend in here, and that meant appearing to be friendly. "Wear to what?"

Zuzu brightened. "To the first-year formal! Didn't you hear about it? It's usually later in the term, but the Academy was apparently worried about all of us 'bonding' so they made it earlier."

"A formal? Is that like a party?" Orelia asked. She thought back to the words *Go home Edgers* written in the main corridor; she had a feeling the Academy was going to need a lot more than a party to make everyone get along.

"Yes! Do you want to borrow something to wear? I brought way too much, considering how much time we spend in uniform. Come see!"

"That's not necessary. I'm not much of a *party person*," Orelia said, realizing she'd never said those two words together—in any language—in her entire life.

"Just have a look, and then you can decide." Zuzu grabbed Orelia's arm and pulled her toward her bedroom.

Zuzu's tiny room was the same size as Orelia's, but it

contained at least four times as many objects. Every surface was covered with clothes, grooming supplies, and various trinkets. "Here," Zuzu said, digging into one of the piles on her chair. "I have a green dress that's going to do amazing things to your eyes."

"To my eyes?" Orelia repeated skeptically. She tried to imagine a garment that came equipped with a magnifying device or some other tool to enhance vision.

"Absolutely. Look!" Zuzu yanked something from the bottom of the pile, which promptly collapsed and spilled off the chair onto the floor. She held the item up for Orelia to admire. "You have to try it on."

Orelia resignedly accepted the green dress from Zuzu, then went to her own room to change. The dress was so tight that Orelia had to take shorter steps, which seemed foolish to her. Clothing was supposed to *enhance* your body—protecting you from ice rain, liquid magma, and flesh-eating bacteria. What was the point of wearing something that made it difficult to walk?

She toddled back into Zuzu's room, expecting her roommate to make a similar pronouncement. But as Orelia entered, Zuzu clapped her hands and squealed, "It's perfect! You look *amazing*."

"I'm not sure...." Orelia said, pulling on the hem that ended well above her knees.

Orelia turned and surveyed her reflection in the narrow mirror on the back of Zuzu's closet door. The deep emerald color was certainly striking, although Orelia didn't know why anyone would wear a garment that seemed designed to attract attention. What if you needed to hide from your enemies? Or a hungry razor-beaked jagraw?

"It's too small," Orelia said, gesturing at the fabric hugging her hips.

"Are you kidding?" Zuzu said with a laugh. "I'd kill to look like you in that dress."

Like most of the Quatran girls she'd seen at the Academy, Zuzu was slimmer than Orelia, whose rounder hips and fuller chest provided much-needed energy stores for her planet's four-hundred-day winter. On Zuzu, the dress would be much looser, which seemed to Orelia ideal for movement.

"You *have* to wear that to the party," Zuzu continued.

"I'm...I'm not sure if I'm going." Orelia was having enough trouble trying to keep a low profile in class, where the rules were fairly logical and consistent. It'd be foolish to attend a nonmandatory social function and face a whole new set of perils. What if she accidentally did or said something that made it clear she hadn't grown up in the Quatra System?

"Oh, you're going. We all have to go. We can't let the Tri kids think that the school still belongs to them." Zuzu took a step back and cocked her head to the side as she surveyed Orelia with a smile. "Besides, it'd be a shame if you never wore that dress. You look beautiful."

To her surprise, Orelia felt something inside her soften. No one had ever called her beautiful before. *She must have some ulterior motive*, Orelia thought. Quatrans didn't just do nice things for strangers.

"You know what? Just leave it on for a bit and see how you feel. You can decide what to do later."

Orelia nodded and walked out of Zuzu's room, desperate to banish the troubling thoughts hovering at the edges of her mind. She couldn't afford to let the actions of a few kind Quatrans make her doubt her mission. She was here to save the Sylvans from annihilation no matter the cost.

CHAPTER 10

VESPER

Vesper smoothed her skirt, then strode into the dining hall. Dinner had quickly become her favorite meal at the Academy; since uniforms weren't required, it was the one time she didn't have to wear clothes emblazoned with her attention-grabbing last name or her disappointing assignment.

She also loved how the room looked at night, when the Academy's circadian lights dimmed to simulate dusk. The chandelier had been brought all the way from Tri three hundred years ago, a relic from a different age, when cadets had been training to subdue rebellions on the outer planets instead of preparing to fight the Specters.

As she headed toward her usual table in the middle of the

hall, dodging attendants zipping back and forth with trays of appetizers, Vesper glanced at the portraits lining the walls. For the first few days, she'd found their stern expressions disconcerting; they bore an uncanny resemblance to the look on Admiral Haze's face when Vesper told her she'd been made pilot instead of captain. But after her squadron's series of promising practice sessions that week, the painted faces felt less censorious and more representative of the seriousness of the cadets' endeavors here, of the centuries-long tradition of excellence.

Vesper was pretty sure that Arran was some kind of math genius. And even though she'd barely spoken, Orelia was clearly highly intelligent. Vesper's opinion of their captain, Rex, hadn't improved much on further acquaintance. But although he was arrogant, he wasn't incompetent, and Vesper was starting to feel more hopeful about their chances.

As usual, her friends from home had saved her a seat. A small part of her felt guilty about always sitting at a table of Tridians, but after a long day of classes, studying, conditioning, and squadron practice, she was too tired to make the effort required to talk to new people. Besides, she doubted any of the Settlers wanted a Tridian at their table. Ever since last week's vandalism incident, the atmosphere had felt even tenser than before. The Devaks, Loosians, and Chetrians seemed to look at every Tridian with suspicion, which the cadets from Tri found highly offensive. But whenever Vesper found herself tempted by similar indignation, she recalled the looks on her squadron mates' faces when they saw the graffiti—Rex's stony rage, Orelia's stoic silence, and Arran's mixture of hurt and confusion.

"Vee, there you are," Ward said, placing his hand on her arm. "We were just talking about how well your squadron's been doing at practice. You must be excited for the first real battle next week."

Out of the corner of her eye, Vesper saw Brill smirk, but she chose to ignore it. Despite Vesper's squadron's high practice scores, the team's makeup struck Brill as endlessly amusing. "We've certainly been improving."

"Sorry I'm late." Vesper turned to see her friend Dash slide into the last open seat.

"Evening, Dash," Frey said. "I heard your squadron had some trouble in the simulcraft today. How many times did you explode?"

"You of all people should know better than to listen to rumors," Dash said as he reached for a roll.

Frey raised one perfectly arched eyebrow. "Most of the rumors about me happen to be true."

"I don't think any of you have a right to complain in front of poor Vee," Brill said. "I still can't believe you have to deal with a Devak captain. Has it been awful?" There was a note of sympathy in her voice at odds with the gleam of delight in her eyes.

Vesper hesitated. She was still disappointed and frustrated about not being captain, but perhaps there was a chance for her to distinguish herself in another way—as the brilliant pilot who flew Squadron 20 to victory. "We're figuring it out," she said.

"But what's going to happen when they make cuts at the end of the year?" Brill pressed. "Do you think you'll get to stay at the Academy?"

Ward glared at Brill, then reached for Vesper's hand and squeezed it. "If her squadron does well in the tournament, she won't have a problem."

"I'm sure you're right," Brill said sweetly. "After all, your mom can always pull some strings for you, can't she, Vee?"

"That won't be necessary," Vesper said icily as Ward whispered for her to keep it together. She was going to prove her mother wrong. She was going to prove *everyone* wrong.

⌃⌃

Vesper hurried down the stairs as quickly as she could without tripping over her long dress. Her parents were having one of their famous dinner parties tonight, and for the first time, Vesper was allowed to join. The guests were all high-ranking members of the Quatra Fleet or important diplomats, and Vesper was determined to make a good impression and make her mother proud.

She straightened the strap of her purple silk dress and strode into the library. It was cold for early autumn on Tri, and one of the attendants had lit the fire. The crackling flames filled the library with a warm glow that made everything look cheerful, even the animal heads mounted on the walls. Her father's prized trophy, the horned mountain cat, seemed to have a sparkle in his fierce dark eyes.

But the library was empty. From the scattered glasses, it was clear that her parents and their guests had already finished their drinks. "You're late, Ms. Vesper," a voice said from behind her. "They've moved to the dining room."

"What?" She spun around to face the attendant. "Is she angry?"

"I have stopped trying to analyze your mother's emotions," Baz said, moving smoothly around the room to collect the discarded glasses.

Vesper smiled. Baz had been with her family since before she was born, and after so many years, he felt more like a confidant than an attendant. "I should go. Wish me luck, Baz."

"No luck necessary, Ms. Vesper. If your parents' guests aren't impressed with you, it means they have glitches and require reprogramming."

Vesper took a deep breath, but before she could let it out, a voice called from the doorway, "There you are." Vesper turned to see her mother looking impossibly elegant in a black silk gown. Unlike other career officers, Admiral Svetlara Haze never seemed uneasy in civilian clothes—she wore her evening dress with the same confidence as she did her uniform.

Vesper suppressed a sigh. Of course her mother had come to find her. Admiral Haze never left anything to chance, whether she was leading a covert expedition in the asteroid belt or ensuring that her daughter made it to dinner on time.

"I'm sorry. I lost track of time during conditioning," Vesper said, a note of pride in her voice. Her mother always complained about cadets who showed up at the Academy unprepared for the physical rigors of military life. Although she wouldn't be applying for another three years, Vesper had already started training.

To Vesper's dismay, Admiral Haze's face showed no sign of approval. "Was that before or after you got the results of your multivariable calculus exam?"

Vesper's stomach plummeted down toward the silver shoes she'd been saving especially for tonight. "It was just the midterm. There's time for me to bring my grade up before the final."

"There won't be if you waste all your time on the gravity track instead of studying." Her mother let out a long sigh and crossed her arms in front of her. "Honestly, I expected more of you, Vesper."

Vesper felt her cheeks start to burn. "I'll do better. I promise."

"I hope so." Without another word, Admiral Haze turned around and strode out the door.

Vesper hurried after her, moving as quickly as she could in her new shoes. But before she could catch up, her mother glanced over her shoulder. "I don't think dinner is a good idea, do you? You clearly need the time to study."

The words struck Vesper like a blow, and she stopped in her tracks. She'd been looking forward to this dinner for ages. Her mother had even promised to let her sit next to Commander

Stepney, the highest-ranking officer in the Quatra Fleet. "Okay,"
she said quietly. But it was too late. Her mother was already gone.

Baz glided up to her. "I'll bring you something to eat in your
room." Vesper nodded. "Don't let your mother upset you."

"I'm not upset, Baz," Vesper said, turning away as she spoke.
With thirteen years of facial-recognition data at his disposal, he
could always tell when she was lying.

⪡

"Besides, Vesper will get the grades she needs to continue
on the officer track," Ward said, still holding her hand.

Brill nodded as she took a dainty sip of soup. "Absolutely.
It just puts *so* much more pressure on you with exams and
everything. Not that I'm worried. If anyone can do it, it's
you, Vee."

Frey shot Vesper a sympathetic look, then made a show of
clearing his throat to change the subject. "We should leave
the tournament aside for a moment and talk about what
really matters." He made an exaggerated show of scanning
the dining hall. "Which outer-planet delicacy I'm going
to sample at the formal tomorrow. The obvious answer is
a Chetrian, of course. All those miner muscles. But then

again, they spend so much time swimming on Loos, and it has the most wonderful effect on their calves." His voice grew slightly dreamy. "And their abs."

Brill jabbed him with her elbow. "No fantasizing about Settlers at the table, Frey. Besides, I have something far more important to discuss." She glanced around the dining hall dramatically, then lowered her voice. "I thought it'd be fun to liven things up once the battles start, so I'm organizing a little betting ring."

"Seriously, Brill? This again?" Dash said. Last year at their old school, Brill had done something similar, having students bet on who'd be admitted to the Quatra Fleet Academy. Things had gotten heated, and a few friendships had been ruined.

"If you don't like it, you don't have to participate." Brill shrugged. "I think it adds an extra bit of excitement. Besides, it's too late to stop now. More than a dozen people have already placed their bets for week one. Of course, I'm going to adjust the odds every week based on squadron rankings and practice scores."

"How do you have time for all this?" Frey asked, staring at Brill with a mixture of skepticism and amusement.

"I'll make it work. Though being captain is exhausting—there's so much to keep track of. You're actually really lucky, Vee, that you can just focus on piloting."

Vesper ignored the jab. She'd put Brill in her place when they faced off in a few weeks.

Brill extended her arm toward Frey with her palm facing up and gave him an imploring look.

"Not now," he said through clenched teeth.

"Come on," Brill said, wiggling her fingers. "No one's looking."

With a sigh, Frey reached into his suit pocket, produced a tiny purple pill, and slipped it into Brill's hand.

"Thank you," she said sweetly, as if he'd just given her a pencil instead of a dangerous illegal drug.

"Anyone else?" Frey asked wearily. "Ward? Vee?"

Vesper hesitated. Her squadron's battle was coming up soon—the day after the formal—and it'd be nice to guarantee that she'd be in top form. She wondered if perhaps the risks of vega dust had been overblown. After all, everyone else had apparently been taking it for years. She didn't need much, just enough to sharpen her focus and reflexes in the simulcraft. If she piloted her squadron to victory, then maybe it wouldn't matter that she didn't make captain.

She'd find another way to prove to her mother and everyone else that she belonged here. Finally, she extended her hand and let Frey place the pill in her palm. She nodded, then slipped it into her pocket. If she kept flying as well as she had today, there'd be no need for the dust, but it made sense to hold on to it just in case.

CHAPTER 11

ARRAN

Arran stood up and surveyed his reflection in the mirror one final time. He didn't have any "evening attire"—hardly any of the cadets from the outer planets did. But he figured his nicest shirt and trousers would be fine. He just hoped he wouldn't run into Dash tonight. Once Arran had come to terms with the fact that the dinner invitation had likely been a joke, he'd skipped the dining hall that night and had managed to avoid catching Dash's eye in class the next day. Arran was thankful that Dash hadn't tried to speak to him either, which meant that Larz Muscatine's son had probably moved on to a new victim. Or, even better, had decided to leave the Settlers alone.

As they'd discussed, Arran stopped to pick up Sula so

they could walk to the formal together. She looked very pretty in her gray skirt and white blouse, but they still stood out in the sea of cadets in dark suits and brightly colored dresses making their way through the corridor. "Don't worry about it," Sula whispered to Arran. "You look so handsome, no one will notice you're not in a suit. In fact, you'll probably start a new trend."

"I'm sure you're right. Tomorrow, when I put on my uniform, the badge will say *Arran Korbet. Style icon. Squadron 20.*"

Sula laughed. "So where is this thing?"

"In the ballroom."

Sula rolled her eyes. "Come on."

"No, I'm serious!" Arran said. "There's actually a ballroom."

"Why, in the name of Antares, would they build a *ballroom* in a space station?"

"I guess that was considered a necessity four hundred years ago." For centuries, the Quatra Fleet Academy had been a very different place—more of a playground for the Tridian elite. That was during a time of relative peace in the Quatra System, after Loos, Chetire, and Deva had been settled but before the rebellions began and well before the first Specter attacks.

An attendant was standing guard at the entrance.

Someone had affixed a bow tie to the closest thing the machine had to a neck. As Sula and Arran approached, it spoke. "Evening attire is required for tonight's event, sir," the attendant said with a surprising amount of scorn. Arran could almost sense a sneer on the machine's smooth, featureless face.

Heat rose to Arran's cheeks, though he knew it was ridiculous to feel belittled by a robot. He shifted uncomfortably from side to side, then stopped, worried about scuffing the shoes he'd taken such care to shine before the party.

"That's not true," Sula said, stepping forward to stand next to Arran. "We were explicitly told that formal wear was encouraged but not required."

Arran nodded. Apparently, since so few of the outer-planet cadets had brought evening attire to the Academy, the rules had been relaxed.

"My instructions have not been updated," the attendant said. "I encourage you to return to your rooms to change."

Arran felt something inside him deflate. It would be difficult to wear a suit he didn't own. He'd never seen anyone wear one in F Territory except for the pompous mayor.

A striking girl wearing an exquisitely tailored suit appeared next to them. It was Vesper, though Arran barely recognized her out of uniform. "Just ignore him," she told Arran and Sula airily. "Someone forgot to upload the new dress code. Don't worry about it."

Without waiting for the attendant's response, Vesper nodded at Arran, then strode into the hall, waved at a friend on the other side of the room, and disappeared into the crowd. Sula and Arran exchanged a wordless glance, then followed her inside.

The large oval-shaped room before them was dimly lit. An enormous glass chandelier hung from the high ceiling, and candle-like bulbs flickered on each table. Attendants glided smoothly back and forth, carrying trays with exotic-looking beverages. About three-quarters of the cadets were in formal wear—Tridian and Settler cadets who'd been savvy enough or wealthy enough to bring the right clothes with them. The remaining quarter wore whatever they'd managed to cobble together.

Three boys walked by, laughing and clinking their glasses without spilling a drop. Each looked perfectly at ease in the suits that probably cost more than Arran's mother's yearly salary. He tried to imagine what it'd be like to feel so comfortable, to know that you belonged.

Arran had felt uneasy around the Tridians ever since

discovering the vandalism. Who'd done it? Was it that haughty-looking girl who'd sneered at him when they'd bumped into each other in the corridor? Was it one of the boys who'd laughed at him on the track that day? Or, worse, was it one of the friendly Tridians? One of the people who said hateful things only behind closed doors? A knot formed in his stomach as a new theory took shape. Could it have possibly been *Dash*? While unlikely, it did seem like something Larz Muscatine's son would do.

"Maybe this was a mistake," Sula said, staring at a girl in a dress made of shimmery purple and green feathers.

"That's ridiculous," Arran said, trying to sound airy and relaxed. "This is our school too. We can't let them intimidate us. Come on," he said, tugging on her sleeve. "Let's get something to drink."

"Okay." Sula let out a long breath. "Just *promise* you won't abandon me."

"I promise. Though I probably shouldn't stay very long. We have our first battle in the morning."

"I know." Sula smiled. "You wouldn't stop talking about it at lunch."

"Sorry," Arran said, blushing. "I'm just excited." Their past few training sessions had gone really well, and he couldn't wait to see how his squadron worked together under pressure.

"Do you see any of the other Chetrians?" Sula asked.

Arran scanned the room. "No," he said. "Do you think they chickened out?"

A voice reached out from the din. "Sula!" A girl with dark brown skin wearing a pink dress strode toward them. "I'm so glad you're here. Weezie has the *best* idea for our new attack formation. You have to come with me." She smiled at Arran. "Sorry, top-secret squadron business. You understand."

"Do you mind?" Sula said, eyes darting between him and her squadron mate. "I know I *just* made you promise not to abandon me."

Arran glanced around the room again, trying to find at least one familiar face, but he didn't see anyone he knew. He didn't want Sula to worry, though. "It's really fine," Arran said, trying to keep the anxiety out of his voice. He was training to fight the Specters, for Antares's sake. He could handle a few minutes at a party on his own.

Sula shot him a grateful smile. "Okay, thanks. I'll be right back."

"Have fun." He tried to keep his own smile firmly in place until she'd disappeared.

Arran pretended to check a message on his link. It was too awkward to keep standing at the entrance, scanning the room for a sign of welcome that would never materialize, but walking around looking lost might be even worse.

Maybe he could pretend to go use the bathroom. But which way was that? An attendant glided by, carrying a tray full of drinks. "Excuse me," Arran said, "where is the—" But the attendant zipped past without acknowledging him.

"Here, I bet you could use one of these."

Arran turned to see Vesper standing in front of him holding two glasses full of pale pink liquid. Each was topped with a slice of red fruit Arran didn't recognize and a cluster of dark green leaves.

"Thank you," Arran said gratefully. He reached for one of the drinks, taking care not to let any of it slosh over the rim.

Vesper clinked her glass against Arran's. "Unity and prosperity," she said, reciting the traditional Quatra Fleet toast before taking a sip. Arran did the same and was surprised by the rush of sweetness. He took a larger sip. They didn't have anything like this on Chetire.

"Good, right? Don't get too used to it, though. They only serve pearlberry juice on special occasions." Vesper glanced over her shoulder, then lowered her voice. "My friend Frey added a little nitro spirit to these, so don't drink it too quickly."

Arran looked at the glass again, slightly startled. He'd never had anything with alcohol in it before. "Don't worry," Vesper said with a smile. "There's not much. You can add more if you want, though." She paused for a moment. "My friends are all over there. Come hang out with us for a bit."

Arran hesitated. He appreciated the friendly gesture, but he could hear the uncertainty in Vesper's voice.

"Thanks, but I'm fine," Arran said, trying to sound more confident and cheerful than he felt.

"I mean it." Vesper smiled and tugged on his sleeve. "It's ridiculous that none of us hang out with people from other planets."

"You're right." Arran nodded. "This is a serious diplomatic mission. Okay, lead the way, Ambassador Haze." He was glad for the excuse to join Vesper and her friends, at least until he found Sula again. Over the course of the past week, he'd found himself warming to Vesper more and more. She was intense and direct, but unlike the other Tridians, she didn't seem surprised by the talents and abilities of her Settler squadron mates. He just hoped she and Rex wouldn't butt heads tomorrow. Sometimes, their conflict pushed both of them to perform better. More often, it caused them to lose focus.

Arran took a deep breath as he followed Vesper over to a group of Tridians, all of them in suits and evening dresses. *It's fine*, Arran told himself. *Just stay calm and don't let them intimidate you.*

He scanned the group, and his heart slammed against his chest.

Dash was with them.

He wore a dark suit that fit his tall, slim body more closely than his uniform—the narrow jacket showed off his flat stomach, and the black trousers made his legs look even longer than usual. He hadn't spotted Arran yet and was absorbed in conversation with a smiling Tridian Arran recognized as Vesper's boyfriend, Ward.

Arran's stomach twisted with a combination of embarrassment and nerves, his mouth going dry as he searched his brain for a game plan. Should he say hi? Or just ignore him altogether?

When they reached the group, Vesper gestured toward Arran. "This is Arran, from my squadron. Arran, this is Ward, Brill, Dash, and Frey."

Everyone nodded or waved except for Dash, who stared

at Arran with an expression he couldn't quite identify. Not irritation or disdain, but something almost along the lines of *hurt*. Arran felt an unexpected twinge of guilt. What if Dash's invitation hadn't been a joke? What if he'd gone to dinner that night looking for Arran?

Without saying a word, Dash turned back to Ward and resumed talking, his smile suggesting nothing other than the ironic amusement that came so naturally to the Tridians. Of course it'd been a joke. Arran had been a fool to think otherwise.

"Frey's the one who can upgrade your drink if you want," Vesper said, gesturing at a handsome boy with smooth dark skin and high cheekbones.

"I'm fine, thank you," Arran said, wishing he knew how to sound as confident and careless as they did.

A blond girl in a spotless white dress, the one Vesper had introduced as Brill, cocked her head as she surveyed him curiously. "I thought everyone on Chetire drank."

Arran stared at her for a moment, unsure how to respond. "Some do, some don't. Just like on Tri, I imagine."

Vesper shot her friend a warning look, but Brill ignored her. "But aren't people always going on and on about people on Chetire drinking themselves to death? I mean, I get it.

It's cold, and there's nothing else to do. I'm sure I'd be obliterated most of the time if I lived there."

"Cut it out, Brill," Vesper said, then shot Arran an apologetic look as Frey shook his head and said with a laugh, "We can't take her anywhere."

An attendant glided up to the group with a tray of fruit Arran didn't recognize. There was no way to grow produce on Chetire outside climate-controlled greenhouses, which made it too expensive for most people.

The others each took some, so Arran followed suit and spent the next few minutes chewing on something tart and prickly as he listened to the Tridians gossip about people he didn't know, speculating on how they'd fare in the tournament and who'd catch the attention of Commander Stepney. A few times, Vesper stopped to explain to Arran whom they were talking about, but after a while, she got too caught up in the conversation to keep making asides.

Arran did his best to look relaxed and interested, but all he could really think about was his rumbling stomach. He'd been too nervous about tomorrow's battle to eat much at dinner, so when another attendant arrived with more refreshments, Arran was relieved to see something he recognized—a bun of some sort. He picked it up and took a large bite.

Bitter black liquid burst out, splashing Arran's face and burning his eyes. Across from him, he heard Brill shriek while Frey gasped, and Vesper and Ward smothered laughs. Heart pounding, Arran tried wiping his face with his napkin, but it only seemed to make things worse. Everything suddenly went blurry.

"Are you an idiot?" Brill snapped.

Arran blinked. The room came back into focus, and his stomach clenched when he saw Brill, her hair and her white dress splattered with black. "I'm so sorry," Arran said, forcing the words out of his tightening throat.

"Apparently, they don't have octopods on Chetire." Frey flashed a tight smile. "The body is full of ink. That's why we eat only the legs." He pointed at his own plate. The round brown thing Arran had mistaken for a bun was flipped over, revealing eight spindly legs he hadn't noticed.

"Everything's *fine*," Vesper said, passing Brill her napkin.

Brill shooed her hand away. "That's not going to help," she hissed.

"I'm sorry," Arran said again, glancing at Dash, who was staring at him with another inscrutable expression. "Can I get you something? Water?"

Brill glowered at him without saying anything.

"I guess I'd better go clean up. I'm sorry." He spun around and hurried away, grateful that the blood rushing in his ears kept him from hearing whatever the Tridians were saying about him.

This time, the attendant at the door said nothing as he passed. The hallway was deserted, he noticed with relief. He didn't want to see anyone right now.

He slouched against the sleek metal wall, tilted his head back, and closed his eyes.

He'd been a fool to think he stood a chance here. Doing well on a math test had nothing to do with what actually went on at the Academy. It was a mistake for anyone to believe that they could scoop up a few Chetrians who'd scored well on an exam, dump them in a place where they hadn't been welcome for the past five hundred years, and expect them to succeed.

"You okay?"

Arran opened his eyes and saw Dash staring at him with concern. "Yes, I'm fine," he said, turning away so Dash wouldn't see the shame in his face.

"Do you want to clean up and then come back inside for a bit?" Dash asked tentatively.

"I'm pretty tired. I think I should probably head back and get some rest."

"Are you sure you're okay? Do you want me to walk you back to your room?"

He was looking at Arran with a combination of kindness and sympathy that only a master manipulator would be able to fake, but then again, that's exactly what Larz Muscatine was famous for. "No, thanks. I'm fine."

Hurt flashed across Dash's face. "Sorry, did I do something wrong? I thought…" He paused to take a breath. "I was looking for you the other night."

Part of Arran was desperate to believe him, but another part was still reeling from the Tridians' laughter. He couldn't allow himself to look like a fool again. "If you need someone to prove your father's point about ignorant Settlers, you should keep looking."

Dash cringed and closed his eyes, as if Arran had just hit him. "You don't know anything about that," he said softly.

"We get the news on Chetire," Arran said, unable to keep the venom out of his voice. "Your father said Settlers posed a greater security threat than the Specters."

Dash shook his head. "No, I mean you don't know any-thing about my relationship with my father."

Arran could see the pain in Dash's face, but it wasn't enough to keep the bitter words from tumbling out. "Oh, so what—you agree to disagree? Do you have a rule about not discussing politics over dinner?"

"I swear, I'm nothing like him. I barely even see him." Dash's voice cracked slightly, and suddenly, the suspicion and anger that had been building in Arran's chest began to drain away.

"I'm sorry," Arran said, letting out a long breath. "I should've asked you about it instead of making up some story in my head."

To Arran's relief, Dash smiled, and Arran felt a fizzy tingle in his stomach. "I don't know," Dash said. "I kind of like the idea of you thinking about me. I just want to make sure they're mostly good things." Dash took Arran's hand, sending a jolt of electricity through his entire body. "Let's go get you cleaned up, and then we can head back inside."

For a moment, all Arran could focus on was the feel of Dash's hand, the warm pressure banishing all other thoughts in his head. But as Dash began to lead him down the hall, Arran hesitated. "Aren't you embarrassed to be seen with me after what happened? Your friends must think I'm an idiot."

Dash made a noise somewhere between a laugh and a snort. "*Embarrassed?* That was fantastic! Brill has been insufferable lately, and she got exactly what she deserved. Now let's go. Anyone who scored 233 on that exam can handle a few stuck-up Tri kids."

Arran smiled. "I scored 223."

"I know. But I've awarded you ten bonus points."

"For what?"

Dash raised an eyebrow, then grinned, revealing the dimple that made Arran melt. "For not realizing how adorable you are. It's pretty charming."

"Adorable," Arran repeated as warmth flooded his chest. "I'm not sure *adorable* is what a self-respecting Quatra Fleet cadet should be aiming for."

"Well, then it's a good thing you're not a pilot, because your aim is terrible. You crash-landed on adorable, and there's no going back." He reached over and gave Arran's hand a quick squeeze. "Now come on. I have a perverse desire to see how you tackle dessert."

CHAPTER 12

CORMAK

It certainly didn't look like any party Cormak had ever been to. No one had passed out on a couch. No drunken fights had broken out. And there wasn't a pile of gas masks by the door. He supposed he could see the appeal. There were nights when you just didn't feel like punching a surly acquaintance in the face and then braving a walk in the poisonous night air to get home.

The party was in an enormous wood-paneled room that must've cost a fortune to build in a space station. It was ridiculous what these people spent money on; the chandelier alone would probably pay for a year's worth of drinking water in Tower B. But he couldn't deny that it had a certain charm. Soft light suffused the room and made everything glow, from the ornate glasses on the refreshment table to the faces of the cadets.

It all seemed so elegant and serene, it was almost impossible to believe that at any moment Quatra Fleet guards could rush in to seize Cormak and drag him away. He'd barely been able to sleep the past few days, and yesterday he had woken up in such a state of panic, he'd actually snuck down to the launch dock to see if there was any chance of stealing onto one of the military cargo ships that periodically transported supplies from Tri. To his dismay, he'd been stopped almost immediately by one of the guards, who made it clear that she wouldn't accept his "I was lost" excuse more than once.

"What's going on?"

Cormak jumped to the side, heart racing.

"Sorry! I didn't mean to scare you."

He turned to see a pretty girl with thick, wavy black hair and deep brown eyes looking at him with concern. From her relaxed posture and long elegant dress, it was clear she was from Tri.

He took a deep breath and tried to regain his composure. "No, I'm sorry. I was...thinking about something else."

She smiled. "Yeah, I could tell. I imagine this party feels a little strange to you."

"What part? This?" Cormak squinted at his glass, which was full of a weird pink liquid topped with leaves. "Yeah, on Deva, we don't make *water* dress up for parties."

"It's not water. It's pearlberry juice. And if you want"— she glanced around the room, eyes flashing—"I can get you some nitro spirit to give it a bit more kick."

Cormak raised an eyebrow. "Now, this *is* strange. Where I'm from, pretty girls don't materialize out of thin air and offer to get you drunk."

She laughed, but before she could respond, someone else appeared at Cormak's side. "Nice try, Lu," Vesper said, raising an eyebrow as she surveyed the other girl. "But getting my captain drunk isn't going to help you win tomorrow."

"Is *that* what you were doing?" Cormak asked with a grin. "Very crafty."

The girl whose name was apparently Lu shot him an embarrassed smile. "I'll be over there if you change your mind," she said, nodding at a group of her friends giggling nearby.

After she walked away, Cormak turned to Vesper. "I liked hearing you call me your captain. It demonstrates a lot of personal growth, Vesper. I'm proud of you."

He expected her to scowl at him, but instead she flashed

a smile that was probably sixty percent amusement, forty percent irritation. A definite improvement. "I hope you're planning to go to sleep soon," she said. "We have a big day tomorrow, and we all need to be at the top of our game."

"As long as you listen to me, we're going to kick Squadron 4's ass."

An attendant glided over carrying a tray of brightly colored candy twists. "Thank you," Vesper said, taking a blue one. After letting his hand hover over the selection for about ten seconds, Cormak took five in assorted colors. As he took a bite of what turned out to be lavender chocolate, his monitor beeped.

"*High blood-sugar levels detected. For more information on optimal nutrition, say* nutrition."

"Dismiss," Cormak said under his breath before taking another bite. He had to hand it to these Tridians. They might be monumentally disconnected from reality, but they knew their desserts.

"*Most recent scans suggest fatigue. Based on your schedule for tomorrow, 8.25 hours of sleep recommended for optimal performance.*"

"*Dismiss,*" Cormak said again.

Vesper shot him a curious look as she lowered herself

into one of the spindly wooden chairs that surrounded the small tables scattered around the room. "I just don't think you understand how important these battles are."

He sat down in the chair next to her. It was even less comfortable than it looked. "I'm pretty sure I get it. It's all anyone can talk about here." Once word had gotten out about his squadron's high practice scores, complete strangers started bombarding him with questions about their training techniques.

"It's all *I've* been thinking about for pretty much my whole life. Everything I've ever done—all the tutors and the training—it's all been in preparation for this." Vesper's voice grew quieter, and she looked away as she spoke. "Everyone's always seen me as the admiral's second-rate daughter. I thought I could change their minds if I made it to the Academy and won the tournament…as a captain."

The playful barbs that had been forming in Cormak's head turned to dust. Yes, she was a rich, spoiled Tridian who'd had it easy in some ways. But he certainly knew what it was like to have people doubt you, to let them convince you that you'd never amount to anything. "I suppose your mom expects a lot from you. It sounds like a ton of pressure," he said carefully.

"It can be," she said, turning back to him with a questioning look, as if unsure whether he was luring her into a trap. "But I didn't just want to be captain to make my mother happy. I wanted it for myself. Squadron captains have the best shot at staying at the Academy for the second and third years, and entering the fleet as an officer. You get to make a difference right from the start. You get to *matter.*" Vesper had the same intense expression Cormak recognized from the simulator, but this time there was a hint of something else. Longing.

He nodded. He understood the fear of losing the future you'd imagined for yourself. For the first time in years, he'd been able to imagine a life beyond the despair that blanketed Deva. But that dream was quickly turning into a dead end.

"I get it," he said slowly. "This is important to me too. I'm not going to let anyone down."

"I'm glad to hear it," Vesper said, pressing her lips together to contain a smile.

"Here you are!" a boy with light brown hair said as he strode toward them, dressed in a suit that even Cormak could tell was expensive, though he wore it with careless ease.

"Ward," Vesper said as she stood up. "What are you doing? I thought you said you were going to bed."

Ignoring the question, Ward stepped forward and extended his arm. "Ward Shipley. Nice to meet you."

Cormak stood as well. "Rex Phobos." After a week, saying his brother's name had grown easier.

"Ah, the captain. Everyone is *very* curious to see how you all do tomorrow. Brill's placed the odds on your winning at five to one."

"Really?" Vesper brightened. "I bet by next week it's going to be ten to one."

Ward grinned and pulled Vesper toward him. "This one," he said affectionately, rubbing her arm. "She's so competitive. I love it. Though I can't say I like all this betting talk. It cheapens the tournament." He looked at Cormak expectantly, as if waiting for him to agree, but Cormak's thoughts were elsewhere.

Five to one, Cormak thought. A smile tugged on his lips as a plan took shape in his head. It was a crazy plan, sure, but it was a crazy plan that had gotten him into this predicament in the first place, and it was going to take an even crazier one to get him out of it.

"I'm going to bed," Cormak said abruptly. "Nice to meet you, Warp."

"It's Ward," Vesper corrected.

"Right, of course. See you tomorrow." He hurried away, ignoring their bewildered expressions.

The corridor was nearly deserted, though he did pass one couple making out in front of the common room and a girl humming to herself, staggering slightly as she walked barefoot holding her shoes.

Cormak scanned into his suite, nodded at his roommate, Basil, who was slumped on the couch, and walked straight into his own room. It was about the same size as his bedroom back in Tower B, but that's where the similarities ended. There was a wooden dresser and what even Cormak had to admit was a pretty cool desk with curved legs and silver handles on the drawers. He still couldn't fathom why anyone had thought it a good use of time and money to furnish a school in space with Tridian antiques, but he wasn't going to complain.

Without bothering to undress, Cormak fell back on the bed, sighing as he sank into the feather-soft, spotless white comforter. He'd never seen anything that clean and bright on Deva, where everything from fingernails to food to socks always had a coating of red dust. It was easier to keep things clean in space, where there was no dirt—and where robots did all the laundry.

At five-to-one odds, anyone who bet against Cormak's squadron tomorrow could make a killing…if his squadron lost. And as captain, he was uniquely qualified to ensure that happened.

He pulled out his Academy-issued link and entered the call code he'd memorized long ago.

"Who the hell is this?" a familiar voice barked a few moments later.

"Sol. It's Cormak," he said, smiling as he imagined how Sol would look if he knew where he was calling from.

"Cormak fucking Phobos. You've got some nerve, kid. You drop off the face of the planet, and then you call in the middle of the night? Do you have any idea what time it is, shithead?"

"I don't, actually," Cormak said pleasantly. "I'm not on Deva at the moment."

"And what does *encrypted number* mean? I've never seen an encryption that works on my link. Are you in prison? You'd better be calling from prison, because otherwise I'm going to find you and kill you. Do you know how much money you've cost me in missed deliveries? Where do—"

"Listen, Sol," Cormak said. "I'm not coming back to Deva." That part was true. He was either headed for a career in the

Quatra Fleet, or he was going to spend the rest of his life rotting in a Chetrian prison. Either way, Sol would have to find a new runner.

"Then what the hell do you want?"

"I need a favor."

Sol snorted. "You think I'm going to do *you* a favor after you screwed me over like this?"

"You will when I tell you how much I'm going to pay you for it."

CHAPTER 13

ORELIA

This was a mistake, Orelia thought, heart pounding as she scanned the ballroom. How had she let Zuzu talk her into this? Attending the formal was a waste of precious time. The messages from Sylvan were becoming more anxious, and although she'd spent the past week recording the location of various stars, she needed more data before she could begin making her calculations. And then she still had to figure out a way to transmit the coordinates.

There was a command center in the Academy that linked up directly with the Quatra Fleet headquarters on one of Tri's two moons. If she could sneak inside and gain access to the system, she might be able to send an encrypted message to Sylvan. But the command center was protected by a variety of security features, and the only way to get inside was to impersonate a high-ranking instructor with the appropriate clearance. In the meantime, she was stuck in a room full of laughing, drinking, chattering Quatrans who'd kill her if they knew what she really was.

As Orelia looked around, it was clear to her why the Quatrans had run through their own planets' resources so quickly and why they were so keen to pillage another's. Everywhere she looked were signs of the enemy's wasteful decadence. Food imported from the far ends of the solar system instead of freeze-dried nutrients. Drinks so full of sugar, they couldn't possibly be hydrating. And all of it under the light of an enormous glittering glass contraption that didn't even illuminate the room properly.

"Isn't it amazing?" Zuzu said as she looked around, awestruck. After finally convincing Orelia to go to the party with her, she'd changed her outfit four times before ending up in the first dress she'd tried on.

"It's dark."

"All the better for sneaking off with certain squadron mates." Zuzu was convinced that Orelia's squadron captain, Rex, was the best-looking boy at the Academy apart from their "uncomfortably attractive" counterintelligence instructor. "Is Rex here? Can you introduce me?"

Orelia surveyed the crowd. "I don't see him," she said, relieved that she wouldn't have to make any awkward introductions. Despite all her preparations and all the observations she'd made since arriving at the Academy, there always seemed to be some detail she got wrong during social interactions.

Zuzu excused herself to go investigate the refreshments, promising to return quickly. But Orelia didn't mind—she'd spent most of her life on her own. She looked around the crowded ballroom, watching clusters of cadets erupt in laughter, pairs engaged in earnest conversation, and a few instructors watching the proceedings with detached amusement. They all looked so *happy*—blissfully unaware that they were being trained to murder innocent Sylvans.

"Having fun?"

Startled, she turned to see Zafir standing next to her in his Quatra Fleet dress uniform—sharply creased trousers and a jacket with two rows of shiny buttons. He was smiling, but there was something in his eyes that suggested he never fully relaxed, that he was always on watch. "Yes, it's quite a party," Orelia said.

"I'm glad to hear it. You looked a little perplexed. Not that I blame you. When I was a cadet, I always found these formals slightly bewildering." He paused. "I'm making it sound like I was here ages ago."

"When did you graduate?" Orelia asked, wondering how long Zafir had been a counterintelligence officer. Did he know about the attacks against Sylvan, or was that information kept secret within the upper ranks of the fleet?

"Three years ago," he said. "Though I'm not supposed to talk about that. Admiral Haze doesn't want my students to know how close we are in age."

That would make Zafir twenty-two, just a year older than Orelia actually was, though her false documents claimed she was seventeen. "Why did you find parties bewildering?" She knew it was foolish to extend the conversation longer than necessary, but her curiosity got the better of her.

"It just seemed strange to me, the idea of putting on fancy clothes to hang out with the same people we spend every waking hour with." He shook his head. "Clearly, I'm a big hit at parties." He seemed different outside the classroom. Slightly less assured. And there was a note of self-deprecation in his voice that, to her surprise, made her want to put him at ease.

"You have to be better than I am. I've never been to a party before."

He raised an eyebrow. "Really?" *Fool*, she chastised herself. Why would she hint at her unusual upbringing in front of the counterintelligence expert? But to her relief, he seemed more amused than suspicious. "Well, you're making quite a debut. That's a very nice dress."

Before she could respond, Zuzu appeared at Orelia's side clutching a plate of unusual-looking appetizers. "I should let you two enjoy the party," Zafir said with a nod. "Have fun."

"Antares, he's good-looking," Zuzu said, blushing as she watched Zafir walk away. "Do you want any of this?" She gestured at her plate.

Orelia shook her head as she scanned the room. She hadn't recorded the stars' positions from this wing of the Academy and wanted to take advantage of the opportunity. "Excuse me," she said. "I need to find the bathroom."

"Sure," Zuzu said, looking slightly abashed at Orelia's curtness.

"I'll try to find Rex for you," Orelia said with what she hoped was a warm smile.

Zuzu smiled back and smoothed her skirt. "Sounds good."

Orelia slipped into the chattering crowd and made her way toward the large window on the far side. She glanced over her shoulder to make sure no one was looking, then activated the camera on her link.

She checked again to confirm that no one was paying attention and snapped a few quick photos, feeling the knot in her stomach loosen slightly. If she kept this up, she'd soon have enough data to start her analysis.

"Orelia! You're here!" Arran called as he bounded toward her. A wide smile stretched across his face, and despite the strange black marks on his shirt, his eyes were shining. Instead of his usual slouch, which always reminded Orelia of a sea creature retreating into its shell, Arran moved with confidence and assurance. "You look beautiful," he said, his grin growing even wider.

She tried to tamp down the thrill of pleasure his words unlocked. She wouldn't let herself become one of them—superficial, vain, materialistic. She refused to return to Sylvan tainted. Besides, *beautiful* wasn't a word you used to describe other people. It should be reserved for the resilient trees that survived the long, hot Sylvan summer when the seas rose and covered nearly two-thirds of the land masses.

"Where did you get that?" Orelia asked with curiosity, pointing to the pink drink in his hand.

"The attendants are going around with trays of drinks, and you can just take one! As many as you want! You don't have to pay for them or anything."

Orelia cocked her head. "How many of these have you had exactly?"

"They don't have alcohol in them." He shook his head solemnly. "But…" He looked around again and whispered, "You can add nitro spirit. I'll show you." He grabbed Orelia's hand and started to tug her forward, sloshing some of his drink over the rim of the glass.

Orelia pulled away. "I'm fine. I'll get one later." She needed to take a few more photos before she could return to her room to analyze the data.

Before she could escape, a tall boy with fair skin and dark hair appeared at Arran's side. "There you are," he said, smiling at Arran with an expression that made her feel both happy and lonely at the same time.

"This is Dash," Arran said, gesturing at the dark-haired boy. "Dash, this is Orelia."

"Nice to meet you," Dash said. "Arran was just telling me

about his genius intelligence officer. You must be excited for tomorrow."

Excited wasn't exactly the right word, since winning the tournament meant nothing to Orelia. Yet she had to admit that they'd been performing well during their practice sessions. When Vesper and Rex weren't wasting time with their pointless shows of dominance, the squadron was focused and efficient. Orelia had never been part of a team before, and to her surprise, there'd been moments when she'd almost enjoyed it.

"We'd be lost without Orelia," Arran said, beaming at her. "I've never seen anyone who can analyze information as quickly as she can."

"I think you deserve a little treat after all that hard work," Dash said. "Come with us."

"No. I'm fine," she said. "I'm not staying long."

"*Orelia*," Arran said, looking at her so seriously, she almost laughed. "You have to come with us."

Orelia hesitated. She glanced toward the door, then looked away when she realized that Zafir was standing nearby. Would he find it strange that she was leaving so early? She'd already revealed too much; she couldn't risk drawing any additional attention to herself. Unsure of what to do, she allowed Dash and Arran to lead her to the drinks table, where they procured for her a lavender beverage that, at Arran's insistence, Dash topped off with clear liquid from a flask in his pocket.

The boys raised their glasses, so Orelia did the same. "Unity and prosperity," Dash said.

"Unity and prosperity!" Arran echoed, clinking his glass against Dash's before doing the same to Orelia's.

She took a tentative sip. The lavender liquid was sweet and frothy, but when she swallowed it, she tasted something pleasantly herbal. "This is nice," she said. Arran and Dash both laughed. "What? What did I say?"

"Nothing," Dash said with a smile. "You sounded so *surprised*. Just don't drink it too quickly. And maybe have something to eat as well."

"Ooh, *yes*." Arran tugged on Dash's sleeve. "Let's get something to eat. But not octopods," he said gravely, turning to Orelia. "You do *not* want to eat one of those."

She followed them through the crowd to a table laden with a variety of bite-size foods, none of which she recognized. "Just be careful," Arran whispered loudly. "Some of it attacks."

She randomly selected a few items, then the three of them found a cluster of chairs and sat to eat, their plates balanced on their laps. "You know what makes Orelia such a good intelligence officer?" Arran said thoughtfully as he nibbled on a piece of cheese. "She's so *quiet*. Like, you almost forget she's there, and then *bam!* She produces some piece of information that changes everything."

"I think I need to see this in action," Dash said.

"I suppose if I'm that good, you'll never see me in action," she said, smiling despite herself. She took another sip of her drink, enjoying the warmth spreading through her chest.

"You'll see it firsthand when we crush your squadron," Arran said.

Dash raised an eyebrow. "I wouldn't get your hopes up."

As she listened to Arran and Dash's playful banter, she felt her anxiety about her mission drain away. Dash excused himself, and a short while later, he returned holding a second lavender drink for Orelia that she accepted without protest.

"So, Orelia," Arran said confidentially as he inclined his head toward hers. "Who should we invite to join us? Is there anyone you have your eye on?"

I have my eye on all of you, Orelia thought before realizing what Arran meant. "No, there's no one," she said despite the strange, unexpected image taking shape in her mind: Zafir in his dress uniform.

"I'm not sure I believe you," Dash teased. "You're blushing."

"Who is it?" Arran asked, grabbing her hand. "Rex? Vesper?"

"No one," she repeated. Arran pouted and she smiled.

This is fun, she thought. She liked these boys even if they were Quatrans. But a few seconds later, a wave of nausea crashed over her, and the dull ache that'd been forming near her temples began to spread throughout her head.

"Are you okay?" Arran asked, suddenly concerned instead of giggly.

"Yes, fine. I think I just need to go to bed." Orelia rose to her feet, and to her confusion, she felt the room start to spin. "Oh no," she said as she staggered to one side.

"Easy there." Dash jumped to his feet to grab her arm, and then Arran took the other. "We'll walk you back."

"No, I'm okay." She tried to shrug herself loose but just ended up falling to the side again. It was like someone had suddenly changed the gravity settings, throwing off her equilibrium.

Arran whispered something to Dash and then took

her hand. "Come on," he said, gently tugging her forward. "Everything's fine."

He led her through the crowded ballroom, now a dizzying swirl of color, laughter, and light. Another wave of nausea slammed into her, and her stomach started to cramp. "I think…I think I ate something bad," she said hoarsely as Arran led her into the corridor.

"I think you just had a little too much to drink. Don't worry. Just drink a lot of water before you go to bed and you'll feel better in the morning. What floor is your room on again?"

When they reached her suite, she was relieved to find the living room empty. She didn't want Zuzu, let alone their other suitemates, to see her looking so undignified. "Thank you," Orelia said, grabbing onto the side of the couch to steady herself. "I'll be fine. You can go back to Dash."

"I'll go in a minute," Arran said. He instructed her to change and get into bed. Too tired and dizzy to object, she complied, and a few minutes later he came into her room holding a large glass of water.

"Drink this." Arran handed her the glass and then sat at the foot of her bed, looking around the room. "Not really one for decorating, are you?"

In contrast to Zuzu's room, which was plastered with pics, clothing, and knickknacks, Orelia's room had no personal items except for the two sets of clothes she'd brought with her from Sylvan. "No, not really."

"It's minimalist. I like it." But as Arran surveyed the room, his face fell slightly. "Didn't you bring anything to remind yourself of home?"

She shook her head, then winced as the pounding returned. "It's easier this way." But the truth was that she'd had nothing to bring. Her room in the military compound on Sylvan had been barer than this one.

Arran stared at her curiously for a moment, then smiled as he rose to his feet. "Sleep well, Orelia. I'll see you tomorrow."

As she sipped the water, the nausea subsided slightly, and she felt a strange mixture of gratitude and confusion. "Why are you helping me?" she asked.

He cocked his head to the side, as if he didn't understand the question. "You're my squadron mate. And my friend."

"Thank you," she said, then closed her eyes as the nausea returned, accompanied by something even worse. Guilt.

CHAPTER 14

VESPER

Vesper woke up with excitement tingling in her stomach. Today was their first battle, and she couldn't wait to emerge victorious from the simulcraft. Her squadron had been receiving top scores during the practice sessions, but the only number that really counted was their rank at the end of the tournament.

Vesper walked quickly through the residential wing, smiling and nodding at people who waved or called to her, but she didn't stop to talk. It was time to focus and get into the zone with the rest of her squadron. But to her surprise and irritation, only Orelia and Arran were inside the simulcraft when she arrived.

"Where's Rex?" Vesper asked, forgoing pleasantries.

"I'm sure he's on his way." Arran glanced at the count-down clock on the screen. "We still have five minutes."

"Right…" Vesper started pacing back and forth. "Okay, I think there's a good chance it's going to be a rescue mission, so our strategy will be pretty simple—we just need to be faster than the other squadron. That's good, because speed has never been an issue for us."

Arran nodded politely, although she could tell he was mostly humoring her. Orelia was already seated in her chair, looking drawn and even more quiet than normal.

The door hissed open and Rex entered. His uniform was wrinkled and his brown skin looked unusually ashen. "Are you okay?" Vesper asked, squinting at his slightly bleary eyes.

"I'm wonderful. So sweet of you to ask." He spoke slower than normal, and instead of bounding toward the captain's chair and doing some obnoxious spin, he trudged over and lowered himself gingerly.

"Are you ill?" Vesper asked, more accusingly than she'd meant.

Rex rolled his shoulders a few times, then cracked his

knuckles. "Never better. Just getting ready to kick some Squadron 4 ass."

"Good," Vesper said, choosing to give him the benefit of the doubt. Rex knew how important this first battle was. He'd rise to the occasion even if he was feeling under the weather. "Now, remember, their captain is Pru Kamal. I used to see her in the simulcraft at my old school, and she's incredibly good at misdirection. So if this ends up being a combat mission, don't get complacent just because it looks like she's using a standard attack formation. She always has another plan."

"Yeah, I know," Rex said, wincing slightly. "You told me that about a dozen times this week."

"I also told you to get here *on time*, but that clearly didn't sink in."

"I *am* here on time."

"Three minutes before the mission starts isn't *on time*." Vesper knew she wasn't helping matters, but she couldn't control the frustration bubbling up inside her. They'd had a whole conversation last night about how much this meant to her. Why was he acting like none of it mattered?

He winced again. "Can you lower your voice, please?"

Vesper stared at him as cold dread seeped down her spine. "Are you *hungover?*"

Rex spun his chair around so he was no longer facing her. "Maybe. So what? There was a party last night. That's what happens. You were also drinking."

The dread was incinerated by flares of anger. Vesper yanked Rex's chair around. "That is *not* what happens," she snapped, no longer caring what Arran and Orelia thought about her. Rex was sabotaging their futures as well. "I guarantee you that no one else competing today is hungover."

"Okay, Vesper, that's enough." Arran shot her an admonishing look. "We all stayed out too late last night. There's no reason to attack Rex."

"I'm not *attacking* him," she said, slightly taken aback by Arran's unusually cold expression.

"Yes, you were. But bullying him isn't going to make us perform any better, and it's definitely not going to make you captain, so just take it easy, okay?"

The words landed like a punch to her chest. "I'm not... I wasn't..." She searched for the right words to help Arran realize he was looking at everything all wrong. She was just trying to win. That's what everyone wanted; that's what would be best for all of them.

The lights dimmed, and a voice rang through the speakers. *"Your battle will commence in thirty seconds. Please take your places."*

With a sigh, Vesper lowered herself into her seat and tried to chase away the guilt gnawing at her. She didn't have time to worry about hurt feelings at the moment. All that mattered right now was winning.

She turned to the dashboard, allowing the glowing lights to soothe her. This was where she belonged even if she wasn't in the captain's chair.

"Welcome, Squadron 4 and Squadron 20. Today's battle will be a rescue mission. You will be presented with identical scenarios and then race to see who completes the operation first. Here is your task. A commercial shuttle was forced to make an emergency landing on Gaspar, one of Chetire's moons, and is quickly running out of life support. Your objective: Depart from Deva, fly to Gaspar, evacuate the survivors, and deliver them safely to Chetire. Your missions begin…now."

"Right, a rescue mission, just like I told you," Vesper said, though she realized she was talking more to herself than the others. The screen filled with pink haze. "What the hell? Where are we?"

"Home sweet home," Rex said drily. "Arran, what's Gaspar's gravitational pull?"

Out of the corner of her eye, Vesper saw Arran swiping rapidly on the screen. "About seventy-four percent of Tridian gravity."

"Orelia, any complications?"

"There's a storm in the Devak mesosphere right above us. We have three options. We can wait for it to pass, we can try to fly around it, or we can fly right through it."

"What do you suggest?"

"We should fly around it. That way, we'll minimize damage to the ship without wasting too much time."

"Let's go for it. Take it away, Vesper."

She was relieved to hear the firmness in his voice. At least he was feeling better. Vesper activated the thrusters, her heart pounding with a combination of excitement and nerves. She grinned as the ship soared through the thick pink air. To avoid the storm, she stayed in the stratosphere for longer than normal, flying at a slightly shallower angle. Once Orelia gave her the all clear, she straightened out and increased her speed until the Devak atmosphere grew thin, eventually giving way to the thermosphere.

"What's Squadron 4 up to?" Rex asked.

Orelia leaned forward to examine the radar screen more closely. "They're about fifty thousand mitons ahead of us."

"What?" Vesper jerked her head around to face Orelia and Rex. "How the hell did that happen?"

"They must've gone straight through the storm," Orelia said with infuriating calm. "They probably sustained considerable damage."

"Shit." Vesper banged her hand against the dashboard. If they didn't catch up soon, they were screwed.

"Is there anything we can do to make up time?" Rex asked.

"I'm doing my best," Vesper said tersely as she activated the backup thrusters. It was an enormous waste of fuel but worth the risk.

"It's highly risky," Orelia said. "But we could try using Chetire's gravity well to gain speed heading toward Gaspar."

"Like slingshot around it?" Rex asked, sounding curious.

"Absolutely not," Vesper said without turning around. Using a gravity assist was one of the most advanced piloting moves you could perform. Real fleet pilots spent years training on simulcrafts before they ever attempted it.

"I don't know...." Rex said, fatigue creeping back into his voice. "It sounds like it might be worth trying."

"There's no *trying*," Vesper said, glaring at him over her shoulder. "If we mess up, which we will, instead of slingshotting around Chetire, we'll burn up in its atmosphere." She turned to Orelia. "Can we catch up if we stick to our current trajectory?"

"If we land faster than they do and retrieve the stranded passengers more quickly, then, yes, we have a chance."

"Good," Vesper said, feeling the excitement return. "Arran, will you conduct mineral analysis of Gaspar's surface? We need to find somewhere soft to land."

"We're doing the gravity assist," Rex said.

"What?" Vesper whipped her head around again. "No way."

"Vesper, that's an order." There was no playful challenge in his voice; he was serious.

"Why are you doing this? It's suicide." She looked from Orelia to Arran, desperately hoping that one of them would back her up, but they both avoided her eyes.

"It's not suicide. A good pilot could pull it off. Now, please proceed as instructed."

"This is bullshit," she muttered under her breath as she turned back to the screen. Rex had no right being captain. He didn't know anything about flying, let alone leadership. He didn't care about winning. All he cared about was putting her in her place.

Arran read off her new coordinates, the ones that would, supposedly, allow her to approach Chetire at the perfect angle so they could use its gravitational pull to shoot around it at a dizzying speed. "You can do this," Vesper whispered to herself as Chetire appeared in the distance.

The tricky part was getting close enough to the surface to feel the gravitational pull but not so close that they'd bounce off the atmosphere and turn into a giant fireball. At this speed, there was no margin for error.

The icy planet grew larger on the screen. "Okay," Vesper said, trying to sound more confident than she felt. "Let's do this."

Arran had made a calculation based on their speed, Chetire's mass, and its gravitational pull. So far, he'd never made a math error, and Vesper was sure the trajectory he'd suggested was the right one. Now it was up to her to follow that path—to approach Chetire at just the right angle.

She took a deep breath to steady her trembling hands and initiated her approach. The simulcraft jerked, and they suddenly gained speed. *It's working*, Vesper thought. *I'm actually doing it.* There was a sharper jerk, and the simulcraft started to rumble. *"Warning. Temperatures reaching dangerous levels. Warning. Temperatures reaching dangerous levels."*

"I'm on it," Arran called. "Initiating emergency engine cooling." Out of the corner of her eye, Vesper saw his hands fly across the screen. "Shoot," he muttered under his breath.

The screens on all sides suddenly filled with flames. "No!" Vesper banged the dashboard again. "Shit, shit, shit!"

The screens went dark. *"Mission failure. Your craft was incinerated in Chetire's atmosphere. There were no survivors."*

Vesper spun around and leapt out of her chair. "What the hell was that, Rex? I *told* you that was going to happen."

"You're blaming this on *me*?" Rex said with a sneer that made his face nearly unrecognizable. "You waltz in here thinking you can order us around because *of course* a Tridian knows more than some clueless Settler, and then it turns out that you can barely fly."

Her skin practically sizzled as a tide of fury rose within her. "Barely fly? I can pull off maneuvers you've never *seen* before."

"Yeah, but not when it counts. When the pressure was on, you choked."

"Okay, that's enough," Arran said, glaring at Rex. "We all did our best. That's what matters."

"No, it's not," Vesper said, beginning to tremble. "What counts is winning."

Without another word, she moved unsteadily toward the door. With each step, her rage drained away, leaving something far worse in its wake—the horrifying realization that Rex was right. Yes, he'd made a stupid decision, but ultimately, she'd been the one who choked. Once again, when it really mattered, she'd let herself down.

CHAPTER 15

CORMAK

Brill had told Cormak to come to the library at 32:30 to collect his winnings. He hadn't been to the library yet, and he ended up taking a few wrong turns before finding himself in a wide, quiet corridor. It had to be one of the exterior rings of the Academy since a panoramic window ran along one of the walls, which revealed clusters of stars and the craggy edges of a passing asteroid. Even for Cormak, who had grown up on a perpetually cloud-shrouded planet, it was a little disorienting to see the stars during what his body was trained to believe was daytime.

The library, when he finally found it, was unlike anything he had seen before. For Cormak, the word conjured an image of a cramped, windowless room in the Sector 23 town hall where a rusted attendant would look up information for you. Yet this room was full of *books*. Thousands of them. Looking around, Cormak was filled with enough wonder to momentarily push aside the guilt that had been festering in his stomach all day. But he knew the reprieve wouldn't last long. Every time he thought about the anguish in Vesper's face, a new cloud of shame engulfed him.

He stepped toward the closest bookcase, which stretched from floor to ceiling, and let his hand hover above one of the spines. It was embossed with gold letters in a language Cormak didn't recognize.

"You're allowed to touch them, you know." Cormak let his hand fall to the side and spun around. Brill, the Tri girl who'd organized the betting ring, was sitting in a leather armchair, surveying him with amusement. She was wearing glittery gold eye makeup that reminded Cormak of the gilded book he'd been looking at, and her blond curls were styled in a way that was possible only with time, money, and lots of showers.

"I know," Cormak said, yanking the book off the shelf. He pretended to flip through it casually, unwilling to reveal the thrill it gave him.

"Do you read Ungai?"

"What?"

She nodded at the book in his hands. "That's written in High Ungai. Mine's not very good. I studied it for only a few years."

Cormak replaced the book on the shelf. "That's a shame," he said. "Ungai's a beautiful language." He hoped it was true.

Brill rose gracefully from her chair and stretched her arms over her head. Something about the movement suggested that it was more for Cormak's benefit than her sore muscles. She'd already changed out of her uniform for dinner, and her short black dress rose up her thighs when she lifted her arms.

Cormak watched impassively. He'd known lots of girls like her, and giving them the attention they craved never ended well. He caught Brill searching for a glimpse of admiration in his face, and when she didn't find it, her expression hardened slightly.

"You did a great job this morning," Brill said. "Vesper totally believed you were too hungover to focus. You're quite the actor."

"Thanks," he said, wincing slightly. Betting against his own squadron had earned him a huge amount of money—just enough to pay Sol to hack into the medical clinic back on Deva and swap Cormak's files for his brother's before they were re-sent to the Academy. It was the only way to avoid expulsion and an arrest for treason. But that didn't make the memory of Vesper's anguished expression any easier to bear.

"Let's see....How much did you win? Four hundred skyor?" She opened a dainty gold purse and began riffling through it. "I don't have that much on me. Can I just transfer it to your account? What's your ID number?"

Four hundred skyor. It was more than he'd ever possessed in his entire life. "I don't know it offhand." He had a vague recollection of his dad opening a commerce account for him when he was a kid, but that was the last he'd heard of it.

"You don't know it?" Brill repeated, incredulous. "How is that possible? How do you get through the day?"

"I don't do a ton of shopping," Cormak said drily.

Brill's eyes widened. "No, of course you don't." The faux sympathy in her cloying voice roiled his stomach.

He took a deep breath, unwilling to get worked up in front of Brill. "I'll get you an account number for the transfer. But in the meantime, can you do me a favor and keep this arrangement to yourself?" He tried to keep his voice light, as the more desperate he seemed to Brill, the more likely she was to use this information against him.

"Your secret's safe with me," she said sweetly. She turned and sauntered away in a manner that made it clear she hoped Cormak was watching. Ignoring her, Cormak searched the library for the most secluded corner he could find, then called Sol on his link.

"You have the money?"

"It's nice to hear your voice as well, Sol. I'm doing great. Thanks so much for asking." Cormak sank into an armchair and stretched out his legs.

"I don't have time for this, Phobos."

"Relax. I have your money. Just give me an account number, and I'll transfer it today."

Sol made a sound somewhere between a snicker and a grunt. "You writing this down?"

"Absolutely. Go ahead." Cormak smiled, relishing the fact that Sol no longer had the power to chew him out for using his brain instead of a pen. "You'll let me know when you've uploaded the new data?"

"As soon as the money comes through. Though I gotta tell you, kid, this sounds real suspicious even to me. Where the hell are you?"

"Gotta go, Sol. Thanks for everything." Cormak ended the call, then twisted around so his legs were hanging over the side of the armchair. He'd done it. Sol would replace Rex's medical records with his own, and then everything would be fine. The knot of anxiety growing in his stomach for the past week finally began to loosen, and he let out a long sigh. He was going to get to stay at the Academy. Hell, he'd probably even graduate.

He just wished he could forget the look on Vesper's face when he'd let her down.

CHAPTER 16

ARRAN

"How's it going, 223?"

Sergeant Pond had just dismissed their engineering class, and Arran was gathering his things when he looked up and saw Dash smiling at him.

It'd been three days since the formal, which had turned out to be one of the best nights of Arran's life. After putting Orelia to bed, he'd returned to the ballroom where he and Dash had flirted all night. Arran had lost track of the number of times Dash had touched his arm or brushed his knee against Arran's leg. He'd been so sure that Dash would kiss him at some point that after Dash had said a friendly good night and walked away it had taken hours for the ache in Arran's chest to fade away. Arran knew that, technically, he could've kissed Dash, but the thought of making the first move left him more nauseated than the shuttle ride had. He couldn't risk the pain and shame of rejection—not again.

"Not too bad," Arran said, doing his best to sound friendly but not overly invested.

"Listen," Dash said, lowering his voice conspiratorially. "Are you free after dinner? I've thought of the *best* way to prank Brill."

Arran couldn't stop a smile from spreading across his face. "I think I'm free," Arran said vaguely. "Who else is coming?"

"I think tonight's a job for you and me. Sound good?"

You and me. "Sounds good."

"Cadet Korbet," a voice called over the clamor of footsteps and chatter. Arran turned to see Sergeant Pond nodding at him. "Drop by my office before dinner. I want to talk to you."

Arran nodded. "Yes, sir," he said, doing his best to sound nonchalant despite the tendril of anxiety twisting around his stomach. Had Pond noticed that Arran hadn't been paying attention in class?

Pond dismissed him, and Arran and Dash walked out of the classroom together. "What was that about?" Dash asked.

Arran shrugged, trying to keep the anxiety at bay. "No idea."

Dash nudged Arran's shoulder. "I wouldn't worry about it, 223."

Arran smiled, marveling at how the simple act of walking from one class to another could suddenly become the best part of the day.

A few hours later, Arran was in the administration wing, searching for Pond's office. His anxiety had only worsened over the course of the afternoon as he tried to figure out why he'd been summoned. "Where is Sergeant Pond's office?" he whispered to his monitor.

"Sergeant Pond is your engineering instructor. If you need assistance with an engineering assignment, a research attendant will be glad to assist you. For directions to the library, say library."

"I need to find his office," Arran said, trying to keep the irritation out of his voice. The last thing he needed right now was for a faculty member to catch him sniping at his monitor.

"Continue down the corridor for approximately six centimitons.... You've arrived at your destination."

Arran paused in front of Pond's door to collect himself,

then took a deep breath and knocked. "Come in!" a voice bellowed. The door opened with a hiss, and Arran stepped inside. The office was smaller than the classrooms but full of so many intriguing items that he didn't know where to look first. On the far wall was a holopic of a slightly younger Pond standing next to Ayo Hobart, the president of the Quatra Federation. Next to Arran was a series of topographical maps, including one of the D'Arcy mountain range on Chetire. But most striking of all was the enormous piece of machinery suspended from the ceiling, part of a fightercraft made out of a black metal Arran had never seen before. As he took in more details, his curiosity gave way to unease, and grim memories crawled out from the back of his brain. Two years ago, the news memos had been full of pics of these ships—an insect-like swarm of them had darkened the sky before the devastating attack on Haansgaard. It was how the Specters had managed to kill so many Chetrians in such a short amount of time.

"I assume you know what that is," Pond said gruffly, rising from his desk.

"It's a piece of a Specter ship," Arran said. Without meaning to, he'd lowered his voice, as if afraid to disturb anything hidden within the craft. Even though Arran knew full well that there was nothing inside, he couldn't quite shake the prickle of fear on the back of his neck.

"I've been told it's useless," Pond said almost fondly. "That's why I was allowed to take it with me."

"What do you mean, useless?" Arran asked, looking up at the ship fragment.

"Anytime we recover a piece of Specter technology, no matter how many similar samples we've seen, we always send it to the counterintelligence lab for analysis. You never know what you might learn about the bastards from a seemingly innocuous piece of equipment. After the most recent attack, we found an undetonated bomb that turned out to be a treasure trove. It was covered in fragments of Specter DNA. That's classified information, of course, but now that you're a Quatra Fleet cadet, you have the security clearance for it."

Security clearance. The words made Arran's chest swell with pride. He couldn't wait to tell his mother. Not what he'd learned, of course. But even the fact that there were things he couldn't tell her would make her joyously happy. He imagined her at the graduation ceremony on Tri. How she'd beam when she saw Arran in his uniform, perhaps onstage receiving a prestigious award.

"Take a seat, Arran." Pond gestured at a chair, then

returned to his own behind his desk. "I wanted to see how
you were doing. I know it hasn't been an easy transition for
the Settlers." He didn't sound nearly as gruff as usual; in
fact, there was a hint of concern in his voice.

"I'm doing okay," Arran said.

"Good, good. I'm glad to hear it. And, rest assured, hateful behavior will never be tolerated at the Academy." There
was a long pause, and Arran shifted uncomfortably, wondering what Pond was waiting for him to say. Finally, Pond
cleared his throat and continued. "I've noticed you spend
quite a bit of time with Cadet Muscatine."

Arran sat up straight and tried to hide his confusion as
his brain raced to figure out why this could possibly matter
to Pond.

"I think you should be careful around him. I assume you
know who his father is."

For a moment, Arran was too startled to speak. "I do," he
said carefully, wishing he knew what Pond was getting at.
"But I don't see what that has to do with our…friendship."

Pond sighed, then offered Arran what he probably
believed was a supportive smile. "Forgive me, but I find
it difficult to believe that Larz Muscatine's son would be
friends with a Chetrian."

"He's not his father," Arran said more sharply than he'd intended.

"Listen," Pond said, raising both hands into the air in a gesture of surrender. "I like the Muscatine boy and would be delighted if it turns out that you're right. But in the meantime, I think you should be careful. Get to know some of the other cadets so if things go badly with him, you don't feel like you're on your own."

"Why would things go badly?" The moment the words left his mouth, Arran's entire body tensed. Like he'd just thrown a bad punch and was bracing for the impact of a more capable opponent's fist. He'd never spoken to a teacher this way before.

Pond seemed unperturbed by Arran's tone. "These things are more complicated than I think you realize. Just take care of yourself, Korbet. That's all I'm asking."

"I'll take that into consideration, sir. Is that all?"

"That's all."

Arran rose from his chair and strode out, using all his self-control to restrain his bubbling anger. Pond had no right to interfere in Arran's personal life like this. Did he think Arran was too much of a Chetrian rube to understand what was going on? He *knew* who Dash's father was, and after a lot of thought and consideration, he'd made a conscious decision to get to know Dash the person, not Dash the estranged son of Larz Muscatine.

"Elevated heart rate detected."

"Yeah, I know," Arran huffed. Why did every single thing in the Academy, sentient or otherwise, act like he couldn't take care of himself?

"New message from Dash Muscatine... Hey, it's me...Dash. Just wanted to see how your meeting with Pond went. Call me, or I'll just see you at dinner."

Arran grinned as the sound of Dash's voice chased away all the frustration welling up in his chest. Dash was the first boy who'd ever seen Arran as anything more than a shy, awkward, forgettable nobody. The first boy who found Arran's intelligence attractive—who made Arran *feel* attractive. He wasn't going to let anyone sabotage that.

CHAPTER 17

ORELIA

Orelia's heart began to pound as she made her way toward the administrative wing. This was the moment she'd been training for. She'd finally collected enough celestial data to determine the Academy's secret location in the asteroid belt between Tri and Loos. All she had to do now was transmit the coordinates to Sylvan—though that was easier said than done.

She peered around the corner. Down the hall was an unmarked door that led to the command center, and as expected, security guards were patrolling outside.

A moment later, the timed alarm Orelia had progammed down the hall began blaring. The guards rushed toward the sound, and Orelia quickly made her way to the command center. The guards would soon realize there was no emergency, so she had no time to waste. She came to a stop in front of the door and pulled out the ID she'd "borrowed" from Captain Russo. Her biological engineering professor was one of the few people who had security clearance for the command center. She held the ID up to the scanner and let out a long breath as the light turned green and the door hissed open.

She crept forward and found herself in a dark, round room that reminded her of the simulcraft—crammed with monitors and blinking lights—except that the large window was full of real twinkling stars, not simulated ones. In the center of the room was the command console.

After a few minutes of fiddling with the unfamiliar system, she prepared to send an encrypted message with the station's coordinates to the military base on Sylvan. She felt a rush of excitement, and for a moment, she couldn't do more than grin as she pictured General Greet receiving the transmission, her commanding officer's smile flickering across her normally stern face.

Yet before she could hit send, cold dread began to spread through her veins. She thought about Zuzu, asleep in their suite, who had been nothing but kind to her since she arrived at the Academy. She thought about Arran and the way he had taken care of her after the formal. Did these people really deserve to die?

Stop it, Orelia told herself. It wasn't up to her who lived and who died. The Quatrans had sealed their fate long ago when their leaders decided to attack Sylvan. Millions of people were counting on her. She didn't have a choice.

Orelia pressed send, then held her breath until the words *Transmission successful* flashed across the screen. She closed her eyes and fell back against the wall with a sigh. All she had to do now was keep her identity secret until the Sylvan ships arrived at the Academy, one of which would extract Orelia before the attack.

She hurried out of the command center, turned the corner, and froze. There were two people striding toward her. *Just stay calm*, she told herself. *There's no rule against going for a walk in the middle of the night.*

But as the echo of stomping footsteps grew louder, her heart began to pound a desperate alarm. Two guards, a short, stocky man and a tall, grim-faced woman, were marching down the corridor in Quatra Fleet security uniforms. *They know.* Orelia took a deep breath and tried to quell the panic rising within her. *You've already completed your mission. It doesn't matter if you don't make it home. There's nothing they can do to change that. If you die, you'll die a hero.*

"Is everything okay?" the female guard asked gruffly.

"Fine," Orelia said, proud that her voice didn't quaver despite her racing pulse. "I couldn't sleep so I went for a walk."

"You're not authorized to be in this area," the man said.

"I got a little lost. I'm sorry," Orelia said, doing her best to sound like a helpless and confused first-year cadet instead of a highly trained operative who'd been poring over maps of the Academy since her arrival.

The man pressed something on his link, then frowned as he listened to an update Orelia couldn't hear. "You're not wearing your monitor."

"I always take it off when I go to bed." Her chest tightened as she reviewed every step she'd taken that night, praying that she hadn't left any clues behind. If she was caught, there'd be no trial, no opportunity to plead for her life. The Quatra Fleet couldn't let anyone know that a Specter had infiltrated the Academy. They'd execute her in secret and destroy the evidence. It would be like she had never existed.

The two guards exchanged glances. "What's your name?" the female guard asked.

"What's going on here?" a deep voice called. Orelia turned to see Zafir walking up behind her.

He was wearing a T-shirt with loose trousers that hung on his hips, revealing a sliver of toned stomach, and his dark curls were damp.

The male guard glared at Zafir. "Everything's under control. Please keep moving," he said, clearly mistaking him for a cadet.

Zafir fixed the guard with an unreadable stare, and the man shrank back slightly. "I'm an instructor here, and I'd like to know what you're doing with my student." He appeared calm, but there was a note of steeliness in his voice that made Orelia want to lean away.

"She was wandering around a restricted area in the middle of the night. We just need to ask her a few questions," the woman said.

This is it, Orelia thought. She glanced at Zafir, expecting to see his face harden with suspicion as he surveyed Orelia. But to her surprise, he simply folded his arms across his chest, revealing sinewy arm muscles she hadn't noticed before. "I'll handle it. You can continue with your patrols."

Recognition seemed to dawn on the woman's face, and she shot her partner a warning look before turning back to Zafir. "Sorry, we didn't recognize you," she said as the man glared at him. "Apologies, Lieutenant Prateek."

The male guard started at the sound of Zafir's name, and Orelia remembered what the boy in her counterintelligence class had said—*I heard he's kind of terrifying.* She didn't normally find Zafir intimidating, but right now, she was grateful that his icy stare wasn't directed at her.

The guards saluted and continued down the corridor. Orelia sighed inwardly, though she did her best to hide her relief. "Sorry about that. I...I couldn't sleep." She tried to keep her voice light, but it was hard to imagine that someone couldn't sense the guilt rolling off her, chilling the air like mist.

"You're not in trouble," he said, his voice much softer than it'd been with the guards. "Are you all right? Here, sit down." He gestured toward a bench against the wall and motioned for her to join him as he took a seat.

"I just didn't expect the guards to be so intense," Orelia said. That was another lie. If Sylvan guards had caught an unauthorized person in a restricted zone, the intruder would be shot on sight.

"Don't worry about them. If they bother you again, just let me know and I'll handle it."

She nodded again and swallowed. She wished she *could* let Zafir handle it. She wished her problem—her guilt over transmitting the Academy's coordinates—was something he could solve with the same brusque confidence he'd used to dismiss the guards.

"What's wrong?" he said softly. He hesitated a moment, then placed his hand on her arm. She stiffened at the unfamiliar sensation, and he withdrew it immediately. But the sympathetic expression on his face didn't change.

"I'm just a little homesick," Orelia said, hoping that would be enough to throw him off the scent.

"You're from Loos, right? You must miss the ocean."

Orelia thought of the flooded forest where she'd gone for a conditioning swim every morning during the summers, inhaling the scent of salt and pine as she ran her hand along the tree trunks embedded with seashells.

Orelia nodded, grateful that she was telling a partial truth. "I love to swim." She missed the way the water cradled her body, making her feel weightless and cocooned at the same time.

"Me too. Have you seen the ocean tank? It's full of salt

water so you can float on your back and stare up at the stars. It's the only time you can forget you're in space."

"I haven't seen it. Are students allowed?" She'd love to dive in right now, letting the water wash away her guilt and worry.

"Only during officially monitored training sessions. But if you just happen to show up one evening while I'm there, I promise to turn a blind eye. I have a soft spot for Loosians. I served with a number of them during my last tour."

"Do you miss being in the field?" she asked, recalling what her classmate had said about Zafir giving up a promising career to teach.

"I do," he said with the hint of a smile, as if amused by the question. "I like teaching, but counterintelligence can be tough. Not everyone's mind works that way." His smile grew. "Yours seems to, though. Your papers demonstrate a remarkable ability to put yourself in the enemy's head."

Her heart began to pound a frantic alarm, warning her to change the subject, but she ignored it. "Why do you think they're attacking us?" she asked. She had to find out how much Zafir knew. Did he truly believe that the Sylvans had attacked first, or was he knowingly teaching lies?

"We can't know for sure, but I think the dominant theory

makes sense—that they've run through the resources on their volatile planet and are looking to pillage ours." His tone was light, but there was the faintest shadow of fear in his eyes.

He doesn't know, Orelia thought. *Or is he just perpetuating that lie?*

"So why'd you retire from active duty? It sounds like the fleet needs you more than ever," Orelia said.

"I didn't officially retire. I'm just taking a leave of absence. The war against the Specters is going to hinge on intelligence as much as it does on weapons and strategy, and I want to make sure the next generation of intelligence officers has the best training possible." She appreciated his candor. There was no boasting or any false modesty. He knew he was talented, but instead of looking for accolades, he decided to focus his efforts on where he could do the most good. "Do you think that's foolish?" he asked.

"No, I think it's noble. What you want isn't as important as what others need." Orelia had learned this lesson the hard way, but she was nonetheless grateful for it.

Zafir surveyed her curiously for a long moment before he spoke. "I agree," he said quietly. There was another stretch of silence, but there was nothing awkward about it. It was comforting to know that someone here saw things the same way she did, even if they were on drastically different paths.

Zafir yawned, and he stretched his arms over his head. "I'd better go to bed," he said, then patted her knee. This time, she didn't pull away and instead felt herself relax under the comforting weight. "Will you be okay?"

"Yes, fine," she said, feeling a strange flicker of warmth in her chest. There was something in Zafir's expression that hadn't been in Arran's face that night when he'd helped her back to her room. Something beyond concern or tenderness.

"Good." He stood and then reached for her hand. Without thinking, she allowed him to help her to her feet, shuddering slightly as the warmth of his hand spread through her body. He released her hand, and as they walked down the hall, her skin didn't stop tingling.

CHAPTER 18

VESPER

I can't do this anymore. The words thudded against her skull like a frantic, trapped bird. *I can't do this.* Dread and panic congealed in her body, weighing her down until she couldn't move. She stood frozen in the middle of the hallway about five doors away from the simulcraft where her squadron was gathering for their second battle. Today they were going up against Brill's squadron, and Vesper couldn't stomach the prospect of facing her after a loss.

Ever since their first battle, when she'd screwed up the gravity assist, she'd been choking, making foolish, amateur mistakes in every practice session. She'd bungled what should've been a simple landing by coming in at the wrong angle. The next day, she hadn't executed a basic evasive maneuver quickly enough, allowing the enemy to blow up their ship about four minutes into the exercise.

There was only one horrifying explanation for it: She didn't have what it took to win.

If her squadron lost again, it was all over. Her mother had made it very clear—if her squadron didn't perform extremely well in the tournament, it would be nearly impossible for Vesper to stay at the Academy.

She heard voices echoing down the hall behind her and recognized Brill's tinkling laugh. Vesper's breath caught in her chest, and her heart lurched into a panicked sprint. *I can't breathe*, she thought. She tried to inhale, but something was blocking her airways. She tried again, but no oxygen reached her lungs.

The voices behind her were growing louder. *I can't let them see me like this*, she thought as the world started to spin. Gasping, she managed to stagger into the girls' bathroom and leaned back against the wall, letting out a long sigh as the silence engulfed her like an embrace.

Her heart rate had slowed slightly, but her skin still felt prickly and hot. She took another deep breath, walked over to one of the sinks along the wall, and placed her hands under the faucet. The sensor noted her elevated body temperature and adjusted accordingly, sending cool water out of the tap that Vesper splashed on her face gratefully. But as the panic subsided, it was replaced by a dread that reached so deeply into her bones, the sensor would never detect it. And there was no water in the solar system hot enough to scour it away.

She glanced at the clock. Four minutes until the battle began. She couldn't do it. She couldn't go in there. Better her squadron lose because they didn't have a pilot than because she was deadweight.

The mirror reflected a face she barely knew. Red eyes, grayish skin, and a fearful expression. Even if she skipped the mission, she couldn't go back to the hall looking like this. She patted her pockets, hoping she'd left her complexion glaze in this uniform. Vesper rarely wore makeup at school, but she couldn't face her classmates looking this weary, this defeated. She shoved her hand deeper into her pocket, and her fingers brushed against something small and hard. It was the pill Frey had given her. The vega dust.

She closed her eyes, imagining what it would feel like to have the drug coursing through her veins, sweeping away all the doubt and anxiety. Her fingers tingled as she thought about grasping the controls, her brain and her muscles once again moving in sync as she piloted their craft to victory. She pictured herself walking down the hall with her head high, having proved once and for all that she deserved to be here.

It's not like I have anything to lose, she thought, bringing the pill to her lips. All the things she'd heard about vega dust, all the terrifying side effects, they couldn't be any worse than this—the constant panic, the feeling like she was fading away.

"What the *hell* are you doing?"

She spun around and saw Rex, hardly recognizable without his smug, cocky grin. He stared at her in confusion for a moment before his eyes landed on the purple pill, and his face hardened into anger. "Drop it," he ordered.

A flare of indignation rose within her. He might've beat her out for captain, but that didn't mean he got to tell her what to do when they weren't in the simulcraft. "What are you doing here?"

"We were worried about you. Our battle starts in less than five minutes. Orelia and Arran sent me to find you. They saw you duck in here."

"They sent *you*. To get me from the girls' bathroom,"

Vesper said disbelievingly as they walked toward the door. "Why didn't Orelia come?"

"They knew I was the only one who could handle you."

"*Handle* me?" She wasn't someone to be *handled*, especially not by a cocky Devak. She lifted her hand to her lips and opened her mouth, wondering what she craved more—the rush of the chemicals entering her system or the satisfaction of his shocked expression.

"Don't be ridiculous." He closed the distance between them with a few steps and grabbed her wrist.

"Let go of me," Vesper said, wrenching away.

He held her arm gently but firmly. "Not until you give me whatever's in your hand."

Something deflated inside her, and she suddenly felt nothing but overwhelming fatigue. "Fine," she said, opening her fist. "It doesn't matter. It's not like it would've made a difference."

Rex plucked the pill from her palm and examined it. "Vega dust? Seriously, Vesper? What were you thinking?" His voice had lost its accusatory edge.

"I…I can't do it." She couldn't believe she was saying this aloud, and to Rex of all people. Until two minutes ago, she would've rather stripped naked in front of the whole Academy than admit failure.

"Do what?"

"Fly. Compete. All of it." Vesper shook her head. "You're all better off without me. I choked during the gravity assist, and it's only gotten worse. You were right. I *did* waltz in here thinking I knew more than the rest of you. But I was all talk. I don't have what it takes."

Rex winced slightly as a look of pain flashed across his face. "I never should've said that. I'm sorry."

"But it's true."

"No, it's not," Rex said, sounding more earnest than she would've thought possible. "I only said that because I was mad at myself. I made the wrong call. It was my fault, not yours." He took a deep breath, and the familiar mischievous glint returned to his eye. "The truth is—and I can't believe I'm saying this—that you on an off day are still about ten times more impressive than most people on their best days. Flying with you is like watching some evil genius at work. Your strategy, your focus, your ability to stay four steps ahead of your competition—it's impressive, and if I'm being honest, kind of terrifying."

Despite herself, Vesper smiled. "You don't look terrified."

"You know what really scared me? Seeing you with that pill. You don't know what that stuff can do to you. You don't know how many lives I've seen ruined—lives with a hell of a lot less potential than yours." He shook his head solemnly. "Now can we please go? Orelia and Arran will kill me if I don't bring you back in time."

Vesper raised an eyebrow and shot him a withering look.

"See? Terrifying. Now come on. Can't have you wasting all your evil-genius energy before the mission even begins." He placed his hand on her arm and guided her out. To her surprise, she waited a full five seconds before shrugging it off.

CHAPTER 19

CORMAK

Cormak bounded down the hall, buoyed by a giddy high unlike anything he'd felt before. He still couldn't believe they'd actually *won*. He and Vesper had slid into their seats just as *Commence mission* flashed across the screen, and from that moment, it was like watching a different girl. Or, rather, like watching the girl who'd impressed him during their first practice session. Her flying was daring and assured, and whenever he glanced over at her, her eyes glittered with fierce determination.

He felt lighter than he had in weeks. He'd transferred the money to Sol's account, and the next day, Sol had confirmed that he'd swapped out Rex's medical records with Cormak's before the files were sent to the Academy. Everything was going to be okay. For the first time, he allowed himself to imagine a future for himself here. Captain of a winning squadron. If they kept it up, he'd be able to join the Quatra Fleet as an *officer*—the first in Deva history.

To celebrate Squadron 20's first win, Admiral Haze had invited the four of them to dinner that night. A formal dinner in her private dining room. Cormak had planned to just wear his uniform, as that was all he had apart from a few ratty T-shirts and one pair of frayed pants. But when Arran heard that plan, he suggested that Cormak borrow something from Dash like he had. So now here he was, heading to dinner with an admiral of the Quatra Fleet wearing Arran's boyfriend's tux. He'd expected to feel like an idiot in it, or worse, a fraud. But when he'd turned to the mirror for a final check, he'd been pleasantly surprised. He looked like a promising cadet, like someone who deserved to have dinner with the admiral.

Not so promising, however, that he didn't get lost on the way there. Cormak made the mistake of assuming that the admiral's dining room was near her office when, in fact, it turned out to be in an entirely different wing of the Academy. "I said Admiral Haze's dining room," Cormak muttered to his monitor.

"Students are not permitted in the private dining room. For directions to the student dining hall, say dining hall.*"*

"Dismiss," Cormak said with a sigh. By the time he reached the entrance, slightly sweaty and out of breath, he was ten minutes late. Luckily, there were only two people waiting in the wood-paneled room, Orelia and Arran.

"Squadron 20 is looking spiffy tonight," Cormak said as he walked toward them, grinning. Like Cormak, Arran was in a dark suit, and Orelia was wearing a pretty dress that made her green eyes look nearly turquoise. "Where's Vesper? She hasn't been taunting Brill for the past eight hours, has she?"

"I'm not sure, but you won't find me stopping her." Arran grinned. "Everyone did great work today. Well done, Captain."

Cormak made a show of shrugging off the compliment, but inwardly, he was proud of his performance in the simulcraft too. He was learning when to make snap decisions and when to defer to the others, when to push them to work even harder and when to tell them to take it easy.

Cormak looked around the room, taking in the ornately carved furniture, gem-colored glass lamps, and old-fashioned maps of the solar system. Everything about it felt over-the-top and ridiculous; yet, as he accepted a drink from a passing attendant and then took a savory-smelling appetizer from another, he had to admit that he'd take the fussiest room in the Academy over Deva any day.

The door slid open, and Cormak straightened his jacket; this was his chance to make a good impression on the admiral. But instead of Admiral Haze, Vesper walked in alone. She wore a long, shimmery dark blue dress, the color he'd always imagined the night sky to be on planets where you could actually see the stars. The fabric, whatever the hell it was, clung to her tall, muscular body, emphasizing curves normally hidden by her uniform. Not that that usually made a difference for Cormak. When you grew up on a planet where you couldn't go outside without jumpsuits, you got pretty good at identifying hot girls in shapeless clothes. But there was something about Vesper. When she was in the simulcraft, eyes blazing, hands moving lightning fast over the controls, you forgot to check out her other assets.

Cormak grabbed another glass from the attendant's tray and carried it over to Vesper. "How are you feeling?" he asked, handing her the drink.

"Better. Good." She nodded. "Really good, actually." She glanced at the couch where Arran and Orelia were talking and lowered her voice. "Thank you for your help earlier. I don't know what I was thinking back there."

"Don't worry about it. We all psych ourselves out sometimes. Though, I have to say, it was *much* more fun watching you psych Brill out." Today's battle had been a combat mission, and the objective had been to destroy the enemy's base while still guarding your own. Vesper kept luring Brill into traps by initiating what looked like standard attack patterns, then switching gears at the last moment. But the best part was that she seemed to be reading his mind as well. Whenever Cormak started to give what he believed to be a brilliant, inspired command, he realized that Vesper was already executing it. Everywhere he turned, there she was, two steps ahead him. For Cormak, outsmarting everyone around him had been a matter of survival, and luckily, he hadn't met many people who could keep up. It was strangely satisfying, if slightly irritating, to feel someone so connected to his thoughts. Like dancing—if your partner were armed with 140 megatons of explosives.

He braced for a barb, expecting her to say that psyching him out was even more fun. But to his surprise, she was smiling. A real smile that he hadn't seen before.

I want her to look at me like that all the time, Cormak

thought, startling himself with the unexpected notion. He'd never had much time for girls, but the ones he'd hung around with back on Deva had always been laid-back types—easygoing girls who wouldn't demand any more energy or attention than he could afford to give. Yet while Vesper was the opposite of easygoing, her intensity didn't feel draining. There was something electric about her that made everything more exciting.

"Sorry to keep you all waiting." Cormak spun around to see Admiral Haze gliding into the room in a gauzy black dress that somehow made her look even more intimidating than usual. "Thank you all so much for joining me tonight. And congratulations on your big win!"

Cormak glanced over his shoulder at Vesper. The smile he'd just seen was gone, replaced by something stiffer, more guarded. "Mother, may I present my squadron mates? This is Orelia, intelligence; Arran, tech; and our captain, Rex."

"It's a pleasure to meet you all," Admiral Haze said, smiling at each of them before letting her gaze land on Cormak. "I'm glad you're here, Cadet Phobos. From what I've heard, you were very nearly left behind on Deva."

"Yes, I got unexpectedly…delayed." He flashed her the sheepish smile that usually won him a few extra days with the rent or convinced a jaded freight pilot to siphon some fuel into Cormak's tank.

It didn't seem to have quite the same effect on the admiral.

"Rex needs to work on his first impressions," Vesper said. She suppressed a smile but wasn't able to extinguish the gleam of amusement in her eyes. "But he improves upon further acquaintance."

"I'm sure that's true," the admiral said in a tone Cormak couldn't quite read. "Now, if you'll all follow me—I've just been informed that dinner is ready." Without another look at Cormak, she turned on her heel and swept away, her long skirt streaming behind her.

The admiral's dining room was considerably smaller than the hall where the cadets ate but even more ornate. Hanging from the ceiling was an enormous chandelier with so many glinting crystals, it looked like a preening Tridian girl in one of her fancy dresses. As he sat down, Cormak half expected the chandelier to whisper something about grimy Settlers.

Two attendants zipped around the table, and a moment later, each person's glass was filled with a fizzy, deep purple liquid.

"Unity and prosperity," Admiral Haze said, raising her glass as she gave the traditional Quatra Fleet toast.

"Unity and prosperity," the cadets echoed.

Everyone clinked glasses, Cormak a bit overzealously. He ended up sloshing some liquid onto the sleeve of his borrowed suit. *Sorry*, Cormak mouthed to Arran as he used his napkin to blot it.

As they ate their appetizer, an unexpectedly sweet but oddly enjoyable blue soup, Admiral Haze asked them about their backgrounds, their classwork, and their plans for the future. She asked Orelia questions about growing up on Loos and seemed impressed when Arran mentioned that he'd taught himself Cyrilia. "And what about you, Rex?" Admiral Haze asked, lowering her spoon and looking at him expectantly. "I imagine you must've been pretty pleased to make captain. Did you always see yourself as a leader?"

Cormak suppressed a snort and nearly choked on his blue soup. He swallowed, then managed to stammer, "No... not exactly." Unless by "leader" she meant "errand boy for one of the most wanted criminals in the solar system."

"You were assigned captain over Vesper, so you must have demonstrated some special talents on the aptitude test, and I'm very curious about what those might be." The admiral paused thoughtfully, and out of the corner of his eye, he saw Vesper tense. "Did you lead any athletic teams back on Deva?"

"I did not," Cormak said with a polite smile.

"Were you the president of any societies at school?"

"My school didn't exactly have *societies*," he said as Arran and Orelia exchanged nervous glances.

"That's a shame, though you were probably grateful for all the extra time to study. Did you win any special awards?"

Cormak considered claiming Rex's awards but decided against it lest he get caught in the lie. "No. I didn't actually do much to distinguish myself until I took the Academy's entrance exam."

Admiral Haze shot him a tight smile. "That just makes your captain assignment all the more remarkable, wouldn't you say?"

Cormak shifted in his uncomfortable chair. He'd always prided himself in knowing the right thing to say in tense situations, but in the past, they'd generally involved whiny rich people, careless water dealers, and apathetic pols. Admiral Haze belonged to a different category.

Before he could respond, Vesper spoke up. "Rex is an excellent captain. I've never met anyone with such great instincts." Arran and Orelia quickly chimed in with similar words of praise.

Cormak barely had time to take in his squadron mates' kind words when Admiral Haze continued. "Is that so?" She turned to Cormak and raised an eyebrow. "Tell me, why do you think you were named captain?"

Cormak had had enough. "I'm sorry, am I under investigation here?" he asked, no longer able to keep the edge out of his voice.

"There's no reason to get defensive, Cadet Phobos," Admiral Haze said. "I'm just trying to get to know you."

But Cormak knew better. She couldn't hide her disgust over the fact that a *Devak* had beat out her daughter for captain. Anger and indignation bubbled in his chest. Haze didn't know anything about what it meant to be Devak. She didn't know how hard he and Rex had worked to survive after their parents died. How Rex's thirty-six-hour shifts and Cormak's endless delivery runs across the desert weren't always enough to keep the gnawing hunger at bay.

He couldn't do it. He refused to sit here and listen to this bullshit, admiral be damned. He folded his napkin carefully, placed it on the table, then pushed his chair back and stood up. "You'll have to forgive me. I'm not feeling very well all of a sudden. Good evening, Admiral," he said stiffly. Without waiting for a response, he turned and strode out, ignoring Arran's and Orelia's looks of horror and Vesper's expression of pain.

CHAPTER 20

ARRAN

"We should go," Arran called, his voice echoing through the dark, cavernous zero-gravity chamber. "We're going to be late for dinner!" He and Dash had been studying in the library, but Dash had grown restless and insisted that they needed to "increase blood flow to their brains" by floating around in zero gravity.

Although Arran had a big history assignment due tomorrow, he hadn't put up much of a protest. Ever since his conversation with Pond, he'd found it hard to relax around Dash, and the library had started to feel airless. He knew Pond's warning was ridiculous, yet Arran couldn't quite shake the seed of uncertainty that had taken root in his mind. Perhaps, despite his professed horror of his father's beliefs, Dash was finding it more difficult to reject Larz Muscatine's teachings than he believed. That would explain why, despite all the time they spent together and their undeniable chemistry, Dash still hadn't made a move.

"Five more minutes!" Dash shouted back. Arran released his grip on the handhold to flex his cramping fingers. He'd begun to pull himself along the wall toward the exit, but it sounded like Dash was still floating somewhere in the middle of the dark room. "I've almost mastered a quadruple somersault." They'd spent the past hour practicing different moves, laughing each time they knocked into each other or thudded against the padded wall, but now Arran was hungry and ready to go.

"Come on. They don't let you have the appetizer if you're late." He still didn't understand why the attendants were programmed to *throw away* food rather than serve it to latecomers.

Dash let out a *whoop*, and in the dim light, Arran could see him rotating through the air. There was a dull thud as Dash hit the wall next to Arran. Laughing, he scrambled for a handhold, brushing against Arran's arm as he searched. "Some things are more important than food, you know."

Normally, anything Dash said in that suggestive tone

made Arran's whole body tingle, but this time he pulled away slightly as an image formed in his mind. His mother, pale and drawn, forcing a smile as she encouraged Arran to eat her portion of dinner. "I'm not very hungry, sweetflake, take it."

Sensing that something was amiss, Dash placed his free hand on Arran's arm. "What's wrong? What did I do?"

"It's nothing." Arran shook his head. "It's just that...I wish you wouldn't make fun of me for not wanting to miss dinner."

Even in the dark, he could see Dash's face fall. "I'm sorry. I'm an idiot," Dash said, squeezing Arran's arm. "You're right. We should go to dinner."

"You're not an idiot," Arran said, as the sensation of Dash's touch sent shivers down his spine. "Could an idiot pull off a *quadruple somersault?*"

But his attempt to lighten the mood fell flat. "You know, we've never really spoken about your life on Chetire," Dash said softly.

"Yeah, that's because it's boring." Arran forced a smile. "It was cold. I studied a lot. We were pretty poor, but so were most people. And things are different now. Although it's going to be at least three years until I start earning a Quatra Fleet salary, the general store already extended my mom's line of credit. For the first time, she's also going to have enough to eat."

He expected Dash to smile at this comforting news, but his face only grew graver. "I'm so sorry, Arran. I really had no idea."

"It's not your fault," Arran said. But the moment the words left his mouth, a heavy silence filled the space between them. He knew they were both thinking the same thing. If it were up to Larz Muscatine, Arran would've *never* been accepted to the Academy. He would've spent the rest of his life on Chetire, working a backbreaking job while he watched his mother waste away.

"What about your father?" Dash asked gently.

"He was killed in a mining accident when I was really young. The tunnel he was in collapsed and..." It had been so long since he'd spoken about his father, it was difficult to summon the words. "He and his team were too far under-ground. No one even tried to rescue them. They were just left there to die."

Dash was silent for a long moment. "That's horrible," he said, then squeezed Arran's arm again. "I'm so, so sorry."

"It happens a lot on Chetire. Nearly half the kids in my school had lost a parent."

"That's awful." Dash shook his head. "I can't believe we never talk about stuff like that on Tri. It's all 'write an essay on the importance of Chetrian exports,' not 'discuss all the ways the Tridians are making life miserable for the rest of the solar system.'"

"See what you did?" Arran said as he smacked Dash playfully on the arm. "You made me talk about my childhood, and now I've totally ruined the mood."

Dash shook his head. "You're incapable of ruining anything, 223."

"You know," Arran said tentatively, "you never really talk about your childhood either."

"That's because mine was pretty boring too. I was rich. The weather was pleasant. My dad was an asshole. That's pretty much it."

It was the first time Dash had mentioned his father since Arran had confronted him the night of the formal. "You said that you don't really talk to him anymore. When did that happen?"

"A few months ago. My dad wanted me to start speaking at his rallies, to be the 'voice of my generation' or some magma boar shit like that. And I told him that I couldn't. Not only that I wouldn't, but also that I was physically incapable of spewing hateful lies. That went over about as well as you'd imagine."

"What happened?" Arran asked, just managing to keep his voice steady despite his racing heart.

"He told me I was a brainwashed traitor and that he couldn't stand to look at me."

Dash spoke matter-of-factly, but there was something in his face that made Arran's chest ache. He tried to imagine his mother saying something like that to him, but it was impossible. "Did he kick you out?"

"I'd already been accepted to the Academy, so we basically ignored each other until I left. He told me that if I went, that was it. He'd never speak to me again."

"He wasn't proud that you'd been accepted?" Arran asked, confused. From what he could tell, most of the Tri kids at the Academy had spent their entire lives preparing for the entrance exams.

"He was proud until he learned that the Academy had finally been integrated. He didn't want his son being forced into some 'delusional social experiment.'"

The question that Arran had been trying to ignore for weeks finally clawed its way out. "What would he say if he found out you were...hanging out with me?"

A mischievous smile spread across Dash's face. "He'd be furious."

"And that doesn't bother you?" He knew Dash fiercely disapproved of his father's politics, but Larz Muscatine was still Dash's father.

"No, it doesn't," Dash said, sounding strangely serious again.

"Why?"

Dash let go of the handle and floated toward Arran until their heads were practically touching. "Because..." Dash's breath tickled Arran's face. He came closer, and then his lips were against Arran's.

Although Arran had imagined this moment countless times, it still came as such a surprise that his brain nearly short-circuited, and for a few seconds, he could barely move. An electrical charge surged through Arran's body, burning away every thought except for the sensation of Dash's lips on his. Holding on to the wall grip with one hand, he wrapped his other arm around Dash and kissed him back. Every time his lips brushed against Dash's, it sent a new jolt through his body. Distracted, he felt himself start to float away from the wall and held on tighter, strengthening his hold on the handle and around Dash's waist, his fingers gripping the skin between the top of Dash's pants and the hem of his shirt. Dash gasped, and the sound was enough to make Arran shudder.

A moment later, they were drifting through the air, still locked in a kiss as they clung together. Only two thoughts remained in Arran's brain—Sergeant Pond had no idea what he was talking about, and this was the best moment of Arran's life.

CHAPTER 21

ORELIA

Zuzu yawned and glanced at the clock. "Oh, Antares. I had no idea how late it was. Why did you let me talk your ear off?"

"Sorry, what?" Orelia asked, startled. She'd spent the day in a daze, consumed by a disorienting jumble of emotions. Although she'd successfully completed her mission, her body was slowly filling with a thickening dread.

It was worse in the silence of her room, so after returning from dinner, she'd ended up sitting on the couch with Zuzu as her roommate described, in excruciating detail, her most recent interaction with Rex. He and Zuzu had spent ten minutes talking in the common room earlier that day, an event that apparently required three hours of analysis. Normally, this recap would've struck Orelia as a monumental waste of time, but now, she welcomed the distraction. She'd take Zuzu's innocent prattle over the haunting refrain that echoed through her head when she was on her own. *Everyone here is going to die because of you.*

"It was an interesting story," Orelia said, only half lying. The concerns that had seemed so trivial when she'd first arrived at the Academy—what to wear, who had a crush on whom—had begun to intrigue her. This was what life was like for people who were allowed to have friends, fall in love, experience heartbreak. All the things Orelia had sacrificed to ensure that millions of other Sylvans could have them. Because somewhere, light years away, a Sylvan girl was pouring her heart out to *her* friend, confiding her dreams of a future that would never take shape if the Sylvans didn't stop the Quatrans from destroying their home.

"You're a terrible liar," Zuzu said with a smile.

You have no idea, Orelia thought.

Zuzu yawned again, then stood and stretched her arms over her head. "I'm going to bed. Are you going to study for a bit?"

Orelia nodded. She was going to pretend to study, at least. Anything to delay going to bed and being alone with her thoughts. After Zuzu said good night and disappeared into her room, Orelia pulled up her calculus assignment, but after she stared at the equations for a few minutes, her heart started to race. She couldn't sit here, surrounded by the peacefully sleeping Quatrans she'd sentenced to die.

She remembered what Zafir had told her about the ocean tank, where you could float on your back and stare up at the stars, forgetting you were in space. That sounded exactly like what she needed now. He'd said it was off-limits to cadets after-hours, but since she was already committing espionage, it seemed silly to worry about such a trivial infraction.

Orelia didn't have any trouble finding the ocean tank, which was near the pool where they'd had an aquatic-training session last week. After weeks of prowling the Academy at night, she knew her way around.

From the moment Orelia stepped inside, she knew she'd made the right decision. The only sound was the gentle slosh of water, the crash of small waves. She took a deep breath and smiled as her nose filled with the comforting scent of salt instead of chlorine.

She took off her uniform and left it in a pile on the ground, revealing the Academy-issued bathing suit she'd put on underneath. As her eyes adjusted to the darkness, she inched her way toward the edge of the tank, settling on the ledge, unsure of whether it was deep enough to dive.

Then another sound reached her ears. The quiet splash of a skilled swimmer moving through the water. Startled, she peered into the tank, but it was too dark to see anything clearly. "Hello?" someone called. The voice was low and quiet, and for a moment, Orelia couldn't tell where it was coming from. The echoing words and the echoing water blended together, surrounding her from all sides.

"Zafir?" The name slipped out before she had time to stop herself. "I mean, Lieutenant Prateek?"

"You know you're supposed to call me Zafir," he said, a hint of a smile in his voice. She could just barely make out the instructor's outline swimming toward her.

"How'd you know it was me?" Orelia asked, tugging at the straps of her bathing suit, which covered less of her chest than she would have liked.

"Just a hunch." He sounded more amused than surprised to find her there. "You should come in."

Orelia hesitated. Surely the counterintelligence expert

would be able to detect the cloud of shame hovering over her. Yet she wanted to dive into the water so badly, her need felt like a physical ache.

"Okay," she said, rising to her feet.

"Hold on. Let me go turn off the waves. They can be a little much at first." Despite the anxiety churning in her stomach, Orelia smiled as she wondered what Zafir would think if he ever saw her swim on Sylvan, ducking under the twenty-foot waves that routinely smashed against the sea-wall in the spring.

She could just make out his shadowy outline as he pulled himself out of the tank, fastened something to his leg, then strode off. A few moments later, the sound of the waves grew quieter, and Zafir returned. The only light in the room came from the faintly glowing stars overhead. As Orelia's eyes adjusted to the darkness, the details came into focus. The glint of starlight on Zafir's titanium leg as he walked toward the tank. The tautness of his muscles. The relaxed expression on his face, a far cry from the intense stare that made so many cadets cower.

Standing on his right leg, he removed his prosthesis. It didn't seem to affect his balance because, without hesitating, he raised his arms over his head, crouched for a moment, then sprang into the air, his body creating a graceful arc before he slipped into the water with barely a splash. A few seconds later, he broke through the surface and pushed his wet hair out of his eyes. "Okay," he said, treading water. "All set."

She considered diving in as well but settled for lowering herself onto the edge and then slipping into the tank. Orelia let out a silent sigh as the water surrounded her like a warm embrace, then she ducked under and swam a few lengths. She emerged a few moments later and grinned, relishing the feeling of weightlessness that, to her disappointment, hadn't been a normal part of living in space.

Zafir was floating on his back just like he'd told her he liked to do. There was so much salt in the water, he barely needed to move to stay afloat, his nearly still limbs glistening. Her eyes landed on his left leg, which ended below his knee.

"How'd you lose your leg?" she asked curiously.

Zafir looked at her with surprise, and Orelia realized she'd made a mistake. "I'm sorry. That was rude."

But to her relief, he smiled. "Not at all. It's refreshing, actually. Most people are too afraid to ask. I was stationed at a base near Haansgaard during the last attack."

His casual tone was no different than the one he used during class when he was comparing different code-breaking techniques. Yet the words sent chills down Orelia's spine. She'd spent years hearing about successful attacks against the Quatrans, but in all that time, she'd never once wondered what those targets might entail. *Who* might be inside those targets. She'd come to the Academy to help the Sylvans destroy the Quatrans, but the closer she got to her goal, the more she questioned whether it was the right thing to do.

"That must've been terrifying," she said. Although Zafir's face was placid, she sensed the phantom of fear and pain hovering around him as the memories resurfaced.

Something in his expression changed. "It was," he said quietly. "I don't talk about it often, but—" He smiled as he shook his head. "Sorry. I'm being ridiculous."

"I don't think you're being ridiculous." If anything, *she* was the ridiculous one, going for a midnight swim with one of the Quatra Fleet's most famous counterintelligence officers, a man who had devoted his life to protecting his solar system from the Sylvans. People like her. Yet, for some reason, she felt far more comfortable talking to him than with Zuzu or her squadron mates. Although their motives couldn't be more different, Zafir and Orelia both knew what it was like to devote your life to a cause you believed in. "I think you're brave."

He fell quiet for such a long moment that Orelia wondered if he'd heard her, but then he finally broke the silence. "I never believe people when they say that. It always sounds like they're reading from a script."

"I'm sorry," she said quickly. "I didn't mean..."

He closed the distance between them with a few powerful strokes. "No." He shook his head. "I mean, it sounds different coming from you. I keep thinking about what you said in the corridor that night—'What you want isn't as important as what others need.' I agree with you. It's been a while since I've spoken to someone who understands real..." He stared at something in the darkness.

She swam closer, pulled to him as if he were a magnet. "Sacrifice," she whispered.

He exhaled, then shifted his gaze to lock eyes with her. "Yes." His face was so close to hers, she could feel his breath on her skin.

"Though, at this moment, I kind of wish I hadn't become a teacher."

"Why?" she asked as her heart started to race.

He shook his head, sending droplets of water into the air. "Never mind. I'm being an idiot."

"Are you?" she asked quietly. Then, without waiting for a response, she leaned forward and brushed her lips against his.

He didn't move. He barely seemed to breathe, and for a moment, Orelia thought she'd made a terrible mistake. But then he placed his hand on the side of her face and kissed her again, sending electricity sizzling through her body. Her lips parted, and she shivered slightly as his hand slid down her back, pulling her closer. It felt as if she were seeping into him, like there was nothing keeping her from melting into the water except for the pressure of his hand on her and the warmth of his lips.

"Are you okay?" he asked, pulling away just long enough to whisper in her ear.

Orelia's heart was beating so fast, she could barely speak. "Yes," she breathed. And for the first time since arriving at the Academy, it was true.

CHAPTER 22

VESPER

"One more direct hit, and they're toast," Vesper said, grinning at the damaged Specter ship on their simulcraft screen.

"Toast?" Arran repeated without looking away from his control panel, where he was busy calculating how much fuel they'd need to return to the base.

"You don't know what *toast* is?" Vesper said incredulously as she steered the fightercraft into a sharp dive to avoid one last desperate batch of enemy fire. "It's just bread that's been...toasted." She winced at her awkwardness and braced for whatever retort Rex was about to hurl her way. Over the past few weeks, they'd fallen into an established pattern of banter, which, while she'd never admit it, had become one of her favorite parts of squadron practice.

"I know what toast is," Arran said, rolling his eyes. "We just don't have that expression on Chetire."

"*Toast is bread that's been toasted*," Rex called from behind her, just as she'd expected. "What a pleasure to see the famous Tridian intellect at work. Truly dazzling."

Vesper smiled, grateful that Rex couldn't see it. "What would you rather have me focus on? Describing the way the carbon molecules in the bread's sugars react with the amino acids? Or destroying the Specter ship and winning this battle?"

Even without looking, she could see Rex pretending to consider the question, his brow furrowing with mock thoughtfulness. "I think it's important that pilots be able to multitask."

"Pretty sure I can steer *and* slap that grin off your face at the same time. Should I try?"

"How do you know I'm grinning?" Rex asked. "I could be fighting back tears for all you know. That was a serious threat you just made."

Because I know your expressions as well as I know this craft's engine. "Because you're boring and predictable," she called back.

"Okay, you two," Arran said with more affection than annoyance. "We haven't won yet. Everyone needs to focus. We have to launch that last missile in the next two minutes, or we're going to run out of fuel before we get back to the base."

"Noted," Rex said in his slightly amusing, slightly irritating "captain's voice." "Orelia, are there any other enemy ships in the area?" He paused. "Orelia?"

Vesper glanced over her shoulder at their intelligence officer, who was staring at the screen with a distant expression. Finally, Orelia caught Vesper's eye and blinked. "Sorry," she said, turning to face her control panel. "No...no one else in the area."

"Okay, Vesper, take us in for the kill."

A minute later, the simulcraft screen filled with flames from the exploding Specter ship. Vesper raised her arms in the air and swiveled around to face her squadron mates.

Orelia remained seated, but the boys both leapt out of their chairs. Arran let out a *whoop* and tried to congratulate Orelia while Rex grinned at Vesper. "Nicely done, pilot." Then, to her surprise, he pulled her into a hug, sending a current of electricity through her body. She pulled away, startled. "I'm sorry," he said as he took a step back.

"No, it's fine," she said quickly, wincing inwardly at the hint of embarrassment on Rex's face. "I'm just…sweaty."

"I know." His smile returned. "I'm completely repulsed. But I still have my appetite, thank Antares. Who wants to go to the canteen for a snack?" He turned to face the others, but Orelia had already slipped out of the simulcraft.

"Sorry, I'm meeting Dash to study." Arran glanced at the time and groaned. "I didn't realize I was this late. See you guys at dinner!" he called as he hurried out, leaving Vesper and Rex alone for the first time since the disastrous dinner with her mother.

That night, Vesper had tried to compose a message to Rex apologizing for her mother's behavior, but she'd eventually given up. What was she supposed to say? *I'm sorry my mother insulted you and your entire planet*? She couldn't believe how calm and dignified Rex had remained throughout the whole debacle. He'd been the model of composure when he'd made his abrupt departure, although Vesper could sense it was requiring all his self-control to hold back the fury she'd glimpsed in his eyes.

"Feel like refueling?" Rex asked, slightly more hesitantly than before.

Vesper felt an unexpected rush of heat to her cheeks. She

wished she could say yes. She imagined them at a quiet table in the canteen, their teasing giving way to more serious conversation. She liked being around the playful, brash Rex, but she wanted to spend more time with the other version of him too—the intense, thoughtful boy she sensed lurking behind the bravado. But she was meeting Ward soon and needed to get ready.

"I can't. I...I have to meet with my history instructor," she said, surprising herself with the lie.

"Good luck," Rex said cheerfully. "Some other time."

She nodded, hoping that he couldn't read her expressions as well as she could read his.

"How exactly did you get permission for this?" Vesper asked for what felt like the hundredth time since Ward had showed up at her room in a suit and announced he had a surprise for her.

"I told you not to worry. It's all taken care of," Ward said with a grin. He wasn't wearing a tie, and his white shirt was open at the neck, revealing the sliver of smooth, tanned skin that, in the past, she'd never been able to resist kissing. At the moment, however, Vesper found herself more interested in why they were in the Academy's highly restricted launchport than tracing Ward's collarbone with her lips. Ward nodded as two guards stepped aside to let them enter the vast hangar that held the Academy's fleet of fightercraft.

A young man in a fleet uniform approached. "Cadet Shipley. Cadet Haze. Follow me, please."

"Is the surprise that we're being court-martialed?" Vesper asked with a nervous laugh.

Ward merely smiled and took her hand. As they followed the officer down the long row of fightercraft, Vesper's concern gave way to awe. The streamlined ships were so beautiful, and she could only imagine how impressive they looked flying in formation.

At the end of the term, the highest-ranked squadron would get to carry out an actual operation in a real fightercraft, and the thought of sitting in the pilot's seat as she maneuvered out of the launchport sent a chill down her spine. She could almost hear Rex saying, "Nicely done, pilot," his voice full of admiration.

After they walked what felt like the entire length of the Academy, the officer escorting them stopped in front of a massive craft Vesper had never seen in person before but recognized instantly. It was a Pulsar—one of the fleet's largest, best-equipped battlecraft, capable of traveling to the farthest reaches of the solar system. "This is incredible," Vesper whispered, craning her head back to see more before turning to Ward with a smile. "This is the perfect surprise. How'd you know it was docked here?"

"Oh, we're just getting started," Ward said as the officer pressed his hand against a panel near the entrance.

"You have one hour," the officer said as the door hissed open.

Vesper looked incredulously from the ship to Ward to the officer. "We get to go *inside*?"

"For one hour," the officer repeated.

"Come on, Vee," Ward said eagerly, taking her hand. They stepped inside and headed up a narrow circular staircase. With every step, Vesper's heart beat faster. Members of the Quatra Fleet worked for *years* before earning a spot on a Pulsar crew, and here she was, exploring one on her own.

At the top of the stairs was the command deck—a vast open floor about twenty times larger than the simulcraft. At the moment, the enormous windows looked out onto the launchport, but Vesper could imagine the breathtaking view when the ship was moving fifty thousand mitons an hour along the edge of the solar system. Various controls lined the perimeter, with chairs for the pilot, technology officer, intelligence officer, and, of course, the captain.

"Go for it." Ward gestured at the captain's chair with a grin. "See how it feels."

"What? No way." Vesper inched back. Just the mere thought of sitting in the Pulsar captain's chair felt like high treason.

"Come on." He tugged her toward the chair. "It's fine. I promise."

Gingerly, Vesper lowered herself into the captain's seat, bracing for some sort of alarm to sound. When nothing happened, she placed her hands on the armrests and grinned.

Ward took a few steps back, cocked his head to the side, and surveyed Vesper with a smile. "Very nice. You look like you belong there."

"How did you arrange this?" Vesper asked, still feeling slightly dazed as she looked around the command deck.

"I pulled a few strings." Ward's smile widened, revealing his perfect white teeth. "Dating the daughter of the admiral has its advantages."

"What does that mean? Who'd you talk to?" Vesper sprang to her feet as her confusion began to crystallize into anxiety. She was trying her hardest to shake the cloud of nepotism that cast a shadow on all her accomplishments. The last thing she needed was to be caught getting special treatment.

Ward shook his head with mock disbelief. "Seriously, Vee? Are you such a control freak that you can't let yourself relax for five minutes? I told you, it's all taken care of."

"You're right." She made a show of closing her eyes and taking a deep breath. "This is amazing. Thank you." It didn't get better than this, she reminded herself. She was the luckiest girl in the solar system to have a boyfriend who cared this much about her, who was thoughtful enough to plan such an extraordinary treat.

"It's not over yet. Come on." Ward took her hand and led her up another staircase. "I think this is where they told me to go...." he said as they wandered down a passage that seemed to be lined with sleeping quarters before coming to a stop next to an open door. "Great, here we are."

Vesper peered inside, then turned to Ward in disbelief. "This is the captain's dining room," she said.

"It is indeed. After you, Vee," he said, gesturing for her to go first.

This time, Vesper knew better than to protest, and with a smile, she stepped inside. The dining room reminded her of her family's library, though instead of animal heads, the walls were adorned with maps of Quatra and the surrounding solar systems. Lamplight provided a soft glow, and when Vesper peered at one of the fixtures for a closer look, she realized it was a Tridian antique that had been retrofitted to be bolted into the ship's wall. "Pretty swanky for a military ship," she said, impressed.

"The Pulsar's designed for trips that last five years or more, so I guess they want the officers to be comfortable." Ward wrapped his arm around Vesper's waist. "Though as long as you were here with me, I wouldn't care how long we were gone for."

She raised an eyebrow. "What would people say if they discovered that the captain was dating a member of her crew?" Vesper imagined herself a few years older, exchanging a knowing smile with a handsome officer on the deck of her fightercraft, enjoying their shared secret. Except, to her surprise, the first face she saw wasn't Ward's—it was Rex's.

You've just been spending too much time at practice, Vesper told herself. *It's normal to get confused.*

"No idea. I'm more concerned with what people would say about the captain dating his pilot."

"You *just* said how good I looked in the captain's seat," Vesper said, jabbing Ward in the ribs.

"You looked very good. But it goes without saying that I'd look even better." He jumped to the side and laughed as Vesper directed another blow his way. "Hmm...assaulting your superior officer. I might have to send your dinner to the brig."

"Dinner?" Vesper repeated. She looked around the room and realized that the table at the far end was covered in silver serving dishes. "Wait? Is that for *us*?"

"It is indeed. And it looks like we have"—Ward tapped his link—"exactly forty-eight minutes to eat and get out of here before our friend downstairs shoves us out of the airlock."

"Ward..." she said softly as they sat down. "This is incredible. *You're* incredible."

An attendant appeared and filled their water glasses. "You deserved a treat," Ward said. "You've been such a great sport about losing captain, but I didn't want you to forget about the future you've always dreamed of. The future you deserve." He raised his glass.

"Thank you," she said.

"Unity and prosperity," Ward said as he clinked his glass against Vesper's while she echoed the toast. "You look beautiful. It's nice to see you so relaxed."

Vesper tried not to think about what Rex had told her that day in the bathroom: *Your strategy, your focus, your ability to stay four steps ahead of your competition—it's impressive.* There'd been a look of admiration in his eyes. But what did that matter? Ward was allowed to appreciate different things about her.

"And to your second victory," Ward said, raising his glass again. "You know, people are starting to think your squadron has a real chance at winning the whole thing. And I think everyone knows who's really responsible."

Vesper took a sip of the soup the attendant had just ladled into her bowl. "What do you mean?"

Ward gave her a knowing look. "I mean, everyone knows that it's not the Devak captain who's behind your wins."

Vesper lowered her spoon and placed it on the edge of the bowl as she looked at Ward with surprise. "Rex is doing a great job. He's inexperienced, but he has really good instincts. I've said so before."

"Come on, Vee," Ward said with a laugh. "I promise Stepney doesn't have this place bugged. You don't have to perform all the time."

"What's that supposed to mean?" she asked, unable to keep a hint of frostiness from creeping into her voice.

"I mean, you don't have to pretend like you're not making up for a lot of deadweight. It's one thing to have a Settler tech officer and intelligence officer. But a Settler captain? You know the Academy only did that so no one complained."

Part of her longed to agree with him. It was tempting to give in to Ward's certainty, to agree that, yes, *of course* Vesper had outscored Rex on the aptitude exam. That she'd lost captain because of political reasons, because it looked bad for the admiral's daughter to captain a squadron full of Settlers. Yet she knew it was a lie. "I'm not pretending anything," she said carefully, anxious not to ruin the surprise Ward had planned for her. "Rex deserves to be captain. I'm not saying I didn't *also* deserve it, but he's not getting any special treatment."

Ward ran his hand through his hair, a gesture that used to soften Vesper during their arguments but had little effect this time. "*Of course* they're getting special treatment. When did you become so naïve? Haven't you started to wonder why your squadron keeps getting such high scores?"

"What are you suggesting?" Vesper tried to keep her tone light and playful, as if they were just bantering as usual. But she couldn't ignore the apprehension building in her chest.

"Come on." He leaned back in his chair. "Don't make me say it. I don't want to sound like an asshole."

"I think it's too late for that," she said with a tight smile.

Ward closed his eyes and took a deep breath, as though he were trying to summon reserves of patience. "You've been flying really well. No one questions that. But your squadron's scores just don't make sense. Mine has never broken seventy, and you consistently score in the low eighties."

"And it never occurred to you that maybe, just maybe, it's because we're *better* than you?"

"Sure. Eventually. But how could three Settlers who'd never set foot in a simulcraft until a few weeks ago suddenly be outperforming kids who've been training their whole lives? You have to admit, it's pretty suspicious." He saw the frustration in her face, and his voice softened. "You know what, forget about it. I'm sorry, Vee." He reached across the table for her hand. "Will you forgive me? I'm just tired and stressed. Please don't let it ruin our evening. I love you."

The words normally sank into her chest and wrapped themselves around Vesper's heart like a hug, but this time they bounced off her skin. Still, she smiled and said, "I love you too."

After all her years of practice, Vesper always knew how to say the right thing.

CHAPTER 23

CORMAK

"Nice work today," his theoretical-physics instructor, Lieutenant Riguero, said. Cormak was glad the classroom was empty so there was no one to see him blush. He couldn't remember the last time a teacher had given him a compliment. When he was younger, his instructors had always been irritated by his constant stream of questions; they assumed he was trying to challenge their authority, not that he was merely curious. Once he got older, he'd stopped asking questions altogether.

But things were different at the Academy. Instead of rolling their eyes when he spoke up, his instructors brightened, eager to discuss. Today, he and Lieutenant Riguero spent ten minutes debating dark matter, and at the end of class, she'd actually *smiled* at Cormak. The last time he'd tried to debate a teacher, she'd told him he was a wiseass who'd never amount to anything. It hadn't bothered him in the moment—he'd always known he was a wiseass who'd never amount to anything. The only person who seemed to think otherwise was Rex, but Cormak figured his kindhearted big brother was deluding himself. *You're way smarter than I am, and you can do whatever the hell you want.* When Cormak had read that line in Rex's message, he'd felt a bittersweet pang amid the crushing pain; it had been comforting to see that his brother, though misguided, had never abandoned his faith in him even at the very end.

Yet the past few weeks at the Academy had gone well enough to make Cormak wonder if, perhaps, Rex hadn't been totally mistaken. He was keeping on top of his assignments and impressing his instructors. Even better, his squadron had been steadily climbing the rankings and seemed to have a real shot at winning the entire thing.

"Good luck with the rest of the tournament," Lieutenant Riguero said, as if reading his mind. "We all expect great things from you, Rex."

A strange sensation washed over him, a combination of pride and sadness. He finally had the chance to do something with his life, and the one person who cared enough to be proud of him was gone. *Gone but not forgotten,* Cormak thought. He was glad to be attending the Academy under his brother's name. He liked that a part of whatever recognition he earned would always go to Rex.

"Please report to the medical center," his monitor trilled in his ear.

"What?" Cormak said aloud, startled. "Why?"

"You've been summoned to the medical center. Please head there immediately."

"Is everything okay?" asked Lieutenant Riguero.

"Yes, fine. I'll see you tomorrow!" He did his best to sound cheerful and carefree, but as he walked down the corridor, he couldn't quell the mounting panic in his chest. Sol had told him he'd been able to hack the Sector 23 clinic's files in time, but what if something had gone wrong?

"Rex!" Cormak turned to see Brill walking toward him, clearly trying to catch up without doing anything as undignified as jogging.

"Hey," Cormak said as she fell into stride next to him, slightly breathless. "I'm kind of in a rush."

"A rush where? Are you avoiding me?" she said playfully.

"Avoiding you?" Cormak repeated, confused. Brill hadn't

crossed his mind since he'd given her the account number for the transfer.

"Listen, a bunch of us are watching a holostory in the screening room later if you want to come." She tossed her blond curls over her shoulder and looked at him expectantly.

"Yeah, maybe," he said, though in his mind, he wasn't sure there would even be a tonight. He paused as they reached the end of the hallway. "Is the medical center to the left or right?"

"It's that way." Brill gestured to the left. "Are you okay? You're all sweaty. Are you having blood drawn or something? Afraid of needles?"

"Yeah, terrified," he said distractedly as he peered down the corridor.

"Do you want me to come keep you company?"

"No." It came out much harsher than he'd intended, and out of the corner of his eye, he saw Brill bristle. "Maybe I'll see you tonight, though," he said, hoping that would be enough to make amends. "Is Vesper going to be there?"

"Don't you spend enough time with her already?" Brill's syrupy sweet voice took on a slight edge. "Besides, she hasn't been much fun lately. If she even shows up at all, she'll spend the whole night talking to Ward. I guess the rest of us aren't worth her precious time."

Cormak remembered the look on Vesper's face after their last win, the way her laugh made something in his chest start fizzing. "I think she knows how to have fun when she's in the mood."

Brill's face hardened, though her smile remained fixed firmly in place. "Of course. I mean, who wouldn't be in the mood to be whisked away on a romantic date by your ludicrously good-looking boyfriend."

"What are you talking about?" Cormak asked.

"Didn't you know? Ward got permission to have dinner in the Pulsar that's docked at the Academy. And I'm sure it's just a rumor"—she lowered her voice conspiratorially—"but I heard they took a private tour of one of the cabins when no one was looking."

Cormak knew Brill was just trying to get a rise out of him, but that didn't keep his stomach from churning at the idea of Vesper with the smug Tridian. "I need to go. I'll see you later."

"Tonight!" she trilled after him.

Five minutes later, he was sitting on an exam table,

sweat beading his forehead as the doctor explained why she'd called him. "We received your medical records from Deva, but I need to take another DNA sample to make sure it matches the information in your file."

"Why?" Cormak asked hoarsely.

"It's Quatra Fleet protocol. It'll just take a minute. Can you extend your arm, please?"

This is it, Cormak thought as he rolled up his sleeve. If Sol had succeeded in swapping Rex's medical data for Cormak's, everything would check out. But if something went wrong, the doctor would know that Cormak was an imposter. This wasn't Deva. There'd be nowhere to hide and certainly nowhere to run. He'd be in Quatra Fleet custody within minutes.

"You'll feel a slight pinch," the doctor said as she rubbed alcohol on Cormak's arm. "Are you all right? You seem a little nervous."

"I'm fine."

"Nothing on your mind?"

Only the looming threat of imprisonment and execution. "Just the final battle," Cormak said. It wasn't really a lie. In his more optimistic moments, he'd actually allowed himself to fantasize about the future. He pictured himself graduating from the Academy—with honors, of course—and then entering the Quatra Fleet as an officer. It was ridiculous. That's not the kind of thing that happened to kids from Devak, especially not dirt-poor orphans who'd spent half their lives trafficking black-market H_2O. The only person capable of beating the tremendously low odds was Rex, and even he hadn't been able to make it off planet. And yet, through a combination of absurdly dumb luck, exceptional timing, and his signature foolhardiness, Cormak had been *this close* to a real life.

"Okay, hold still."

This was it. He took a deep breath and let it out slowly. It was all out of his control now. If his harebrained scheme had worked, he'd know in a minute. But thinking about it now, the chances of that seemed minuscule. Sol could've taken the money and run. He could've made a half-assed attempt to swap out the records and given up. It was time to accept the inevitable. Cormak was doomed.

He felt a pinch on his arm and closed his eyes as the blood flowed out of him, taking his vision for a better future along with it. The crazy thing was that Vesper was part of every scenario he imagined. He saw them standing next to each other at graduation, celebrating their high honors at a fancy party where people would be staring at him with envy instead of disdain, entering the top-secret Quatra Fleet base as newly minted officers.

"I'm going to run the blood sample through the computer. It'll take just a few seconds."

Cormak could only nod. The images in his head weren't anything more than a delusion. It was time to accept the truth. Vesper was going to be a pilot and spend the rest of her life alternating between thrilling missions and glamorous vacations with her smarmy boyfriend. And Cormak was going to be a corpse.

"You're all set, Rex. Thanks for your patience."

He couldn't have heard her correctly. Cormak shook his head, trying to settle the chaotic swirl of thoughts. "Sorry, what did you say?"

"Everything's in order. I just scanned your blood, and your records check out. Good luck with your final battle." She smiled, then slipped out of the room, leaving Cormak frozen on the exam table. *Everything's in order.* It had worked. Sol had done the impossible. He was free.

Slowly, Cormak slid off the table, legs trembling. It was as if someone had pulled a plug in his chest, draining all the anxiety but taking everything else with it. *It's okay,* he thought. *You're going to be okay.* He laughed and spun around, nearly knocking over a table covered with sterile surgical tools. But it didn't matter. None of it mattered.

It took him a few minutes to get dressed since his hands were still shaking. But by the time he walked out of the medical center, his cheeks hurt from smiling. He'd been given a second chance to make something of his life, and this time he wasn't going to let anyone stand in his way.

CHAPTER 24

ARRAN

"Have you seen Vesper or Rex?" Arran panted as he and Orelia finished their fourth lap. They'd started running together a couple evenings a week, and while they normally jogged along in companionable silence, Arran was too anxious about the upcoming final battle to stay quiet. Although he knew his grades were probably strong enough to keep him at the Academy, the only way to guarantee a spot in the second year was to win the tournament. "I wonder how they're feeling."

"I'm sure they're fine," Orelia said, apparently unfazed by both the looming battle and the thick sand covering the ground. The multi-environment track was currently set to desert mode, and the air was hot and thin, as if there wasn't quite enough of it to go around. Everyone who ran by was breathing heavily. "Is Dash upset that we beat him the other day?"

Arran grinned at the memory of a sweat-soaked Dash doing his best to act gracious, shaking Rex's hand and congratulating the rest of Squadron 20 but unable to hide his bafflement. "He was for a bit, but he's gotten over it. I'm pretty sure he's rooting for us to win tomorrow."

"Pretty sure?" Orelia repeated with a smile. "Of course he is. He clearly cares about you." Her expression changed slightly, just like it always did when she talked about emotions, as if the words didn't quite come naturally to her.

"Maybe," Arran said, trying to sound nonchalant despite the flutter in his chest. Ever since their kiss in the zero-gravity chamber, he hadn't been able to think about Dash without his face breaking into an enormous smile. He'd never taken vega dust or anything like it, but he couldn't imagine any drug producing this type of euphoria.

The air suddenly turned moist and cool. "Oh, thank Antares," Arran said. The sand drained away with alarming speed, replaced by thick mud that seeped in from the sides of the track. "Never mind. I don't like this any better." He fought his way through the mud, making a slurping noise every time he lifted a foot.

"The only setting you like is snowstorm," Orelia said, still breathing normally.

"Yeah, well, wait until you come visit me on Chetire, and you'll see why." To his surprise, Orelia blushed. "I'm serious," Arran continued, trying not to wheeze. "It's cold and boring, but I think you'd still have fun." Based on the very little she'd shared, he got the impression that Orelia's life on Loos had been a lonely one, and he couldn't wait to let his mother fuss over her.

"I'd like that," she said. Her voice grew quiet, though not from exhaustion like Arran's had. "Do you think you'll invite Dash at some point?"

Arran also blushed, but since his face was already so red from running, he doubted Orelia would notice. He thought about bringing Dash to Chetire all the time, but part of him was afraid of what Larz Muscatine's son would think of the small, sad home where he'd grown up. At the Academy, it was easy for Dash to forget that Arran was a Settler. But on Chetire, there would be no escaping the reality that Arran came from a place that Dash had been raised to look down on.

"Maybe, at some point."

Arran thought he'd done a good job of keeping his voice light, but it wasn't enough to stop Orelia from looking at him with concern. "What's wrong?"

"Nothing!" he insisted. "I'm just nervous about tomorrow."

"No, it's something else."

For a moment, Arran prayed that the poison gas setting would come next so they'd have to grab gas masks and run in silence. He hadn't mentioned his strange conversation with Sergeant Pond to anyone and wasn't eager to relive it. But the words bubbled up seemingly of their own accord. He told Orelia about Pond's warning, how he didn't think it was a good idea for Arran to get too close to Dash.

"That's ridiculous," Orelia said with more indignation than he'd thought her capable of. "Anyone who's seen you together knows that Dash cares deeply for you."

Arran's rapidly beating heart swelled with gratitude. "I think it's more complicated than that, though," he panted. "Hold on, I need to catch my breath." He staggered to a halt and bent over, resting his hands on his knees. "How are you not tired?" He wheezed, looking at Orelia, who'd barely broken a sweat.

She shrugged. "I did a lot of endurance training on Loos. So what's more complicated?"

Arran jumped to the side to let three mud-covered girls run past, their faces contorted with various degrees of pain. "I know Dash likes me. But you've heard about his father; he's leading the charge to get us kicked out of the Academy."

"But that's not what Dash wants."

"No, of course not. But it doesn't make things any simpler. Dash's father is incredibly powerful, and if he finds out his son is dating someone like me, he could make life really difficult for both of us. I just think we might be getting in over our heads."

The mud drained away, leaving firm dirt in its place. "Come on," Orelia called, starting to run again. "Break's over."

Arran trudged after her, wincing with each step. "It doesn't matter," he said with a groan. "Because I'll probably die on this track before any of that stuff becomes an issue."

With a grin, Orelia spun around and began to run backward. "Will this make it easier for you to keep up?"

"You know, sometimes I wonder if you're the nicest person I know or the most evil. It's hard to tell." Orelia's face fell as she came to an abrupt stop. "Orelia, I was just joking,"

Arran said gently. He had to remind himself to think twice before he teased her, as it was never clear what was going to send her into one of her strange, unreadable moods.

"I know," she said, though there was a hint of relief in her voice. "Anyway, I think you should trust Dash. He knows what he's getting into."

"I'm not doubting *him*. I'm just saying that sometimes you have to accept that there are things out of your control. We're all a product of our backgrounds, you know?"

"And *I'm* just saying that people can surprise you." Orelia paused for a moment, staring straight ahead as they ran. "We're shaped by our pasts, but we're not defined by them. We can all make choices."

Arran let her words sink in. Perhaps Orelia was right. After all, Arran was both a product of his background and an exception to it. A proud Chetrian who beat all the odds and was now in one of the most promising squadrons in the Quatra Fleet Academy. And although Dash had come from very different circumstances, he'd also refused to go down the path others had set for him. He'd been strong enough to make his own choices and would continue to do so. Especially now that he had someone supporting him.

"You're right," Arran wheezed. His lungs were burning,

and he was pretty sure his hamstrings were about to disintegrate, but he felt calmer than he had in days.

"I've found that I generally am."

Arran smiled. "How come *you're* allowed to joke and I'm not?"

"Who said that I was joking." She smirked, then broke into a sprint. Despite his protesting muscles, Arran ran after her. "How are you planning to win tomorrow if you kill your tech officer?" he called. He smiled to himself. Squadron 7 had no idea what was about to hit them.

By the time he entered the simulcraft the next day, Arran found himself feeling slightly less confident. Both squadrons had nearly perfect records, one of which was going to end today.

Rex was already sitting in the captain's chair, looking distracted as he responded half-heartedly to Vesper's prebattle chatter, which seemed a bit more manic than normal. Orelia sat quietly in the intelligence officer's seat, but she somehow seemed even more withdrawn than usual.

"Is everyone okay?" Arran asked, looking around the simulcraft.

"Never better," Vesper said with a slightly strained smile.

"Your mission will commence in two minutes."

Vesper clapped her hands together. "We've got this." She sounded energetic and cheerful, but it wasn't enough to hide her desperation.

"Today, you'll be performing a rescue mission. We've received a distress signal from a team of scientists on a research station above Nevo, a gas giant in the uninhabited Hextra System. Your objective: Travel to Nevo, evacuate the station, and return everyone safely to the base. Your score will be determined by speed, fuel usage, and the condition of your passengers and craft."

As Arran settled into the tech officer's chair, he cracked his knuckles and turned to Vesper. "Don't worry. This is going to be as easy as…toast. That's what that means, right?"

This time, she let out a genuine laugh. "Okay, wiseass. Save all that brainpower for the mission." She turned to face the others. "From what I know about Squadron 7, they tend to be overly cautious, so most of their points come from accuracy instead of speed. If we can be fast *and* accurate, we should be able to beat them easily."

Arran glanced at Rex, waiting for him to point out that

he was the captain, not Vesper. But to Arran's surprise, Rex looked serious and didn't do more than nod. Arran felt more knots of worry form in his stomach. They all had so much banking on this win.

"Commence mission."

"Arran, how do the engines look?" Rex asked, suddenly alert.

Arran scanned the numbers on the fuel and temperature monitors. Sometimes, the system threw a wrench into the mission by having you start with a malfunctioning ship, but this time everything looked normal. "All systems go."

"Good. Orelia, any obstacles?"

Her fingers flew across her screen until an image of the Hextra System appeared. "There's a methane storm in the atmosphere of Nevo—a big one. That might be why they've sent a distress call. But the storm isn't anything we need to worry about until we get much closer."

"Okay. In that case, Vesper, take us away."

She nodded in answer and deftly took off from the launchport. A few moments later, they'd left the base behind.

No one spoke much during the journey to the Hextra System, which, according to Arran's calculations, would take twelve minutes at hyperspeed. As he performed his routine checks on the engines, weapons, and life-support systems, his thoughts drifted to Dash. Would his father be more open to his dating a Settler if Arran's squadron won the tournament? Or would it only make him furious to know that Dash had lost to a majority Settler squadron?

"We're less than one parsec away," Orelia said without looking away from the screen. In response, Vesper took the craft out of hyperspeed, and the world around them came back into focus. "It looks like the research station is floating in the top layer of Nevo's atmosphere."

"That means it'd suffer serious damage in a storm," Rex said. "If their life-support system fails, they'll suffocate."

Arran suppressed a shudder as he thought about his father and the four other miners who'd died slow, painful deaths deep underground.

"Do we know how many people are inside?" Vesper asked.

Arran adjusted the frequency on the transponder. "No, but I'll see if there's a way to communicate with them."

After a few moments of static, a voice came in through the speakers. "Mayday...mayday...This is Nevo Station Alpha....Do you read?"

Rex pressed a button on the captain's control panel on his chair. "This is Squadron 20. We're here to take you home."

"Thank Antares," the voice said, trembling slightly. Arran stared at the speaker, startled by how real it all sounded, and wondered if it was prerecorded or if someone at the Academy was pretending to be a stranded scientist. "There are twelve of us on board, and oxygen is running low."

"Approaching Nevo." Vesper gestured toward a small bluish green sphere in the distance.

"Arran, will we be able to dock?" Rex asked.

Arran pulled up a schematic of the research station. "No...our fightercraft's too big to dock. We'll have to send the rover. But it only fits four people, so we'll need to make a few trips."

Vesper cursed under her breath. "That's going to take forever."

"Yeah, well, sometimes saving lives takes time," Arran snapped, then immediately regretted it. They were all feeling the strain right now, but taking it out on one another was the worst thing they could do. He took a deep breath and exhaled. "Besides, Squadron 7 will also have to make multiple trips. We have time."

As they approached, Nevo grew larger until they couldn't

see anything other than bluish-green gas. "Whoa...that storm is massive," Rex said, pointing at the violent-looking swirl that made the planet look like a roiling ocean.

"There's the research station," Vesper called. "I'll get as close as I can, but we can't risk getting too near the storm." The words were barely out of her mouth before the simulcraft began to rattle. "Okay...I guess we'll wait here."

Arran dispatched the rover, which he'd programmed to dock at the research station. They watched it appear on the screen, then grow smaller as it descended toward the planet.

Rex issued instructions to the head of the research station, and a few minutes later, the rover reappeared with its four virtual passengers. The simulcraft shook again, more violently this time. "The storm's moving toward us," Orelia said. "If we don't leave now, we risk disabling our ship."

"We can't leave now. We've rescued only four people," Arran insisted, feeling slightly breathless as he imagined suffocating to death in an abandoned research station slowly sinking into a gas giant. "We'll fail the mission if we leave the rest behind."

"We'll also fail if we all *die*," Vesper said, her fingers turning white as she gripped the controls.

The simulcraft shook again, and Arran felt his harness dig into his skin. "Vesper's right," Rex said grimly. "This is the best we're going to do. It's time to head back."

Arran glanced over his shoulder at Rex. "Wouldn't rescuing more people *increase* our score? Maybe that's part of the mission. It could be some kind of ethical test."

"If it's an ethical test, then we *definitely* shouldn't try to rescue the remaining scientists," Orelia said coolly. "It's a reckless waste of time. What if everyone on the station dies because we weren't strong enough to leave a few people behind? Saving four lives is always preferable to losing sixteen."

"There's no time," Vesper called. "If Squadron 7 finishes the mission first, they'll win. Is that what you want? To let *them* automatically continue on to the second year instead of us? Because I sure as hell don't."

"Hold on," Arran said as a plan took shape in his mind. "What if we tether the research station to our fightercraft and tow it back to the base? Then we won't have to leave anyone behind."

"How bad is the storm?" Rex asked. "Will we be able to make it to the station and then escape the atmosphere?"

Orelia leaned forward to look at the radar. "Possibly. Our ship can withstand more damage than the rover."

Rex stared into the distance for a moment, then nodded. "Okay, let's do it. Vesper, set a course for the research station."

Without responding, Vesper took the ship into a deep dive. The rattling grew more intense, and the lights in the simulcraft began to flicker. The research station came into view. It had lost power and was drifting toward the eye of the storm.

"Arran, initiate tethering!" Rex shouted over the din.

The ship tilted to the side, and Arran winced as his harness dug deeper into his skin. "I'm not sure this is going to work," Vesper said through gritted teeth. "I can't keep the ship steady enough to tether."

"Yes, you can," Rex said. "This is nothing compared to what I've seen you do."

To Arran's relief, the encouragement seemed to work, and a moment later, the research station was locked to their ship. A prompt came up on Arran's screen, asking if he wanted to take control of the station's systems. He pressed *yes*, then adjusted the ship's life-support settings to make sure oxygen would flow through the tethering mechanism. "We're good to go," he called to Vesper. "Let's get out of here."

They shot forward, and the rattling increased until Arran could feel his bones being jolted out of place. Then all went still and quiet. "Take it away, Vesper," Rex said. "Don't worry about conserving fuel. Let's just make up for lost time."

"Come on, come on," Vesper whispered as she pushed the craft to maximum speed. No one else spoke until the virtual image of the Academy appeared in the distance. It didn't sound like anyone was even breathing. The bay door opened, and Vesper guided the craft into the dock.

Mission complete flashed across the screen. But still no one spoke. If Squadron 7 had also somehow managed to rescue the scientists and make it back sooner, they'd win the tournament.

"Congratulations, Squadron 20. You've received the high score for this mission."

Vesper's joyful scream filled the simulcraft as she leapt from her seat. "We did it!" she shouted, throwing her arms around Rex before embracing Orelia and finally Arran.

"I'm sorry," she said. It was hard to tell if she was laughing or crying.

"You have nothing to apologize for," Arran said, squeezing Vesper's hand.

"I'll be less obnoxious next year, I promise." Behind her, Rex said something about not making promises you can't keep, but this time Vesper ignored his ribbing.

Next year. Arran grinned at the thought, and as if reading his mind, Vesper did the same, her eyes filling with tears as she squeezed his hand in return.

CHAPTER 25

VESPER

Vesper didn't care that she kept bumping into people and walls; she couldn't stop looking down at her uniform badge as she half walked, half ran down the corridor toward the residential wing.

Vesper Haze
Pilot
Squadron 20
Rank: 1st

They'd actually done it. They'd *won* the tournament, and now all four of them were guaranteed to stay on at the Academy.

"Congrats, Vesper!" an older cadet called as she passed.

"Thanks!" she said, still barely able to look up.

"Well done!" A girl Vesper knew from her old school patted her on the arm as she passed.

"Thank you," she said, tearing her eyes away from her badge just long enough to flash the girl a smile. She sped up, walking as quickly as she could without breaking into a run. Word was clearly spreading fast, and she wanted to be the one to tell Ward the good news. She'd thought about messaging him, but she was eager to see the pride and excitement in his face. Despite their slightly strained dinner the other night, she knew he'd be thrilled for her.

As she entered the residential wing, Vesper forced herself to slow down and walk normally. With dignity. And with as much modesty as she could muster. She knew there were people who'd want to chalk her win up to nepotism, and she couldn't risk giving them any additional reasons to resent her. But as she rounded the bend that led to Ward's suite, her excitement got the better of her, and she broke back into a run.

Breathless, she pressed the buzzer next to the door, and about thirty seconds later, the door hissed open. "We did it!" she squealed, throwing her arms around Ward. "We won!"

"That's awesome, Vee." He patted her on the back, then let go to lean against the wall.

"Let's go inside," she said. "I want to give you the play-by-play."

"You know, now's not a great time. I think a few of my roommates are napping, and I need to finish that history paper before dinner." He must've seen the hurt and confusion in her face because he smiled and said, "Come on, don't look at me like that. You know I want to hear all about it. Can't we talk later?" He smiled again, this one slightly stiffer than before.

"Why are you acting like this? What's wrong?"

He sighed and rubbed his temples in a gesture that made him look somehow older and wearier. "Nothing. I'm trying my best to be happy for you. I really am. But you also have to understand that while you're prancing around as princess of the Academy, I'm trying to deal with the fact that I'm completely screwed."

"What are you talking about?" She placed her hand on his arm, but he jerked it away.

"My squadron came in *eighth*," he said with exaggerated patience. "There's only so much you can do as captain when half your team is barely literate."

Vesper recoiled as surprise and disgust curdled her stomach. "What the hell, Ward? Do you know how ridiculous you sound?"

"No, I don't. I'm sick of this shit. I'm tired of pretending like we're all equal. Just because the administration was bullied into changing the policy doesn't mean that the Edgers are any smarter than they were before. They don't belong here, and we all know it. Why is everyone afraid to speak the truth?"

"No," she said slowly, as her disgust began to bubble into anger. "They didn't suddenly become smarter. They've *always* been as smart as we are. We were just too dumb to realize it. Of course they belong here, Ward."

"When did you turn into some brainwashed pawn just repeating what you've been told? You might be too much of a coward to say it, but I'm not." His lips twisted into a sneer, transforming the face she knew so well into one she barely recognized. "The Edgers need to go home."

Vesper stared at him as a realization swept through her, chasing the anger away and leaving only cold horror in its wake. "It was you, wasn't it? *You* wrote that message."

A tiny, naïve, hopeful part of her prayed that he'd deny it, that he'd look so hurt by the accusation, she'd know she'd made a terrible mistake. But instead he shook his head and let out a bitter laugh. "What does it matter? It's not like it made any kind of difference. The Edgers are still here, aren't they?"

"You're disgusting." Vesper spun around and strode off, walking with as much assurance as she could muster given the waves of shock and fury slamming into her from all directions. How could Ward have done something like that? *Ward.* The boy who sent her sweet messages before bed. The boy who'd spent countless hours at her house, the boy her parents adored. The boy who came up with silly nicknames and loved kissing her. She braced for the pain, waiting for that searing jolt to her chest, but it never came. She felt stung and disgusted by his betrayal, but not heartbroken the way she'd expected.

He can't get away with this, she thought as her resolve hardened, sending new strength through her trembling body. She knew what she had to do.

⌃⌃

"Vesper?" Admiral Haze rose from her chair and surveyed her daughter with a combination of confusion and pleasure. Vesper never dropped by her mother's office unexpectedly.

"I just heard the good news. Congratulations, pilot," she said as she walked around her desk and perched on the edge. "Everything okay?"

"Ward was the one who wrote the graffiti in the hallway," Vesper said, cutting straight to the point.

"Ward *what*?" her mother said, more startled than Vesper had ever seen her. Svetlara Haze was famous for her icy composure; every schoolchild in the solar system had seen the iconic photo of her on one of Chetire's rocky moons, calmly speaking into her link as a massive explosion sent her rover flying into the air behind her.

"Ward was the idiot who wrote *Go home Edgers*. Though maybe I'm the idiot for thinking that I loved him." She slumped into one of the uncomfortable chairs next to the desk, defying her mother to tell her to sit up straight.

"What makes you suspect that Ward is the culprit?"

Vesper stared at her mother incredulously. "Are you kidding me? *Because he told me he did it.*"

She waited for her mother to snap into action, summoning Ward to her office or calling an emergency session of the disciplinary committee. But she simply sighed and rubbed her temples. "That wasn't the smartest move."

"It was *disgusting*," Vesper said, frustration mounting.

"And obviously a violation of about a dozen different Academy rules. You're going to expel him, right?"

"Expel him?" her mother repeated. "Are you really asking me to expel your boyfriend?"

"He's obviously not my boyfriend anymore," Vesper said, narrowing her eyes. "And he can't stay here."

"Listen, Vesper...." Admiral Haze stood wearily and returned to her chair behind the desk. "I know this is upsetting. But I don't think expelling Ward is the answer. Everyone has moved on from the incident, and I'm hesitant to stir up tension again. I'll talk to Ward so it's clear that this behavior is unacceptable. But making an example out of him will just make everything worse."

Vesper's head spun as she stared at her mother in disbelief. "You're just going to let it slide? He wrote *Go home Edgers* on Academy property. What kind of message does that send?"

Above them, one of the moons in the holographic map of the solar system turned red. Admiral Haze glanced at it, and her face hardened. "I know to cadets the Academy can seem like the most important thing in the world—their whole world, in fact—but it's just a tiny piece of a much bigger picture. We're in the middle of a war, and my job is to cultivate

talent and develop the next generation of Quatra Fleet officers capable of protecting our species. Ward is a gifted cadet,
and we can't afford to get rid of him because he made one
stupid mistake. That's why you're all here. To *learn*."

Vesper stood up, trembling with anger, but when she
spoke, her voice was steady. "If this is how we treat one
another, then we might have to ask ourselves at some point
if we're worth saving." She spun around and walked to the
door, ignoring her mother's calls for her to return.

This is complete magma boar crap, Vesper thought as she
strode through the corridor, ignoring everyone who waved or
tried to catch her eye. Everything she'd been told about the
Academy had been a lie. There was no honor code. No one was
looking for "cadets with character." And her mother couldn't
have cared less about Ward's frankly mediocre captain skills.
All she cared about was saving face with everyone back on Tri
and not upsetting influential civilians like Ward's parents.

There was only one person she could bear to look at right
now. One person who'd never lied to her or sucked up to
her. One person who'd understand the fury and confusion
battling within her.

And she knew exactly where to find him.

CHAPTER 26

CORMAK

"I'd like to propose a toast," Dash said, raising his voice over the din. Cormak, Arran, Orelia, Zuzu, Sula, and Vesper's friend Frey had gathered in the common room to celebrate Squadron 20's win, and someone, Cormak wasn't sure who, had convinced an attendant to bring over fancy refreshments. Dash lifted a glass of deep red spineberry juice. "Unity and prosperity."

"Unity and prosperity!" everyone echoed.

"And, of course, to Squadron 20." Dash grinned at Arran, who turned slightly pink.

"To Squadron 20!" Cormak and the others repeated joyfully. Well, most of the others. Frey's smile struck Cormak as slightly forced, but it was clear he was trying to be a good sport about the whole thing. He'd come to congratu-late Vesper, but no one had seen her since they'd left the simulcraft.

It was about an hour before dinner, and the circadian lights had begun to dim, creating a twilight effect in the common room. The glasses scattered on the small tables glinted in the warm light of the lamps, giving the room a cozy atmosphere that Cormak hadn't thought possible in space. Hell, he hadn't realized he'd even *known* the word *cozy* until this moment. But apparently, it had been lying dormant deep in his brain, waiting for the right moment to pop out.

"I'd like to propose another toast," Arran called from the couch, where he was seated with Dash's arm around him. He raised his glass. "To Rex, for his leadership, quick think-ing, and composure under pressure."

"To Rex!" the others echoed.

Cormak hoped the dim light concealed the blush rising to his cheeks. *Rex would've loved this*, he thought.

"And to Arran," Orelia said, raising her glass. She was sitting on the floor, leaning back against the couch, looking more relaxed than Cormak had ever seen her. "For coming up with an ingenious solution."

They all clinked glasses again, and Arran reached down to squeeze Orelia's shoulder.

"What happened next?" Zuzu asked, looking from Orelia to Cormak. "I bet Rex saved the day." She smiled at Cormak, and a remote part of his brain registered that she was very pretty. But it was like hearing music in a distant room, music that was quickly overpowered by a louder, soaring tune as he thought about the person who'd actually saved the day.

As they frantically tried to escape the methane storm, Cormak had pretty much forgotten that it was a simulation. They all had. The only one who hadn't seemed rattled was Vesper. With the engine failing and the craft rumbling, she still managed to pilot the craft to safety, her hands moving across the controls so quickly, she didn't have time to wipe the sweat dripping down her face. Even in the midst of the chaos, Cormak realized she'd never looked more beautiful.

"Do you know where Vesper is?" he asked Frey.

He thought he'd done a good job of keeping his voice casual, but the Tridian's smile suggested otherwise. "I don't know. But I'm sure your pilot will return to you soon. Nothing to worry about, Captain."

Dash shot Frey a warning look, and Cormak felt his

cheeks grow even warmer. Was he some kind of joke to the Tridians? The poor, delusional Devak who foolishly thought he had a chance with the admiral's daughter? He wanted to tell them they had it all wrong. Yet no matter how hard he tried, he couldn't chase away the image of Vesper in the simulcraft.

"When do you find out about the real mission?" Sula asked, sounding both envious and apprehensive.

"I'm not sure," Arran said. "I don't really understand it. They let us take a *real* fightercraft out? Is that a good idea?"

"It's *fine*," Frey said with a dismissive wave. "You'll go out for twenty minutes, pick up some easy-to-find item that's been left for you, and fly right back. The hardest part will be docking, though I suppose that's Vesper's responsibility—oh, look, here's the lady of the hour!"

Cormak turned to see Vesper striding toward them. She was in uniform, and her long dark hair was still damp with sweat. But all Cormak could focus on was her face. Her cheeks were flushed, and her eyes glowed with determination and something else, an expression that had grown less familiar to him during the past few weeks—fury.

"Are you okay?" he said, rising to his feet.

"I need to talk to you."

Before he had time to respond, she'd grabbed his hand and was pulling him toward the door, unbothered by the confused stares and whispers they left in their wake.

"What's going on?" Cormak asked as the common room door shut behind them. The corridor was empty, as most of the other cadets were changing for dinner. But Vesper didn't seem to care one way or the other. He recognized her expression from their first few interactions and knew that when she was in this mode all that mattered was carrying out her mission.

She fixed him with such an intense stare that, for a moment, he assumed her rage was directed at him. "I just found out that Ward's an asshole," she said, her voice steady despite the slightly manic gleam in her eyes. "And my mom's a bigger asshole."

"You're only realizing that now?" he asked, cringing at the memory of Admiral Haze's patronizing jabs.

"Everyone here is a fraud." Her voice grew quieter as she stepped closer. "Everyone except for you."

"What are you talking about? What's wrong?"

"It was Ward who wrote the graffiti, and my mother refuses to do anything about it."

"*Ward?*" Cormak repeated. Frankly, he was surprised

the kid knew how to spell *Edger* without someone coaching him. "Your boyfriend?"

"Not anymore." She cringed, and some of the fury faded from her face. For the first time, she looked almost fragile. "I can't believe I was so stupid."

Without thinking, Cormak reached out and took her hand. "You're many things, Vesper Haze, but you're not stupid. How could you have possibly known he'd do that?"

She stared at their hands, but to Cormak's surprise, she didn't pull away. "I might've known if I'd ever thought about it. He was so clearly the boy I was *supposed* to date that I never took the time to think about who he really was." She closed her eyes and winced. "I wanted to do everything right. I wanted to be impressive."

"You're much more impressive without that idiot, believe me," Cormak said, trying to make her smile. It didn't work. She looked so sad, so hurt, that he was forced to use a different tactic. Sincerity. "Listen, Vesper, you don't need to worry about impressing people. Everything you do is remarkable whether you realize it or not."

She stared at him for a long moment as something shifted in her face.

Then with her trademark assurance, she kissed him.

It came as such a shock that at first Cormak could barely move. But as her lips pressed against his, instinct kicked in. He leaned against the wall for balance, wrapped his arm around her waist, and kissed her back. She sank into him, and he tightened his hold to steady her. He'd kissed a fair number of girls before, but it had never felt like this. There was no fumbling, no wondering what to do next. It was like his lips had already memorized the shape of her mouth and he couldn't keep them from seeking out their favorite spots. Everything about her felt both familiar and electrifyingly new at the same time.

He tilted his head and kissed her cheek before trailing down to her neck.

She let out a gasp, her breath tickling his face as she held on to him. It was too much for him to take, and without thinking, Cormak wrapped his other arm around her, giving in to his body's desperation to be as close to her as possible.

"*Erratic heart rate and blood flow detected,*" his monitor droned in his ear.

"Dismiss," Cormak whispered.

"You want to stop?" Vesper asked, pulling away with a smile.

"Definitely not." He placed his hand under her chin and tilted his head down to kiss her again.

"If your monitor is telling you to rest, you should probably take a break."

"Don't make me issue an order, pilot." He placed his hand on her hip and gently pulled her toward him.

CHAPTER 27

ORELIA

"Are you nervous?" Arran whispered as he and the rest of Squadron 20 followed Admiral Haze across the launchport toward the fightercraft they'd be using for their mission.

"Slightly," Orelia said, though the anxiety eating away at her stomach lining had nothing to do with their short flight outside the Academy. It had been weeks since she'd sent the coordinates, and with each passing day, her guilt had grown more overpowering. It had all seemed so simple when she'd first arrived, full of the excitement and relief that came with successfully infiltrating the Academy. She was living among the enemy—the next generation of killers being trained to attack her people and colonize her planet. It didn't matter that the cadets were being lied to, tricked into believing that the Specters had attacked unprovoked. Whatever the Quatrans' motivation, they were being taught to kill Sylvans and had to be stopped.

Yet the knowledge that a Sylvan ship was on its way to destroy the Academy—and everyone inside—now left her in a constant state of nausea. Hundreds of cadets, including her friends, were going to *die* because of her.

And then there was Zafir. Being in the ocean tank with him had been the happiest she'd felt since leaving Sylvan. She'd replayed their kiss hundreds of times in her head, and it never failed to make her whole body tingle. But then she'd remind herself that of everyone at the Academy he was the best equipped to discover the truth about her. If she wanted to survive until the Sylvans extracted her, she'd have to keep her distance.

"Don't be nervous! This is going to be *killer*." Rex was practically bouncing up and down in contrast to Arran, who'd gone quiet and serious, nodding at everything Admiral Haze said. Orelia kept waiting for Vesper to snap into leader mode and start giving advice, but she seemed strangely subdued, smiling but speaking less than usual.

Perhaps unsurprisingly, the inside of the fightercraft looked exactly like the simulcraft. Except that the view out the windows was real, so instead of simulated stars, all they could see were the walls of the launchport. As they took their seats, Arran closed his eyes and inhaled deeply while Vesper and Rex exchanged excited smiles.

"You all look very much at home," Admiral Haze said, surveying them with approval. "Now, this operation is going to be easy, especially compared with the battles you completed in the simulcraft. Earlier today, we launched a satellite into orbit. All you need to do is locate the satellite on your radar, set a course to retrieve it, and then return to the Academy. The entire process should take less than an hour. Your instructors will be monitoring your progress from the command center, and help is standing by in case anything goes wrong." Orelia felt her stomach fluttering as she imagined Zafir in the command center along with their other instructors, watching with pride as she set off on the mission. "Any questions?"

"We've got this," Rex said, flashing a grin at his squadron mates.

"I leave it up to you, Captain," Admiral Haze said. "Good luck." She placed her hand on Vesper's shoulder, then strode out.

"Squadron 20, this is mission control." A voice crackled

through the speakers. "You're cleared for launch whenever you're ready."

"Everyone ready?" Vesper asked. She cracked her knuckles, then rolled her shoulders.

"Ready," Arran said from his seat. The tremor had disappeared from his voice. He was all focus.

"Ready," Orelia called. Although she didn't much care about impressing any instructors other than Zafir, this outing would provide some welcome distraction. The busier she was, the less time she'd have to wonder when the Sylvans would arrive to destroy the Academy.

"All set there, Captain?" Vesper called to Rex.

"All set."

Orelia waited for him to add something flippant, but it never came. She glanced over and saw him swallow, drumming the arms of his chair as he stared straight ahead.

When the countdown reached zero, the usual mission commence message appeared on the screen. But this time, the windows didn't automatically fill with simulated stars. First, they had to wait for the automated tracks to guide the ship to the edge of the dock.

"End autopilot mode," Vesper said.

"Autopilot mode ending."

Out of the corner of her eye, Orelia saw Vesper ease back the throttle, and then they were airborne.

Arran let out a *whoop* as the Academy grew smaller behind them and the stars grew brighter. "We're really doing this!"

"Antares help us, we are," Vesper said. Orelia couldn't see her face, but she could hear the smile in her voice. *Good,* she thought. She wanted her friends to enjoy themselves as much as possible before... Orelia couldn't complete the morbid thought.

"Arran, are we ready to switch into full speed?" Rex asked.

"All systems go."

"Orelia, any obstacles in our way?"

She checked the radar again just to make sure. "All clear."

"Take it away, Vesper."

Their seats began to shake slightly as Vesper activated the thrusters. "This is awesome!" Rex called. Even without turning to look at him, Orelia could tell he'd started to relax.

After a few minutes, they fell into their usual rhythm, speaking in the shorthand they'd developed after spending countless hours in the simulcraft together. The cabin filled with the sounds that had become as familiar to Orelia as her own breath: Arran muttering to himself, the click of Vesper's jaw as she clenched her teeth in concentration, the tap of Rex's foot as he called out instructions.

"How much farther?" Rex asked.

Orelia leaned in closer to the radar screen. "It's less than three thousand mitons away. At this speed, we'll reach it in another twenty minutes." It was a little disappointing that the mission turned out to be so short. She had no interest in returning to the Academy and facing the excruciating fate that awaited her.

"Excellent." Behind her, she heard Rex crack his knuckles. "As easy as dust cake."

"As easy as *dust cake*?" Vesper repeated. "What does that mean?"

"You've never heard that expression?" Rex said incredulously.

"It's 'as easy as sugar cake.'"

"Yeah, well, we don't have a lot of sugar on Deva. Or cake, for that matter. The only thing that's easy to procure is dust. Hence the saying."

Despite her anxiety, Orelia smiled. At some point over

the past few weeks, their banter had started to feel almost comforting.

They located the satellite easily, and Arran used the command codes they'd been given to access the satellite's maneuvering thrusters and guide it into their hold.

"All right then, pilot," Rex said with a grin. "Take us home."

As Vesper turned the fightercraft back toward the Academy, Orelia noticed something on the radar moving in their direction. She watched it closely for a moment, and a chill passed through her. "No," she whispered as she activated the scanner, focusing the laser beam that allowed them to measure the size and shape of potential obstacles.

"Everything okay, Orelia?" Vesper called, glancing at Orelia over her shoulder.

Orelia's eyes were fixed on the screen, but she couldn't speak. All she could do was stare at the startlingly familiar shape on the screen. *No*, she thought. *It's too soon.*

"What's going on over there, Orelia?" Rex asked, a hint of worry in his voice.

Arran swiveled his chair around and leaned toward her.

"What the hell is *that*?" Vesper snapped.

Orelia tore her gaze from the radar to follow Vesper's pointed finger out the window. The same shape that she'd seen on the screen loomed in the distance, growing larger by the second.

"It can't be...." Rex said hoarsely. Orelia could picture the expression on his face without turning. The look of someone watching his childhood nightmare come to life. For while the large craft hurtling toward them looked perfectly normal to Orelia, to Rex and the others, it was an image that conjured pure terror.

An enormous Specter battlecraft.

"That's impossible," Arran said, as if he could make the ship disappear through the power of logic. "This is a safe zone. The Quatra Fleet patrols the perimeter. There's no way the Specters could penetrate it."

"Everyone relax. It has to be some kind of trick, like the storm from our last battle." Rex's voice was steady and assured, but Orelia could detect a note of fear.

"That was in a simulcraft. They can't create an illusion in *space*," Vesper said, eyes still locked on the ship. It was so close, it now took up most of the window. She pressed a red button on the dashboard. "Academy command, do you read?" There was nothing but static. "Mayday, mayday,

Academy command, do you read?" The static grew louder. Vesper slammed her hand on the dashboard. "Shit. It's not working."

They've scrambled the communications, Orelia realized as panic swelled in her chest. Instinctively, her hand went to the transponder in her uniform pocket. It wasn't connected to their ship's network, so it might still work. And since they were outside the Academy, she'd finally be able to send an outgoing message.

"Can you tell where it's headed, Orelia?" Rex asked more anxiously than before.

Orelia didn't have to check the radar screen to give her answer; she knew exactly where it was going. "The Academy."

"What do we do?" Vesper asked, eyes growing wide as she looked from one squadron mate to another.

"We have to warn the command center," Arran ordered. "Vesper, try again."

Vesper slammed the red button again. "Academy command, come in...come in, Academy command..." Her voice cracked, but there was nothing filling the silence except static.

Arran leapt from his seat and reached over Vesper to

press the button himself. "The Specters are coming for you. You need to do something!" he shouted. "Come on!" He spun around and collapsed back into his chair. "They're going to kill everyone," he said with a gasp.

Just then Orelia saw the ship change course on the radar screen. It was headed toward them. "They've seen us," she said, fear coursing through her.

"Warning...warning...incoming projectile detected. Prepare for impact in 15...14...13..."

"They're shooting at us," Arran said more to himself than the others. He'd gone pale and was staring straight ahead, frozen. "They're shooting at us, and we're going to die."

He was right. Their fightercraft with its small payload of missiles was no match for the enormous Sylvan battle-craft. It would destroy them and then continue on its path to the Academy. By the time Admiral Haze and the other officers realized what was happening and armed the school's fightercraft fleet, it would be too late—the Academy would be wiped out.

Orelia reached into her pocket for the transponder. She never thought she'd dare risk letting anyone else see it, but her squadron mates were too fixated on the Sylvan ship to notice.

Call off the attack. I'm on the fightercraft, she wrote.

"Like hell we are," Rex muttered. "Vesper, get us out of here."

"On it. Hold on, everyone," she called as she took the ship into an inverted dive that took them just outside the missile's path.

Orelia's stomach leapt into her throat, and she closed her eyes. When the dizziness subsided, she looked back down at her transponder.

The ship has received orders not to fire on you again. Keep a safe distance from the Academy, and the crew will retrieve you after the target is destroyed.

"We need to launch our own attack," Rex said, his voice growing steadier. "It's our only chance. Arran, prepare the missiles. Vesper, prepare to fire."

"*No.*" The word tore through Orelia's throat before she had time to stop it.

"What the hell are you talking about?" Rex barked. "The order stands."

Arran's fingers flew across the controls as he scrolled through a series of symbols that were completely indecipherable to Orelia. "Missiles activated," he said, sounding strangely calm, as if he'd convinced himself he was back in the simulator.

"Okay, Vesper, fire at will."

"Wait," Orelia called. "We don't need to fire.... They've turned around."

Vesper leaned forward for a better view. "I think they're heading toward the Academy again."

While everyone stared at the Sylvan ship, Orelia reached for her transponder again.

I'm not the pilot, Orelia wrote desperately. *I can't make them keep a safe distance.*

A moment later, a response appeared. *You've been trained for this situation. Take control of the ship.*

Orelia knew exactly what that meant—she'd been taught multiple ways to render an opponent unconscious.

"We have to stop them," Arran said hoarsely as he stared out the window in horror. Orelia watched as Vesper clenched her jaw and gripped the controls tighter just as she'd done countless times before

"We will," Rex said. "Vesper, *fire*."

Orelia held her breath as the missile tore through the darkness toward the Sylvan ship. "That's a hit," Rex said more to himself than the others. "It has to be."

But Orelia knew it wasn't. The Sylvans' shield system

was too advanced for this type of missile. That's why the attacks on the Quatra System had been so deadly—the Quatra Fleet simply didn't have weapons that could bring down a Sylvan ship.

They watched as the missile made contact only to crack and shatter into a thousand useless pieces.

"Try again," Rex ordered. "We might've damaged the shield. It could work the next time. We have to keep trying."

"They're getting closer to the Academy," Vesper said, panic fraying her voice. "How much time do we have?"

Orelia swallowed. "Depending on what kind of weapon they're using, they'll be in range in about six minutes." But she knew exactly what kind of weapon the Sylvans would be using, and if the squadron didn't figure out a way to stop them in less than two minutes, every single person in the Academy would die.

"Okay, let's try this again." Vesper yanked back on the throttle and the fightercraft surged forward.

"You can't fire at this close a range," Rex warned. He was gripping the sides of his chair so tightly, his arms had started shaking. "We'll blow ourselves up."

"Don't worry, I've got this," Vesper said. She released the

weapon, then took the fightercraft into another steep dive. But there was no explosion to avoid, as once again, the missile was deflected by the shield.

Incapacitate the pilot. That is an order.

Orelia closed her eyes as she visualized what it would take to seize the controls from Vesper. She'd have to snap her neck or strangle her until she passed out all while keeping Arran and Rex at bay. Despite her training, she recoiled in horror at the thought of wrapping her hands around Vesper's throat. She couldn't do it.

I'm with three Quatrans, she wrote back. *They won't let me incapacitate the pilot.*

"They're all going to die," Arran said in an anguished whisper that sent a jolt of pain through Orelia's chest.

I'm ordering you to proceed.

Orelia's breath caught in her chest as icy terror swept through her. This was it. She was going to die. Either her squadron's fightercraft would be destroyed in the blast, or the Sylvans would execute her for not following orders.

"We need a stronger weapon," Vesper called, as if speaking the words aloud were enough to will the weapon into existence.

"We just have to keep trying. How much longer do we have?" Rex asked.

"About four minutes," Orelia whispered, unable to hide her growing horror. If they continued to shoot at the Sylvan ship, it would destroy them. But if they did nothing, they were moments away from watching everyone in the Academy die.

"It's not going to work," Arran snapped. "We need to try something else."

Rex banged his fist against the armrest of his chair. "We don't *have* anything else."

"Wait…yes, we do," Arran said. "We can use the satellite."

"How would that work?" Vesper asked, twisting around to look over her shoulder while Rex sat up straighter in his chair.

"It's a communications satellite, so if we set it to the same frequency as the Specter ship, we might be able to jam their communications system. They'll lose navigational control and won't be able to shoot at us or the Academy."

"Can we really do that?" Vesper asked, looking frantically from Arran to the black windowless Specter ship. "The satellite is still in the cargo bay."

Arran nodded. "We should still have full access to the satellite's systems from when we accessed the thrusters."

The hope in his voice cut into Orelia like a knife. The Sylvans used a spread spectrum, so there was no single frequency to jam.

"We'll try it," Rex said quickly. "We've got nothing to lose. Arran, open the cargo bay doors and vent the atmosphere. That'll push the satellite out."

"Okay...opening."

There was a grinding sound, and through the viewport, Orelia saw the satellite tumbling end over end, covered in glimmering icicles.

"Hold on...." Arran's hands flew across the controls, and the satellite's maneuvering thrusters fired silently, slowly turning it to the proper orientation. "Okay...I'm going to start trying different frequencies. Let me know if anything happens."

There was a long moment of tense silence. "I don't think it's working," Vesper said finally, eyes locked on the Sylvan ship. "It's still heading toward the Academy."

Tell them, Orelia thought. *You have to tell them it's not going to work so they have time to get out of the blast range.*

Arran cursed under his breath. "I can't think of any other options," he said. "One of these should've worked."

"Keep trying." Vesper clenched her jaw and gripped the controls tighter. "I'll make sure we're in position to fire."

"I think we should turn around," Orelia said. "They could fire at us again at any moment. It's not—"

"No," Rex said sharply. "We're not turning around."

"We're running out of time!" Vesper shouted. "It looks like they're preparing to fire."

No, please, Orelia willed silently. She couldn't do it. She couldn't watch everyone in the Academy die. But the only way to stop the Sylvans was to tell her squadron mates about the frequency—something no Quatran could possibly know. And if it worked, it would disable the battlecraft's shield in addition to taking out navigational power. Her squadron would be able to destroy the ship easily.

"We have to do something," Arran said, voice cracking.

Orelia tried to imagine the Sylvans on the ship. Was it a crew she knew from the base? Her stomach lurched as she imagined the young soldiers on their first real mission, carrying out an operation that would help them save their doomed people. Could she really risk their lives to save the Quatrans? But then Orelia imagined Vesper's cries of anguish as she realized her mother and all her friends had perished. She winced at the thought of Arran's heartbreak over Dash. She thought about Zafir, and Zuzu, and all the others who'd showed her only kindness, and her resolve hardened.

"I think they might be using a spread spectrum," Orelia said quietly. "We may have to use a directed energy pulse that saturates all frequencies."

"That's it!" Rex said eagerly. "Arran, can you—"

"I'm on it," Arran called back.

The satellite had finished rotating and was now pointed directly at the Sylvan ship. There was no bright discharge of light or firing missiles. Just a silent confirmation on their screens that the signal was being blasted at full power.

"Please, Antares, come on," Arran breathed.

"They've stopped maneuvering," Vesper said. "I think it worked."

It was over. Orelia had signed her own death sentence. Either the Quatrans would execute her as a spy, or her own people would execute her as a traitor. She tried to take a deep breath, but she couldn't force the air into her lungs.

Rex craned his neck to look at Orelia's radar screen.

"They can't maneuver, but they're still on a direct course for the station. In a few minutes, they'll be in range to take out the Academy. It's time to unload everything we've got. Vesper, *fire.*"

The fightercraft shook as their final volley of missiles shot forward, silently blazing their way toward the Sylvan ship.

A moment later, the fightercraft rumbled as the windows filled with the surreal, terrifying sight of flames engulfing the Sylvan ship. *I'm so sorry,* Orelia mouthed as tears filled her eyes, words that would provide little comfort to the Sylvans who'd just lost their lives.

The fightercraft jerked violently, then went still, and for a moment, no one spoke. No one seemed to even breathe. And then the cabin filled with joyful cries and sighs of relief. "We did it!" Rex said, pumping his fist in the air while Arran muttered to himself, "It's okay.... We're okay...."

Rex reached for Orelia's shoulder. "You're a freaking genius!"

Orelia stared straight ahead. She couldn't force a smile. She couldn't even look at her squadron mates. She refused to watch them celebrate the slaughter even if they'd been acting in self-defense. The one comfort was that she wouldn't have to carry this guilt for long. Someone would wonder how she'd known about the multiple frequencies. Questions would follow. It was just a matter of time before someone discovered her secret, and then she'd get the punishment she deserved.

She'd be killed.

CHAPTER 28

ARRAN

"Squadron 20, this is the command center. Do you read?" A frantic voice crackled through the comm system. It was Admiral Haze. "Squadron 20, come in."

Arran let out a long sigh and rested his head on the control panel. The Specters had scrambled their communications, but now that the enemy ship was destroyed the systems were back to normal. Everything was going to be okay. They'd done it, and now the adults could take over.

"We read you, command center," Rex said shakily.

"Oh, thank Antares," Haze said, abandoning protocol. In the background, Arran could hear dim chatter. He tried to imagine who was there with the admiral and how many people had been alerted about the attack. Sergeant Pond, surely, and all the deans. At what point would they contact the cadets' families? Had someone already gotten in touch with his mother, or was she blissfully unaware that her son had narrowly avoided being blown up by the Specters?

"Are you all okay?" Admiral Haze asked.

"We're fine. Just let us know the next time you send us to destroy a Specter ship. Slightly unconventional training method, don't you think?" Rex's tone was playful, but his face was still drawn from their recent ordeal.

Haze let out a strangled laugh. "Stay where you are. You're getting an escort back to the Academy."

The transmission ended, and for a moment, no one spoke. Finally, Rex broke the silence. "That was crazy."

"I can't believe it," Arran said hoarsely, speaking aloud for the first time. They'd fought the *Specters*. And not only had they survived; they'd saved everyone at the Academy. A few seconds later, and it would've been too late. "They were going to kill everyone."

"But we stopped them," Rex said with a grin. "No one can beat Squadron 20!"

Vesper cheered, and Arran laughed as giddy relief began to spread through his body. He glanced at Orelia, who was staring straight ahead, silent and unmoving. He didn't think she'd spoken since they'd activated the pulse. She was probably in shock. They all were.

Within a few minutes, they were on their way back, surrounded by three close-flying Quatra Fleet fightercraft. "I should always arrive at the Academy like this," Rex said.

"Maybe once, just once, you can try to avoid making an entrance," Vesper shot back with a grin.

"There's no way you can spin this that makes it my fault," Rex said.

"It's not your fault," Orelia said quietly without looking at any of them. "None of you are to blame."

"Yeah, we know," Rex said with a smile as Vesper shot Orelia a strange look.

Arran reached over to place a hand on Orelia's shoulder. "Are you all right?"

She nodded, but she didn't make any attempt to remove his hand.

A dock opened as they approached the Academy. Vesper slowed down and steered the ship through the gap without a hitch, an impressive feat of focus and composure considering everything they'd just been through. Arran's brain whirred as it struggled to process the enormity of what had happened. Where had the Specters come from? How had

they penetrated the Academy's perimeter? He started com-
piling a list of questions to ask Admiral Haze during their
inevitable debriefing, but as soon as the hatch opened, it
became clear that he'd have to wait.

The launch deck was packed with people, including a
group of medics right in front. "Get them to the medical
center," a voice ordered, though Arran couldn't tell where it
was coming from.

"We're *fine*," Vesper insisted, sidestepping a medic trying
to take her vitals.

"Give them some space," another voice ordered; this time
it was one Arran recognized—Admiral Haze's.

She pulled Vesper into a tight hug, then turned to face
the others. "Are you all okay?"

"We're fine. Just a little shaken up," Arran said.

"Speak for yourself. I feel fantastic," Rex said, bouncing
in place. The shock had evidently worn off for him, or else it
was being transformed into manic energy.

Admiral Haze shot him a slightly disapproving look
while Vesper smiled indulgently. "Let's continue this conversation in my office," Haze said, gesturing for the cadets
to follow her.

As they made their way toward the administration wing, Arran scanned the halls for a glimpse of Dash but didn't spot him. None of this would feel entirely real until he got to tell Dash about it.

In any other situation, Arran would've found Admiral Haze's office intimidating. A large ornate wooden desk took up half the room, and above it, a glowing holomap of the Quatra System hovered in the air. Paintings of former Academy heads lined the walls, and the shelves were full of books with titles like *The Beauty of War* and *The Vanquished Enemy*. But his encounter with the Specters had radically changed Arran's standard for "intimidating."

Haze leaned back against her desk and gestured for the others to sit. There weren't enough chairs for everyone, so Vesper remained standing, along with Sergeant Pond and Zafir. "Walk me through what happened," Admiral Haze said without preamble.

The cadets exchanged glances. Arran expected Vesper to launch into an explanation, but she nodded at Rex, signaling him to start.

"Well," he began, sounding slightly nervous. Some of his bravado had faded during the walk to Haze's office. "We'd just picked up the satellite and were on our way back when the Specter ship appeared. It seemed like it came out of nowhere."

"You didn't notice anything on the radar?" Haze asked, looking at Orelia.

Orelia shook her head. "Not until they were already in range."

Zafir stared at Orelia with the same inscrutable expression he sometimes used in class, and she shifted uncomfortably. "We realized they were headed for the Academy," Rex continued. "When we couldn't get in touch with you, we knew we had to try to take them out ourselves."

Unable to stay quiet any longer, Vesper jumped in. "Our missiles couldn't penetrate the Specters' shield, so Arran came up with a genius plan to use the satellite to jam their communications system.

"Really?" Pond said. "Fascinating. How did you know the right frequency?"

"We didn't," Arran explained. "Orelia guessed that they were using a spread spectrum that allowed them to switch frequencies."

"An impressive guess," Haze said, surveying Orelia with a look that Arran couldn't quite read. But then her face softened. "I'm proud of all of you," Haze said before smiling at Vesper. "Very proud."

Pond looked from Zafir to Admiral Haze. "How the hell did the Specters find us?" he asked gruffly.

"We'll have to look into that later," Admiral Haze said in a tone that suggested she didn't want to discuss this in front of the cadets. "You four are dismissed. Just try to keep what happened today to yourselves. We don't want to cause alarm until we have a better understanding of the situation."

The cadets nodded and filed out into the corridor. "So what do we do now?" Rex asked, looking slightly bewildered. "Lunch?"

"You're *hungry*?" Vesper said, shaking her head with a combination of exasperation and amusement.

"It turns out that killing Specters gives you one hell of an appetite," he said cheerfully.

Orelia closed her eyes, and her face contorted with pain. "What's wrong?" Arran asked, squeezing her arm.

"Nothing." She stepped to the side, freeing herself from his grasp. "I'm just tired. I think I should go lie down."

"Are you sure you don't want to eat something first?" Rex asked, looking at her with concern.

"No. I'm fine. I just want to rest."

Vesper reached toward Orelia, then thought better of it and let her arm fall to her side. "I'll walk you to your room."

"That's not necessary," she said stiffly, sounding more like the old Orelia. "I'll see you all later." Without meeting any of their eyes, she strode off unsteadily, clearly walking as quickly as she could on trembling legs.

"Should I go with her?" Vesper whispered.

Arran shook his head. "I think she wants to be alone." A sudden wave of fatigue crashed over him, and he tried to estimate how many more steps he'd have to take until he could fall into his own bed. "I think I should probably rest as well."

"Okay, we'll see you tonight," Vesper said, rising onto the balls of her feet to give him a hug. Arran smiled at her use of the word *we*. He wasn't exactly sure what was going on with Vesper and Rex, but he liked it. And it made him even more eager to find Dash. He'd swear him to secrecy, but he *had* to tell him what happened.

Arran hurried to Dash's room. To Arran's relief, he was there, though when Dash opened the door, he looked oddly pale. "Are you okay?" Arran asked before realizing how ridiculous that would sound once Dash learned about Arran's brush with death.

"Yes, I'm fine. What about you? How'd it go?"

Dash led Arran into the living room, where Arran gave him the short version, watching Dash grow even paler with every word. "I can't believe it," Dash said hoarsely before pulling Arran into a hug.

"Yeah, it was..." Arran searched for words that could possibly do justice to the strange swirl of intense emotions that had consumed him since they'd destroyed the Specter ship. "It was the most terrifying and thrilling few minutes of my entire life." He leaned his head on Dash's shoulder as another wave of fatigue washed over him. "I need to go lie down. Come to my room with me?" He wanted to lay his head against Dash's chest and listen to his heartbeat as he fell asleep.

"I should let you rest," Dash said. His tone was kind, but the words still stung.

"What?" Arran asked, looking up. "No, I want you to come with me."

"I know, but you've just suffered a massive shock. It's probably better for you to be alone."

Arran stared at him incredulously, searching Dash's face for some kind of clue that would explain this strange behavior. "I was thinking about you the whole time," Arran said. "Wondering if I'd ever see you again. I don't want to be alone. I want to be with you."

A fleeting look of pain flashed across Dash's face so quickly that Arran might've imagined it. "You'll feel better after you rest. Come on. I'll walk you back." Dash stood up and took Arran's hand, a gesture that normally filled Arran with warmth. But even the pressure of Dash's hand wasn't enough to chase away the chill Arran felt seeping through him as they walked down the corridor in silence.

CHAPTER 29

VESPER

At the end of every term, the Academy threw a party for the winning squadron, but Vesper had a sneaking suspicion that this celebration would be very different. It had been three days since Squadron 20's mission, and despite her mother's efforts, the Specter attack was all anyone could talk about.

The party was held in the ballroom, and it seemed even more lavish than the welcome dance at the beginning of the term. The only light came from the hundreds of glass-encased candles scattered throughout the large room and the distant stars glinting in the windows. Music and laughter swirled around the elegantly dressed crowd that included the entire faculty, as well as some Quatra Fleet officers.

Commander Stepney himself had made the trip, looking even more dignified than usual in his dress uniform.

"Where's the rest of your squadron?" her mother asked as she swept over to Vesper, her black dress streaming behind her. "Commander Stepney wants to congratulate you all."

A thrill of pleasure coursed through her as Vesper rose onto her toes to scan the crowd. "Orelia and Arran are over there," she said. They were by the drinks table, surrounded by people who were clearly bombarding them with questions about the attack. "I'll grab them and bring everyone over to you."

Her mother nodded. "Find us in ten minutes."

As Vesper wove through the mass of cadets and teachers in their finery, nearly every head turned to look at her. If there was ever any doubt that she deserved to be at the Academy, her victory against the Specters had put it to rest. No one was meant to be here more than she was.

Yet, she had no interest in basking in the glow of victory at the moment. All she wanted was to find Rex. They still hadn't spoken about the kiss. She'd assumed one of them would bring it up, but they'd been busy with the final battle, and then the thing with the Specters had happened. It was all so surreal. Here she was, consumed by a desperate desire to know Rex's feelings when just three days ago she'd been fairly certain she was about to die.

The music had grown louder, and a number of people were dancing—some in groups, some in couples. Vesper made sure to skirt the edge of the open space lest she accidentally get swept up with the dancers. The mere thought of dancing in public made her queasy. For some reason, the coordination that allowed her to dash around the multi-environment track or perform complex maneuvers in the zero-gravity room failed her when she had to sway in time to music. She also had a better chance of avoiding Ward if she hovered near the wall. She'd managed to avoid him since their breakup, and while she knew she'd have to face him at some point, she had enough on her mind tonight.

"Not interested in tearing up the dance floor?"

Vesper turned to see Rex surveying her with an amused smile that made her stomach flutter.

I'd rather set myself on fire than dance in front of you, she thought. "I figured it'd be rude to intimidate everyone with my superior moves. No one likes a show-off."

Rex raised an eyebrow and smirked. "Is that so?"

Vesper nodded seriously. "Yes. I've been meaning to talk

to you about that ego of yours. I think you should try to tone it down."

"I'll take that under consideration moving forward. But tonight's about us, and I plan to make the most of it." He extended his hand.

Vesper stared at it warily. "What are you doing?"

"Let's go. I want to see those legendary moves."

"I don't think so," she said, keeping her voice light despite the knot forming in her stomach.

"Come on. Is Miss 'I can destroy a Specter ship without breaking a sweat' really afraid of *dancing*?"

"Oh, I definitely broke a sweat."

He leaned in and whispered in her ear. "I know. You never look more beautiful than when you're all sweaty in the pilot's seat."

Vesper laughed and swatted him playfully, and it took all her self-control not to kiss him again right there in front of hundreds of people casting curious glances around the room. Instead, she took his hand and allowed him to lead her onto the dance floor.

"Is this some form of revenge for making your life diffi-cult for so long?" she asked.

His lips twitched with amusement. "We're about to find

out." He placed his hand on her waist and then guided her hand to his shoulder.

Rex moved easily from side to side in time to the music, steering Vesper back and forth as he shifted. *I must look like such an idiot*, she thought, cringing as she avoided catching Rex's eye. But when she stole a glance at him, he was smiling.

She smiled back, and he tightened his hold on her waist, speeding up with the tempo. No matter which way he stepped, he moved her seamlessly with him. He lifted his arm, and without thinking, she spun underneath it, laughing. He twirled her again, faster this time. It was just like flying with him in the simulcraft when their thoughts became perfectly synchronized. *Except maybe better*, she thought as his hand moved from her waist to her lower back, sending shivers up her spine. *Definitely better.*

"My mom wants us to go talk to Stepney," she whispered, afraid that if she spoke too loudly he'd let go.

"Now?" The music slowed, and Rex wrapped his arms around her, inclining his head toward hers.

"In a few minutes." She looked up at him, then let out a small laugh. "Though you might want to deal with that stain first."

He glanced down at the small splotch of pink mustard on his shirt and smiled.

"I'll be right back," he whispered into her ear before letting go.

"I'll meet you over there," she said, gesturing to where her mother was talking to Stepney. "I'm just going to grab Orelia and Arran."

Vesper set off again through the crowd, trying to take deep breaths so she'd stop trembling. But before she reached her squadron mates, she heard a familiar voice. "Congratulations, Vee. I heard you put on quite a show the other day."

As usual, Ward was dressed impeccably, yet tonight nothing about his appearance conveyed elegance. Everything seemed overly pressed and starched, just like the tight smile on his face.

"It wasn't exactly a *show*," Vesper said. "We prevented a Specter attack." She knew he was still furious about their breakup, but surely hearing that your ex-girlfriend had saved your life would prompt a little bit of gratitude.

"Oh, I know. It must have been terrifying," he said, his voice suddenly full of concern that didn't quite match the look in his eyes. "It's a good thing Rex decided that this mission wasn't a good one to sabotage."

"What are you talking about?"

Ward nodded toward Rex, who was standing near the drinks table dipping a napkin into a glass of water. "I'm surprised you forgave him. Did he split the money with you?"

Sparks of irritation sizzled in her chest, and she was about to tell Ward to stop wasting her time when he continued. "He bet *against* your squadron for the first mission. That's why he pretended to be sick—though he probably was pretty hungover; those Edgers tend to drink themselves into oblivion. He won about four hundred skyor according to Brill."

Vesper narrowed her eyes. "This is pretty pathetic. Even for you."

"You think I'm making it up?" Ward sniggered. "Go ask him yourself."

She hesitated, unsure what would annoy Ward more— dismissing the accusation and staying where she was or going over to Rex and having him humiliate Ward by denying the whole thing. The second option had the advantage of letting her get away from Ward, so she shot him a fake smile and said, "I'll do it right now."

Although Rex was facing away from her, he must've been watching out of the corner of his eye, because as Vesper approached, he reached for her hand and pulled her toward him. She smiled as she pressed against him, feeling the tension drain away.

"What did Ward want?" Rex asked as he and Vesper made their way through the crowd.

"He was just being an idiot," she said, glad to see that her mother had found Orelia and Arran. "He told me this ridiculous story about your throwing our first battle on purpose."

Rex patted the stain on his shirt with a napkin, and Vesper thought she saw his shoulders tense slightly. "He made that up, right?" she said calmly, ignoring the faint prickle of irritation in her stomach.

"Not completely, no." Rex shot her an apologetic smile.

"So, it's true? You *threw* the battle?" She knew she shouldn't get too worked up—they'd ended up winning the tournament anyway—but that loss had sent her into a serious downward spiral. Every morning, she'd woken up with a weight on her chest that only grew heavier throughout the day. She'd been so desperate that she'd almost taken *vega dust*, for Antares's sake.

She took a deep breath, trying to cool the anger that had begun to bubble inside her. If Rex had thrown the battle, it was probably for a good reason. *Show him that you understand*, she told herself. This was her chance to prove that she wasn't just another rich, out-of-touch Tridian. "Why?"

"I needed the money," he said.

"Okay. For what?" Vesper asked.

Rex looked away. "I can't tell you."

"That's convenient," she said, unable to keep the bitterness out of her voice.

He turned back to glare at her. "I don't know what you're getting so upset about," he said testily. "We won the tournament. It doesn't matter."

"It matters to *me*," Vesper said, her voice cracking. Rex had had the audacity to waltz into that bathroom and make some bullshit speech about *believing* in her when their loss had been all his fault to begin with. "You should have just told me the truth. If I'd known you needed money, I would have understood. Instead, you made me think I wasn't good enough. You knew how insecure I was and you used that against me."

Rex's face hardened. "You can't blame all your problems on me, Vesper. It's not my fault that you fall apart whenever things aren't perfect."

The fury in her stomach sent waves of heat roiling through her body. "Yeah, you're right. It's not your fault, it's mine. Because I should've known better than to trust someone like you." Without another word, she spun on her heel and strode away.

CHAPTER 30

ARRAN

Arran looked around the dining hall with a frown. Dash wasn't at his usual table with his Tridian friends, and he wasn't sitting with his squadron either. Arran glanced down to check his link for what felt like the thousandth time that day. Not only had Dash skipped engineering class, he hadn't responded to any of Arran's messages.

Ignoring his protesting stomach, he hurried out of the dining hall, nodding at the dozens of people who waved or smiled as he passed. Ever since the attack, Arran had been catapulted from the fringes of Academy life into the center, but somehow, he felt lonelier than before. It didn't matter how many new friends he made if Dash wasn't by his side. Arran couldn't come up with an explanation for Dash's strange behavior, but he was determined to get to the bottom of it. Tonight.

"Are you okay?" someone called. He turned to see Vesper hurrying toward him. "You didn't stay for dinner."

"Yes, fine," Arran said quickly. "I just realized I wasn't very hungry. Are *you* okay?" He hadn't noticed inside the dining hall, but in the harsh light of the corridor it was clear she wasn't the beaming, bright-eyed girl he'd last seen at the party the evening before. Based on her sallow skin and the bags under her eyes, he wouldn't be surprised to learn she'd been up all night.

"I'm fine," she said, looking away.

"Have you seen Dash?" Arran asked, changing the subject. "I haven't been able to find him all day."

"Have you checked the screening room? We had one at our old school, and Dash always liked to use it when it was empty, like during dinner."

Arran felt a strange, bittersweet ache in his chest as he thought about how many small details like this he still didn't know about Dash. "I'll look there. Thanks, Vee."

She smiled and squeezed his arm. "See you later. Good luck."

He frowned and was about to ask why he'd need luck, but she was already gone.

⋙

He found the screening room easily, though he wasn't surprised he hadn't noticed it before. He'd only ever seen a handful of holostories, as watching them wasn't exactly a popular pastime in F Territory.

Arran placed his link against the scanner, and the door hissed open. He stepped inside, and in the dim light he could just make out three rows of the most comfortable-looking chairs Arran had ever seen in his life, all facing a screen on which dancing animals seemed to be having some kind of party.

As Arran's eyes adjusted to the darkness, he realized the room wasn't actually empty. Someone was sitting in the front row all the way on the side against the wall. Arran crept forward to find Dash curled up in one of the enormous chairs, lying with his head against the armrest and his long legs draped over the other side. A box of sour coins, his favorite candy, was tucked under his arm. Something in Arran's chest cracked, releasing a wave of affection.

"Is that your dinner?" Arran asked with a smile as he slid into the seat next to Dash.

"What are you talking about?" Dash said with feigned indignation. "Look at the wide array of nutrients! There's green coloring…yellow coloring…a veritable feast."

Despite his playful tone, something about Dash's expression seemed strained. "Where have you been? I was looking for you," Arran said gently.

"I wasn't hungry, so I came here instead."

Arran waited for him to continue with something like *But I was about to message you.* Or *But I was going to come say good night before bed.* But Dash returned his attention to the screen. "What are you watching?" Arran asked after a long moment.

"You don't know *Explorer Friends?*" Dash said without looking at Arran.

"I don't think we got it on Chetire."

Dash cringed. "I'm sorry. I don't know why I keep making stupid mistakes like that."

"I don't think I'd call it a *mistake.*" Arran took Dash's hand and squeezed. "We're still getting to know each other."

Dash squeezed Arran's hand in return, then looked at

him with a combination of pain and pity that made Arran's stomach feel like it was full of fyron.

"What's going on? Why are you acting like this?"

Dash closed his eyes. "I'm sorry," he whispered.

"Sorry about what?" Arran asked in a strangled voice that didn't sound like his own.

Dash pulled his hand free from Arran's grip, and when he opened his eyes, they glistened with tears. "I tried so hard, but it isn't going to work."

"What's not going work? What the hell are you talking about?"

"Someone told my dad about us. I don't know who, but he's furious."

Arran tried to place his hand on Dash's arm, but he shifted out of reach. "I'm sorry," Arran said as cold dread began to coil around his stomach. "But I guess this was going to happen eventually, right?"

Dash shook his head. "Not like this." He inhaled deeply, as if trying to breathe through intense pain. "He told me he'll pull me out of the Academy unless...unless we break up."

Arran stared at Dash, his brain whirring ineffectually, like an overloaded machine. "I don't understand. He can't do that."

Dash let out a bitter laugh. "You don't know him."

"But it's not like he's paying for you to be here." Once they were admitted to the Academy, all the cadets' expenses were paid by the Quatra Federation. "He can't just pull you out of school."

"I know you don't understand what it means to be a general in the Quatra Fleet," Dash said wearily. "One call to Commander Stepney, and I'm out."

"Why are you making all these excuses?" Arran whispered. Before Dash could respond, the cruelest portion of Arran's brain came up with its own explanations.

Because he never liked you that much to begin with.

Because he found someone else.

"They're not excuses," Dash said as an edge crept into his voice. "You think I *want* to do this? It's been killing me."

"So just tell him that we broke up."

"That won't work. Someone will tell my father the truth. I don't have a chance."

The tears that had been welling up in Dash's eyes began to spill down his cheeks. "We don't have a chance."

Dash barely spoke above a whisper, but his words cut into Arran like a white-hot knife slicing his skin and searing everything beneath. "Arran, I'm sorry...." Dash reached for Arran's hand, but that only made the pain worse. *This is the last time he's going to hold my hand*, Arran thought. A wave of loneliness washed over him, colder than anything he'd ever felt on Chetire. Although Dash was sitting a mere six inches from him, it felt like a chasm had opened up between them.

Part of Arran understood Dash's position. After all, Arran had had to fight tooth and nail to get into the Academy to make a better life for himself. On some level, he certainly got Dash's desire to stay in the Academy to secure a future he too had fought hard for. But that didn't seem to matter when it felt like Arran's heart was being torn apart.

"I have to go," Arran said, rising shakily to his feet.

"Arran, wait," Dash pleaded. "This is as hard for me as it is for you."

It took all of Arran's strength not to look back as he walked out the door without a word.

CHAPTER 31

CORMAK

"Do you know what this is about?" Orelia asked as she and Cormak made their way to the auditorium.

Cormak shook his head. He didn't particularly care why classes had been canceled for an assembly. Ever since the formal, he'd had trouble mustering enough energy to care about anything. He knew he was being ridiculous—during the past few days, his squadron had won the tournament *and* saved the lives of everyone at the Academy. He should've felt as weightless as he had in the zero-gravity room. Yet all he could think about was the look on Vesper's face right before she'd stormed off. Her callous words had stung, but not as much as the knowledge that he'd hurt her. Again.

They turned into the central corridor and found themselves in a sea of cadets heading toward the auditorium. The crowd was quieter than usual, which didn't strike Cormak as particularly strange at first; the Specter attack had left the cadets nervous and subdued. But then he realized the real reason for the lack of chatter—the stony-faced, helmeted Quatra Fleet guards along the far wall. There appeared to be more than a dozen of them, guns resting on their shoulders as they watched the cadets.

Orelia inhaled sharply and froze, causing the boy trailing them to crash into her. Cormak grabbed Orelia's arm. "Are you okay?" he asked, slightly alarmed to see his most unflappable squadron mate looking so flustered.

"I'm fine," she said quickly. "The guards just took me by surprise."

"Me too," he said with a nod. If he'd still been waiting for his medical records to clear, the sight of the guards would've given him a heart attack.

He and Orelia spent the rest of the short walk in silence, then followed the crowd into the auditorium. "Whoa," Cormak muttered as Orelia stiffened next to him, staring at the panoramic window that wrapped around the enormous room. The stars that had captivated him during orientation were barely noticeable—all he could focus on were the massive Quatra Fleet battlecraft surrounding the Academy.

"Let's sit over there," Orelia said, and Cormak nodded without looking, allowing her to lead him while he kept his eyes trained on the looming ships. It was only after she'd turned into the fourth row that he realized she was heading for the two empty seats next to Vesper and Arran. He paused, hoping it wasn't too late to backtrack, but Arran had already spotted them and was waving them over.

Vesper hadn't seen them yet. Her eyes were fixed on the empty stage, either oblivious or indifferent to the nervous chatter around her.

To his dismay, Orelia motioned for Cormak to go in first, and unable to come up with a reason to refuse, he slid past a few seated cadets and lowered himself into the empty seat next to Vesper. She tensed slightly but didn't tear her eyes away from the stage.

Fine, Cormak thought. He should've known that Vesper would never see him as anything other than space trash. This was the type of shit that got you killed on Deva— letting a pretty girl convince you to listen to your heart instead of your gut.

He turned to Arran and was about to make a show of ignoring Vesper in return when Admiral Haze stepped onto the stage, followed by Zafir and Sergeant Pond, and the quiet murmuring of the crowd died away. As usual, Haze didn't waste any time getting to the point. "As you all know by now, a few days ago, a Specter ship managed to breach the carefully guarded perimeter around the Academy. The investigation into the security failure is ongoing, but in the meantime, the Quatra Fleet has tripled the security around the Academy. *Nothing* is making it past the new perimeter. You're all safe here…for the time being. However, it's abundantly clear that the Academy's location has been compromised. And there's no doubt that another attack is imminent."

A heavy silence blanketed the auditorium as the cadets exchanged nervous looks. *Another attack is imminent.* Cormak shivered as the words washed over him like the freezing decontamination mist they used on Deva. He recalled the terror and awe he'd felt when the Specter battlecraft had first appeared, then tried to imagine an entire fleet making its way toward the Academy.

He felt Vesper tremble slightly and, without thinking,

nearly reached for her hand before catching himself just in time.

"Over the next few weeks, we'll be planning a massive defensive campaign," Admiral Haze continued, unleashing a wave of whispers. "And it's essential that we have enough officers to carry it out."

Out of the corner of his eye, he thought he saw Vesper glance at him, but he kept staring straight ahead.

"This is a lot to process, but I know that every single one of you will demonstrate the commitment and courage that defines the Quatra Fleet. You're here because you felt a special calling—a duty to protect your family, your communities, your solar system, and your species. And now you'll have the chance to answer that call."

All around Cormak, cadets were sitting up straighter. Admiral Haze was one of his least favorite people in the Quatra System, but that didn't prevent her words from stirring something inside him. He looked over at Arran, who was nodding seriously, but when Arran caught Cormak's eye, he grinned. "Sounds like a job for Squadron 20," Arran whispered.

"Do you think they'd actually assign us to the same crew?" Cormak asked quietly.

"It seems foolish to break up a winning combination. Don't you agree, Vee?" Arran said.

"I wouldn't want to fly with anyone else." Her eyes darted toward Cormak. "It takes a special type of captain to put up with my outbursts."

He hesitated as hope began to fray the knot of guilt and frustration in his stomach. "And it takes a special type of pilot to forgive her captain for being a complete jerk from time to time."

Vesper pressed her lips together, a hint of a smile on her face.

Up on the stage, Admiral Haze stopped to look around the auditorium. "A few months ago, I welcomed you to the Academy as cadets. Today, I look around and see the future of the Quatra Fleet. We've never gone down without a fight, and we're certainly not going to start now. We'll rise to the challenge with courage and conviction." She paused and scanned the room, her voice steely but her eyes ablaze. "Here's to unity and prosperity."

"Unity and prosperity!" the cadets echoed.

Vesper turned to Cormak and they locked eyes. "I'm sorry," he whispered.

"It doesn't matter," Vesper said, shaking her head. "I know you'll never bet against us again."

"Squadron 20? Or...us?" Cormak ventured.

Vesper didn't answer, but her smile told him everything he needed to know.

CHAPTER 32

ORELIA

As she turned into the corridor that led to Zafir's office, Orelia's pulse began to race even faster. She'd been on edge ever since Zafir had sent her a message asking her to drop by his office at the end of the day. At first, the sight of his name on her link had sent a wave of warmth through her body. It would be their first time alone since their midnight swim, and her skin tingled with the memory of his lips on hers. But a moment later, her excitement was swept away by cold fear. She had no idea if he was summoning her to his office as the young man she'd kissed in the ocean tank—or as one of the most decorated counterintelligence officers in the Quatra Fleet.

She wiped her sweaty palms on her pants as the questions that had been rattling in her head reached a near frenzy. Did he want to talk about the kiss or the attack? Or something else entirely? She tried to come up with a plan for each scenario, but by the time she reached his door, she could barely breathe, let alone think.

She forced herself to take a deep breath, then knocked, praying that he wouldn't answer so she could slip away and save the conversation for another time. Or, given what they'd just learned at the assembly, that he'd suddenly become too busy to question her at all. "Come in!" his voice called. Orelia raised a shaking arm to the scanner, and the door slid open.

She'd seen a few of her instructors' offices, but so far, Zafir's was the only one with a window—though the view was hardly the most striking feature. Everywhere she looked were shelves full of vials and airtight containers holding everything from fragments of Sylvan ships, bomb remnants, fuel samples, and what seemed to be a tiny patch of skin suspended in liquid.

"Orelia. Have a seat," Zafir said from behind his desk, motioning toward the chair on the other side. She couldn't read his tone, and the expression on his face was similarly inscrutable.

She sat gingerly at the edge of the seat, unable to keep herself from glancing back over her shoulder at the liquid-filled vial. "You can go take a closer look if you want," Zafir said. "It's pretty remarkable. The xenobiologists were analyzing a fragment of the Specter ship you destroyed and realized that some of the cells were organic and intact. They were able to grow that skin from Specter DNA. So far, it's the closest look we've gotten at them."

Orelia suppressed a shudder as guilt and disgust curdled in her stomach. Those skin cells had belonged to a real person. A Sylvan *she'd* killed.

"I'm okay," she said faintly, hoping it didn't make her sound incurious. Even with all her years of training, she couldn't read Zafir's face. There was no sign that he saw her differently from any other student; she couldn't detect a trace of affection or even discomfort. He was completely impassive.

"Listen." He paused to clear his throat. "I want to apologize for my behavior in the ocean tank the other night. It was incredibly inappropriate, and I'm very, very sorry for putting you in such a position. I promise, it won't happen again."

It was as if his words had wrapped themselves around her rib cage, forcing the air out of her lungs. Logically, she knew it was a good thing that the counterintelligence expert wanted to keep his distance, but that didn't do much to temper the pain radiating through her. It was hard to believe that the young man in the medal-covered uniform was the same one who'd wrapped his arms around her in the water, who'd made her feel like she wasn't entirely alone.

"You don't have to apologize," she said, grateful that some of her training hadn't gone to waste and that she could keep her voice steady.

"Yes, I do." He straightened his collar, as if eager to confirm that he was properly attired this time around. "I'm your teacher, and my job is to create a learning environment where you feel safe. I want you to be able to talk to me, to trust me, without letting"—he paused, looking uncharacteristically flustered—"mistakes like that get in the way."

Orelia stared at him, unsure of how to respond. Swimming in the ocean tank with Zafir was the safest she'd felt since arriving at the Academy, the most comfortable she'd felt with any Quatran. "I understand," she said quietly.

"Good. We're all dealing with a lot right now, and the last thing any of us needs is an extra complication." Some of the discomfort in his face slipped away. "How are you doing?" he asked, assuming the direct, confident tone he used in class.

"I'm fine," she said, though nothing could be further from the truth. She couldn't go more than a few minutes without wondering if she'd known any of the Sylvans on the ship they'd destroyed. She kept thinking about how many families would be in mourning right now. How many mothers had woken up today, gasping under the weight of their crushing grief? How many people had thought of a joke to send their sister or brother, only to remember that their sibling would never read anything again?

"You demonstrated remarkably quick thinking when you realized you needed to send that energy pulse across multiple frequencies."

"Thank you," she said, torn between pride and horror.

"How'd you figure that out?"

"Figure what out?" she asked, stalling as her brain searched frantically for an answer that would deflect suspicion.

"The shield frequency for the Specter ship."

"I think I read something about spread spectrums once," she said vaguely.

"Very lucky indeed." He was smiling, but it wasn't the smile she was used to, the one that made him look younger, friendlier. For the first time, there was no sympathy in his eyes. It had been replaced by something cold.

"You're very well read. Even more so than I realized." He leaned back in his chair. "Would you mind answering a few more questions? It would be incredibly helpful."

Get out, a voice called from the back of her mind as every muscle in her body tensed, ready to spring into action. She scanned Zafir's face for a hint of the person she'd kissed in the ocean tank, but she barely recognized him.

"Of course," she said hoarsely. She'd undergone countless hours of interrogation resistance training, but none of the brutal exercises had prepared her for this desperate panic. "Maybe tomorrow? I'm not sure how useful I'll be right now. I'm pretty tired."

"I'm afraid we can't wait that long," he said, shaking his head. He pressed something on his desk, and the office door slid open, revealing four Quatra Fleet guards, faces obscured by their helmets, guns raised—and pointed at her.

Cold dread pulsed through Orelia's veins as she turned back to look at Zafir.

"See you soon, Orelia."

ACKNOWLEDGMENTS

This book wouldn't exist without the talents of the extraordinary team at Alloy. Thank you for believing in me as a writer and for the privilege of telling stories. Special thanks to Joelle Hobeika, Romy Golan, Lanie Davis, Josh Bank, Sara Shandler, and Les Morgenstein for making my wildest dreams come true. Extra special thanks to Alloy alums Annie Stone, who helped dream up these characters, and Eliza Swift, who guided me as I brought them to life. I owe a particularly enormous debt of gratitude to my brilliant, patient, wise editor, Viana Siniscalchi, who took a jumble of words and transformed them into a book.

I'm grateful to everyone at Little, Brown, especially my editor, Pam Gruber, whose staggering intelligence and insight elevated this story in countless ways. Same to Hannah Milton, who gave thoughtful notes at a crucial stage.

Thank you to the teams at Hodder & Stoughton (especially the whip-smart and hilarious Emily Kitchin) and Hachette Australia.

Thank you to the superstars at Rights People for helping me share my stories with readers around the world, and to my amazing foreign publishers (especially Myrthe Spiteri at Blossom Books for bringing me all the way to the Netherlands!).

I'm lucky to have an unmatched support network. Thanks to my Scholastic family, my dazzlingly talented writing group, and all my incredible friends, especially the LA crew, who received emails with the subject line "sci-fi emergency" in the middle of the night and responded promptly. Extra thanks to Gavin Brown for helping me untangle the mysteries of space, to Nick Eliopulos for his thoughtful, caring analysis of Arran and Dash's storyline, and to my uncle, Peter Bloom, for being my on-call explosions and alien technology expert. And a very special thank-you to Benjamin Hart for his unwavering support, manifesting in countless Blue Apron dinners...and a spectacularly skillful final line edit.

Above all, thank you to my family: my father, Sam Henry Kass, a writer/director whose talent is matched only by his empathy and loyalty; my mother, Marcia Bloom, whose art contains more beauty and wisdom than any novel; and my brother, (doctor!) Petey Kass, whose compassion and humor inspires me every day.

This book is written in memory of three important people I lost in the past two years: my grandmother Nicky Bloom, a physicist who taught me to look at the world with curiosity; my grandmother Nance Kass, an actress and singer who nurtured my love of stories and took me to every museum in New York; and my dear friend David Crist—a gifted writer, deep thinker, and natural teacher who transformed every life he touched. Thank you for sitting next to me on the bus that day in seventh grade so we could talk about sci-fi; I wouldn't be the same person or storyteller without you. This one's for you, Dave.